DESTINATION: VOID

Relays clicked as Prudence shunted the ATT to Com-central. Presently she said: "Short and sweet. Hempstead tells us to cease ignoring communications. We are ordered to turn back. Odd choice of words: 'This is an arbitrary turn-back command.'"

At the sound of Prudence's voice, Flattery went cold. *They know*, he thought. *They know we have created a rogue consciousness.* "Arbitrary turn-back" was the coded order he had both dreaded and longed for.

It was the kill-ship command.

DESTINATION: VOID
FRANK HERBERT
(Revised Edition)

BERKLEY BOOKS, NEW YORK

A different version of this novel appeared in *Galaxy*,
under the title "Do I Sleep or Wake."
Copyright © 1965, by Galaxy Publishing Corp.

DESTINATION: VOID

A Berkley Book / published by arrangement with
the author

PRINTING HISTORY
Berkley Medallion edition / June 1966
Revised Berkley edition / December 1978
Nineteenth printing / May 1983

ISBN: 0-425-06263-5

A BERKLEY BOOK ® TM 757,375
The name "BERKLEY" and the stylized "B" with design
are trademarks belonging to Berkley Publishing Corporation.
PRINTED IN THE UNITED STATES OF AMERICA

I SAW THE pale student of unhallowed arts kneeling beside the thing he had put together. I saw the hideous phantasm of a man stretched out, and then, on the working of some powerful engine, show signs of life and stir with an uneasy, half-vital motion. Frightful must it be, for supremely frightful would be the effect of any human endeavor to mock the stupendous mechanism of the Creator.

—Mary Shelley
on the creation of
Frankenstein

PROLOGUE

IT WAS THE fifth clone ship to go out from Moonbase on Project Consciousness and he leaned forward to watch it carefully as his duty demanded. The view showed it passing the Pluto orbit and he knew that by this time the crew had encountered the usual programmed frustrations, even some deaths and serious injuries, but that was the pattern.

Earthling, it was called. *Earthling Number Five.*

The ship was a giant egg, one-half of it a dark shadow lambent on a starry background, the other half reflecting silver from the distant sun.

A nervous cough sounded from the darkness behind him and he suppressed a sympathetic repetition of that sound. Others were not as self-controlled.

By the time the coughing spasms had subsided, the *Earthling* had begun to make its turn. The movement was impossible, but there was no denying what they all saw. The ship turned through one hundred and eighty degrees and reversed, heading directly back down its outward track.

"Any clue at all on how they did that?" he asked.

"No, sir. Nothing."

"I want you to go through the message capsule again," he said. "We're missing something."

"Yes, sir." It was a sigh of resignation.

Someone else spoke from the darkness: "Get ready for the capsule launching..."

Yes, they'd all seen this enough to anticipate the sequence.

The capsule was a silver needle that looped from the *Earthling*'s stern. It held to the ship's blind spot (who knew what weapons such a ship might produce?) until it was lost among the stars.

From beneath their view a flame darted—the laser relay with its *destruct* message. A purple glow touched the ship's bulbous nose. It held for no more than three heartbeats before the ship exploded in a blinding orange blossom.

"That Flattery model is sure as hell reliable," someone said.

Nervous laughter went around the room, but he ignored it, concentrating on the viewer. Why the hell did they always think it was the Flattery model? It could be anyone on the crew.

Their view closed on the swollen blossom with the collapsing speed of time-lapse which made the explosion's orange light wink out too rapidly. Presently, the movement slowed and their view moved into the spreading wreckage, probing with crystalline flares of light until it found what it sought—the recording box. That and the message capsule were the most important elements remaining from this failure.

Claw retractors could be seen grabbing the recording box and pulling it back beneath their view. The crystalline light continued to probe. Anything they saw here could be valuable. But the light picked out nothing but twisted metal, torn shreds of plastic and, here and there, limbs and other parts of the crew. There was one particularly brutal glimpse of a head with part of a shoulder and an arm that ended just below the elbow. Bloody frost globules had formed around the head but they still recognized it.

"Tim!" someone said.

A woman's voice far to the rear of the room could be heard repeating: "Shit...shit...shit..." until someone silenced her.

The view blanked out and he leaned back, feeling the

ache between his shoulders. He knew he would have to identify that woman and have her transferred. No mistaking the near hysteria in her voice. Some harsh catharsis was indicated. He shut down the holopack's controls, flicked the switch for the room lights, then stood and turned in the blinking brilliance.

"They're clones," he said, keeping his voice cold. "They are not human; they are clones, as is indicated by their uniform middle name of 'Lon.' They are property! Anybody who forgets that is going off Moonbase in the next shuttle. That sign on my door says 'Morgan Hempstead, Director.' There will be no more emotional outbursts in this room as long as I am Director."

CHAPTER 1

We call it Project Consciousness and our basic tools are the carefully selected clones, our Doppelgangers. The motivator is frustration; thus we design into our system false goals and things which will go wrong. That's why we chose Tau Ceti as the target: there is no livable planet at Tau Ceti.

—Morgan Hempstead
Lectures at Moonbase

"It's DEAD," Bickel said.

He held up the severed end of a feeder tube, stared at the panel from which he had cut it. His heart was beating too fast and he could feel his hands trembling.

Fluorescent red letters eight centimeters high spelled out a warning on the panel in front of him. The warning seemed a mockery after what he had just done.

"ORGANIC MENTAL CORE—TO BE REMOVED ONLY BY LIFE-SYSTEMS ENGINEER."

Bickel felt an extra sense of quiet in the ship. Something (not *someone*, he thought) was gone. It was as though the molecular stillness of outer space had invaded the *Earthling*'s concentric hulls and spread through to the heart of this egg-shaped chunk of metal hurtling toward Tau Ceti.

His two companions were wrapped in this silence, Bickel saw. They were afraid to break the quiet moment of shame and guilt and anger...and relief.

"What else could we do?" Bickel demanded. He held up the severed tube, glared at it.

Raja Lon Flattery, their psychiatrist-chaplain, cleared his throat, said: "Easy, John. We share the blame equally."

Bickel turned his glare on Flattery, noted the man's quizzical expression, calculated and penetrating, the narrow, haughty face that somehow focused a sense of terrible superiority within remote brown eyes and upraked black eyebrows.

"You know what you can do with your blame!" Bickel growled, but Flattery's words destroyed his anger, made him feel defeated.

Bickel swung his attention to Timberlake—Gerrill Lon Timberlake, life-systems engineer, the man who should have taken responsibility for this dirty business.

Timberlake, a quick and nervous scarecrow of a man with skin almost the color of his brown hair, stared at the metal deck near his feet, avoiding Bickel's eyes.

Shame and fear—that's all Tim feels, Bickel thought.

Timberlake's weakness—his inability to kill the OMC even when it meant saving the ship with its thousands of helpless lives—had almost killed them. And all the man could feel now was shame...and fear.

There had been no doubt about what had to be done. The OMC had gone mad, a wild, runaway consciousness. It had been a sick ball of gray matter whose muscles turned every servo on the ship into a murder weapon, who stared out at them with madness from every sensor, who raged gibberish at them from every vocoder.

No, there had been no doubt—not with three of their number murdered—and the only wonder was that they had been allowed to destroy it.

Perhaps it wanted to die, Bickel thought.

And he wondered if that had been the fate of the six

other Project ships which had vanished into nothingness without a trace.

Did their OMCs run wild? Did their umbilicus crews fail, when it was kill or be killed?

A tear began sliding down Timberlake's left cheek. To Bickel, that was the final blow. Some of his anger returned. He faced Timberlake: "What do we do now, *Captain?*"

The title's irony was not lost on either of Bickel's companions. Flattery started to reply, thought better of it. If the starship *Earthling* could be said to have a captain (discounting an in-service Organic Mental Core), then unspoken agreement gave that title to an umbilicus crew's life-systems engineer. None of them, though, had ever used the word officially.

At last Timberlake met Bickel's stare, but all he said was: "You know why I couldn't bring myself to do it."

Bickel continued to study Timberlake. What shabby conceit had given them this excuse for a life-systems engineer? Once the umbilicus crew had numbered six— the three here plus Ship Nurse Maida Lon Blaine, Tool Specialist Oscar Lon Anderson, and Biochemist Sam Lon Scheler. Now, Blaine, Anderson, and Scheler were dead—Scheler's exploded corpse jamming an access tube on the aft perimeter, Anderson strangled by a rogue sphincter lock, and lovely Maida mangled by runaway cargo.

Bickel blamed most of the tragedy on Timberlake. If the damn fool had only taken the ruthless but obvious step at the first sign of trouble! There had been plenty of warning—with the first two of the ship's three OMCs going catatonic. The seat of trouble had been obvious. And the symptoms—exactly the same symptoms that had preceded the breakdown of the old Artificial Consciousness project back on earth—insane destruction of people and materiel. But Tim had refused to see it. Tim had blathered about the sanctity of all life.

Life, hah! Bickel thought. They were all of them—even the colonists down in the hyb tanks—expendable biopsy material, Doppelgangers grown in gnotobiotic sterility in

the Moonbase. "Untouched by human hands." That had
been their private joke. They had known their Earth-born
teachers only as voices and doll-size images on cathode
screens of the base intercom system—and only occasion-
ally through the triple glass at the locks that sealed off the
sterile crèche. They had emerged from the axolotl tanks
to the padded metal claws of nursemaids that were servo
extensors of Moonbase personnel, forever barred from
intimate contact with those they served.

Out of contact—that's the story of our lives, Bickel
thought, and the thought softened his anger at Timberlake.

Timberlake had begun to fidget under Bickel's stare.

Flattery intervened. "Well . . . we'd better do *something*," he said.

He had to get them moving, Flattery knew. That was
part of his job—keep them active, working, moving, even
if they moved into open conflict. *That* could be solved
when and if it happened.

Raj is right, Timberlake thought. *We have to do
something*. He took a deep breath, trying to shake off his
sense of shame and failure . . . and the resentment of
Bickel—damned Bickel, superior Bickel, special Bickel,
the man of countless talents, Bickel upon whom their lives
depended.

Timberlake glanced around at the familiar Command
Central room in the ship's core—a space twenty-seven
meters long and twelve meters on the short axis. Like the
ship, Com-central was vaguely egg-shaped. Four cocoon-
like action couches with almost identical control boards
lay roughly parallel in the curve of the room's wider end.
Color-coded pipes and wires, dials and instrument
controls, switch banks and warning telltales spread
patterned confusion against the gray metal walls. Here
were the necessities for monitoring the ship and its
autonomous consciousness—an Organic Mental Core.

Organic Mental Core, Timberlake thought, and he felt
the full return of his feelings of guilt and grief. *Not human
brain, oh no. An Organic Mental Core. Better yet, an*

OMC. The euphemism makes it easier to forget that the core once was a human brain in an infant monster— doomed to die. We take only terminal cases since that makes the morality of the act less questionable.

And now we've killed it.

"I'll tell you what I'm going to do," Bickel said. He looked at the Accept-And-Translate board auxiliary to the transmitter on his personal control console. "I'm going to report back to Moonbase what's happened." He turned from the raped panel, dropped the severed feeder tube to the deck without looking at it. The tube drifted downward slowly in the ship's quarter gravity.

"We've no code for this . . . this kind of emergency." Timberlake confronted Bickel, stared angrily at the man's square face, disliking every feature of it from the close-cropped blond hair to the wide mouth and pugnacious jaw.

"I know," Bickel said, and he stepped around Timberlake. "I'm sending it clear speech."

"You can't do that!" Timberlake protested, turning to glare at Bickel's back.

"Every second's delay adds to the time lag," Bickel said. "As it is, it has to go more than a fourth of the way across the solar system." He dropped into his couch, set the cocoon to half enclose him, swung the transmitter into position.

"You'll be blatting it to everyone on Earth, including you-know-who!" Timberlake said.

Because he half agreed with Timberlake and wanted to gain time, Flattery moved to a position looking down on Bickel in the couch: "What specifically are you going to tell them?"

"I'm not about to mince words," Bickel retorted. He threw the transmitter warmup switches, began checking the sequence tape. "I'm going to tell 'em we had to unhook the last brain from the ship's controls . . . and kill it in the process."

"They'll tell us to abort," Timberlake said.

The merest hesitation of his hands on the tape-punch

keyboard told that Bickel had heard.

"And what'll you say happened to the brains?" Flattery asked.

"They went nuts," Bickel said. "I'm just going to report our casualties."

"That's not precisely what happened," Flattery said.

"We'd better talk this over," Timberlake said, and he felt the beginnings of desperation.

"Look, you," Bickel said, shifting his attention to Timberlake, "you're supposed to be crew captain on this chunk of tin and here we are drifting without any hands on the controls at all." He returned his attention to the keyboard. "You think you're qualified to tell *me* what to do?"

Timberlake went pale with anger. *Bickel defeats me so easily*, he thought. He muttered: "The whole world'll be listening." But he turned away to his own couch, jacked in the temporary controls they had rigged shortly after the first ship brain had begun acting up. Presently, he sank onto the couch, tested the computer circuits, and asked for course data.

"The Organic Mental Cores did not go nuts," Flattery said. "You can't..."

"As far as *we're* concerned they did." Bickel threw the master switch. A skin-creeping hum filled Com-central as the laser amplifiers built up to full potential.

I could stop him, Flattery thought as Bickel fed the vocotape into the transmitter. *But we have to get the message out and clear speech is the only way.*

There came the click-click-click as the message was compressed and multiplied for its laser jump across the solar system.

With a chopping motion that carried its own subtle betrayal of self-doubt, Bickel slapped the orange transmitter key. He sank back as the transmit-command sequence took over. The sound of relays snapping closed dominated the ovoid room.

Do something even if it's wrong, Flattery reminded himself. *The rule books don't work out here. And now it's too late to stop Bickel.*

It came to Flattery then that it had been too late to stop Bickel from the moment their ship left its moon orbit. This direct-authoritarian-violent man (or one of his backups in the hyb tanks) held the key to the *Earthling*'s real purpose. The rest of them were just along for the ride.

At the sound of the relays snapping, Timberlake reached up to a handgrip, squeezed it fiercely in frustration. He knew he could not blame Bickel for feeling angry. The dirty job of killing their last Organic Mental Core should have fallen to the life-systems engineer. But surely Bickel must know the inhibitions that had been droned into the life-systems specialist.

For just a moment, Timberlake allowed his mind to dwell on the sterile crèche and labs back on the moon—the only home any of the *Earthling*'s occupants had ever known.

"Man's greatest adventure: the jump to the stars!"

They had lived with that awesome concept from their first moments of awareness. Aboard the *Earthling*, they were a hand-picked lot, 3,006 survivors of the toughest weeding-out process the Project directors could devise for their Doppelganger charges. The final six had been the choicest of the choice—the umbilicus crew to monitor the ship until it left the solar system, then tie off the few manual controls and turn the 200-year crossing to Tau Ceti over to that one lonely consciousness, an Organic Mental Core.

And while the 3,006 lay dormant behind the hyb tanks' water shields in the heart of the ship, their lives were to remain subject to the servos and sensors surgically linked to the OMC.

But now we're 3,003, Timberlake thought with that sense of grief, of shame and defeat. *And our last OMC is dead.*

Timberlake felt alone and vulnerable now, faced by their emergency controls. He had been reasonably confident while the brains existed and with one of them responsible for ultimate ship security. The existence of emergency controls had only added to his confidence ... then.

Now, staring at the banks of switches, the gauges and telltales and manuals, the auxiliary computer board with its paired vocoder and tape-code inputs and readouts—now, Timberlake realized how inadequate were his poor human reactions in the face of the millisecond demands for even ordinary emergencies out here.

The ship's moving too fast, he thought.

Their speed was slow, he knew, compared to what they should have been doing at this point . . . but still it was too fast. He activated a small sensor screen on his left, permitted himself a brief look at the exterior cosmos, staring out at the hard spots of brilliance that were stars against the energy void of space.

As usual, the sight reduced him to the feeling that he was a tiny spark at the mercy of unthinking chance. He blanked the screen.

Movement at his elbow drew Timberlake's attention. He turned to see Bickel come up to lean against a guidepole beside the control console. There was such a look of relief on his face that Timberlake had a sudden insight, realizing that Bickel had sent his guilt winging back to Moonbase with that message. Timberlake wondered then what it had felt like to kill—even if the killing had involved a creature whose humanity had become hidden behind an aura of mechanics long years back when it was removed from a dying body.

Bickel studied the drive board. They had disabled the drive-increment system when the second OMC had started going sour. But the *Earthling* still would be out of the solar system in ten months.

Ten months, Bickel thought. *Too fast and too slow*.

During those ten months, the computed possibility of a total ship emergency remained at its highest. The umbilicus crew had not been prepared for that kind of pressure.

Bickel shot a covert glance at Flattery, noting how silent and withdrawn the psychiatrist-chaplain appeared. There were times when it rasped Bickel's nerves to think how little could be hidden from Flattery, but this was not one of those times. Out here, Bickel realized, each of them had to become a specialist on his companions. Otherwise, ship pressures coupled to psychological pressures might destroy them.

"How long do you suppose it'll take Moonbase to answer?" Bickel asked, directing the question at Timberlake.

Flattery stiffened, studied the back of Bickel's head. The question . . . such a nice balance of camaraderie and apology in the voice . . . Bickel had done that deliberately, Flattery realized. Bickel went deeper than they had suspected, but perhaps they should have suspected. He was, after all, the *Earthling*'s pivotal figure.

"It'll take 'em a while to digest it," Timberlake said. "I still think we should've waited."

Wrong tack, Flattery thought. *An overture should be accepted.* He brushed a finger along one of his heavy eyebrows, moved forward with a calculated clumsiness, forcing them to be aware of him.

"Their first problem's public relations," Flattery said. "That'll cause some delay."

"Their first question'll be, why'd the OMCs fail?" Timberlake said.

"There was no medical reason for it," Flattery put in. He realized he had spoken too quickly, sensed his own defensiveness.

"It'll turn out to be something new, something nobody anticipated, wait and see," Timberlake said.

Something nobody anticipated? Bickel wondered. And he doubted that, but held his silence. For the first time since coming aboard, he felt the bulk of the *Earthling* around him and thought of all the hopes and energies that had launched this venture. It occurred to him then what a mountain of hard-headed planning had gone into the project.

He sensed the sleepless nights, the skull sessions of engineers and scientists, the pragmatic dreamers tossing their ideas back and forth across coffee cups and butt-mounded ashtrays.

Something nobody anticipated? Hardly.

Still, six other ships had vanished into silence out here—six other ships much like their *Earthling*.

He spoke then more to keep up his own courage than to argue: "This isn't the kind of thing they'd let go by the board. Moonbase'll have a plan. Somebody, somewhere along the line, thought of this possibility."

"Then why didn't they prepare us for it?" Timberlake asked.

Flattery watched Bickel carefully, aware of how that question had touched him. *He will begin to have doubts now,* Flattery thought. *Now, he will start asking himself the really loaded questions.*

CHAPTER 2

The holoscan you are watching at this moment
is of our Bickel model, our most successful
"Organ of Analysis." He is charged to explore
beyond the imprinted patterns of consciousness which humankind inherits with its genes.

—Morgan Hempstead
Lectures at Moonbase

TIMBERLAKE ADJUSTED a dial on his console to correct a
failure of automatic temperature adjustment in quad
three ring nine of the ship's second shell. "We should've
been buttoned down in our hyb tanks and on our way
over the solar hump to Tau Ceti long ago," he muttered.

"Tim, display the time log," Flattery said.

Timberlake hit the green key in the upper right corner
of his board, glanced at the overhead master screen's
display from the laser-pulse time log.

Ten months—plus.

The indefinite answer made it seem the *Earthling*'s
computer core shared their doubts.

"How long to Tau Ceti?" Flattery asked.

"At this rate?" Timberlake asked. He risked a long
glance away from his board. The stare he aimed at

11

Flattery betrayed the fact he had not thought of *that* possibility, making the trip the hard way—long and slow with a crew active all the way.

"Say four hundred years, give or take a few," Bickel said. "It's the first question I fed into the computer after we disabled the drive increment."

He is too crystal sharp, Flattery thought. *He bears watching lest he shatter.* And Flattery chided himself then: *But the job Bickel has to do requires a man who can shatter.*

"First thing we'd better do is bring up one replacement from the hyb tanks," Bickel said.

Flattery glanced to his left where Com-central's other three action couches lay with their cocoon arms open, empty and waiting.

"Bring up only one replacement, eh?" Flattery asked. "Live in here?"

"We may need occasional sleep-rest periods in the cubby lockers," Bickel said and he nodded toward the side hatch into their spartan living quarters. "But Com-central is the safest spot on the ship."

"What if Project orders us to abort?" Timberlake asked.

"That won't be their first order," Bickel said. "Seven nations invested one hell of a pile of money and effort and dreams in this business. They have a purpose which they won't give up easily."

Too crystal sharp, Flattery thought. And he asked: "Who're you nominating for dehyb?"

"Prudence Weygand, M.D.," Bickel said.

"You think we need another doctor, eh?" Flattery asked.

"I think we need Prudence Weygand. She's a doctor, sure, but she can also function as a nurse to re-place . . . Maida. She's a woman and we may need female thinking. You have any objections to Weygand, Tim?"

"What's my opinion worth?" Timberlake muttered. "You two've decided it, haven't you?"

Bickel already had turned toward his own action couch. He hesitated at the petulance in Timberlake's voice, then went on to the couch, pulled the full-vacuum suit from the rack beneath the couch, and began suiting up. He spoke without turning: "I'll take over here while you and Raj bring her out of hyb. You'd both better suit up, too, and stay suited. Without an OMC at the controls—" He shrugged, finished sealing the suit, and stretched out in his action couch. "I'll take the red switch on the count."

Timberlake was caught up then in the changeover. The master board swung across on its travelers, stopped as it made junction with Bickel's console.

"What if Moonbase answers while we're in the tanks?" Flattery asked. "We won't be able to stop the dehyb and come up for a—"

"What's to do except record the message?" Bickel asked.

He began adjusting hull-integrity sensors, finished that, checked the Accept-And-Translate system, swung the AAT board close beside him where he could see its telltale when Moonbase replied.

Flattery shrugged, got out his own full-vacuum suit. He noted that Timberlake already was suiting up—but with a fumbling reluctance.

Tim senses Bickel taking absolute command, Flattery thought, *but he doesn't know the necessity for it . . . and he cannot bring himself to like it. He will, though.*

Bickel satisfied himself the ship was functioning as well as it could without the homeostatic control of an OMC. He sank back to watch the board as the others left Com-central. The hatch seals hissed and there came the metallic slap of the magnetic locks as the hatch closed and resealed itself.

Now, Bickel felt the ship around him as though he had neural connections to every sensor revealed on his board. The *Earthling* lay spread out for him—a monstrous juggernaut . . . yet fragile as an egg—a tin egg.

Against his will, Bickel's attention drifted toward that dead light on the lower left corner of his board—the light that should have been glowing a live yellow to denote that all was well with the OMC.

But all was not well with the OMC; the unsleeping *brains* had failed.

They were stress-tested for every conceivable situation, Bickel told himself. *Something inconceivable happened. Or did it?*

Timberlake's question nagged at him. *"Why didn't they prepare us for it?"*

The master board above him grew a line of yellow lights that told him the ship's gravity center had shifted. A wild shift in the gravity field had torn colony cargo from its holddowns and killed Maida. Gently, to avoid oscillations, Bickel began adjusting controls to bring the field back into line.

How much simpler it would have been to get along without gravity, he thought. But medical science had never really solved the problem of the human physical deterioration that resulted from existence in prolonged null-gravity. The balance mechanism of the inner ear still was the most susceptible. Four to five weeks without gravity brought permanent damage for some subjects. So they lived with the minimal field system—the gravity-field mechanism that had developed an unexpected deadly bug out here.

The telltale lights began to wink out.

Bickel followed the balance readjustment carefully. They had only the most tenuous theory on what caused that field to shift this way. They suspected local anomalies as they moved through the solar system's own gravitational field.

The last telltale went dark.

Bickel sank back onto the couch, drew a deep, ragged breath. Perspiration covered his body and he felt his suit system laboring to compensate.

This watch on Com-central could become a particular kind of hell, Bickel realized. The suspenseful responsibility, duel with an unknown death, wore you down. You controlled only the most essential ship functions from here. Monitor instruments had never been intended for this work. Fine adjustments and delicate repairs had to be ignored until they reached that point of gross demand where a crewman had to be sent out to direct the servos in their work.

An increment of damage could be computed—the kind of damage, one thing added to another, where the ship itself would cease operating. There was a death point for the ship out ahead of them and it could be computed as a function of damage.

Bickel avoided feeding the problem into the computer. He knew his own limits. Precise knowledge of that unknown moment would hamper him unless it became a matter of immediacy. They had months yet—perhaps the full ten. And ten months was forever, the way things now stood. The ship was far more likely to meet disaster in some other form; he could feel it.

Something about the Tin Egg was sour—Big Sour. It did not make sense to Bickel that a man had to sit here in Com-central, the strain of responsibility increasing with each heartbeat, waiting and knowing some mechanism or balancing function of the ship was headed for trouble—yet unable to meet the problem with more than a gross, clumsy makeshift.

With the OMCs, this ship balance had been a finely tuned neuro-servo reflex, almost automatic—as homeo-static in response as that of a healthy human body.

Bickel added his own corollary question now to the one Timberlake had posed: *Why were all the eggs put in one basket?*

CHAPTER 3

What matters most is the search itself. This is more important than the searchers. Consciousness must dream, it must have a dreaming ground—and, dreaming, must invoke ever-new dreams.

—Morgan Hempstead
Lectures at Moonbase

As SHE AWOKE, Prudence thought: *We made it!*

Excitement filled her at the thought of stepping out onto a virgin world with all its strange newness and never-before problems. Six failures were worth it. The seventh try was a charm. We have succeeded. Otherwise . . . otherwise . . .

Her mind bogged down in sluggishness. *Otherwise* was a concept with several pathways out of it.

The tingle-ache of dehyb ran along the muscles of her arms and legs, produced transient knots of pain. She knew as a doctor the reasons for the pain, could rationalize the fact of it: human *hybernation* was a far different process from animal hibernation. Not a drop of water could remain in the body—and you went so close to the borders of death that some contended you were suspended *within* death.

She tried to sit up.

It was then she saw Timberlake and Flattery looking down at her where she lay on the lab shuttle. Their expressions brought *otherwise* to full focus. For a moment, she looked beyond them to the tubes and stimulant plugs that had been removed from functional contact with her body.

Flattery restrained her. "Easy now, Dr. Weygand," he said.

Dr. Weygand, she thought. *Not Prudence. Not Prue. Dr. Weygand. Cold formality.*

She began losing that first elation.

Then Flattery began explaining in his soft, soothing voice and she knew her elation had to be put away. The contingency problem had arisen. She had been awakened for that.

"Just tell me who we lost," she said, and her throat hurt from its months of disuse.

Timberlake told her.

"Three dead?" she said. She didn't ask how they had died. The other problem, the contingency for which she had been prepared, took precedence over mere curiosity.

"Bickel requested you be brought out of hyb," Flattery said.

"Does he know why?" she asked, ignoring the strange look Timberlake shifted from her to Flattery.

"He rationalized it," Flattery said, and he wished she'd withheld these questions until they were alone.

"Of course he did," she said. "But has—"

"He hasn't posed the problem yet," Flattery said.

"Don't push him," she said, and glanced at Timberlake. "Forget what you just heard here, Tim."

Timberlake scowled, suddenly withdrawn and wary.

Flattery bent over her right arm with a slapshot hypo in his hand.

"Must you?" she asked. Then: "Yes, of course."

"There's nothing for you to do right now except recuperate," he said, and pressed the slapshot against her arm.

She felt the mechanism's kick and, presently, the soft

spread of narcosis. Flattery and Timberlake became wavering figures haloed in light.

At least Bickel is still alive, she thought. *We do not have to replace him with a backup—take second best.*

And just before sinking into the downy cloud of sleep, she wondered: *How did Maida die? Lovely Maida who . . .*

Timberlake watched the film of withdrawal wash over her light blue eyes. Her breathing took on soft regularity.

As life-systems specialist, Timberlake had checked the computer-filed tape flag for every person on the Tin Egg. He recalled now that Prudence Lon Weygand was classed superb as a surgeon—"Superior 9 in tool facility." And the scale went only to 10. He reflected now on her strange conversation with Flattery and realized the tape had not told the full story. She obviously had ship functions beyond surgeon-ecologist . . . and at least one of these functions concerned Bickel.

"Forget what you just heard here, Tim."

Timberlake could still hear that cold-voiced command and he knew it did not square with the emotional index on Prudence Lon Weygand's tapes. There, she was listed as "Place nine-d green" on the compassionate vector. In the close-quarters living of this umbilicus crew, that emotional index posed problems because of its tightly linked sex drive. With a sense of shock, Timberlake took a closer look at her feed-tube spectrum on the hyb chart, saw that she had been fed the sex-suppressant anti-S drugs even under hyb. She had been kept ready.

Ready for what? he asked himself.

Flattery closed and locked her litter cocoon, said: "She'll sleep until she's almost back to normal. We'd better get her a full-vac suit out of stores. She'll need it when she comes out."

Timberlake nodded, made a last check on the few remaining life-systems linkages into her litter. Flattery was acting very odd—mysterious.

"You can ignore all that conversation as she woke up," Flattery said. "Common dehyb confusion. You know how it is."

But she was fed anti-S drugs in hybernation, Timberlake thought.

Flattery nodded toward the hatch into Com-central, said: "John's been almost four hours alone on the board. Time he got some relief."

Timberlake finished his inspection of the litter gauges, turned, led the way through the hatch.

Seeing the wary, thoughtful look on Timberlake's face, Flattery thought: *Damn that woman's big mouth. If Tim says the wrong thing to Bickel now it could muddy the whole project.*

CHAPTER 4

The legal status of the clone as property
cannot be questioned. This is a decision we
have taken as a species for the survival of the
species. The clone is a spare-parts bank and
much more. The clone falls outside the legal
prohibition against experiments upon humans
without their informed consent. Clones are
property and that's that.

—Morgan Hempstead
Lectures at Moonbase

BICKEL HEARD Flattery and Timberlake enter Com-
central, but was forced to keep his attention on the big
board. An odd timed pulse had appeared in the primary
loops of the navigational analogue banks of the
computer. It appeared and vanished with no apparent
cause. Each oddity of computer function forced a review
of that basic question: *Why had the OMCs failed?*

Was this strange pulse a thing for which the brains
were unprepared? How could it be when every last OMC
circuit tested open-and-operating?

The answer to the OMC failure lay in the psychological
area, Bickel felt. The seat of the problem was in that one

place where they could not stick their probes—in the gray matter that once had been part of a human.

Well, I know how we have to tackle this mess, Bickel thought. *But will the others go along?*

Bickel heard Flattery slide onto his own action couch, risked a glance at the man. Flattery might be difficult to handle. Flattery was an M.D. and ship-trained, yes. He could stand a watch, repair the simpler servos and sensors, and obey the ordinary precautions that spelled out life-systems security. There was another Flattery, though: the psychiatrist-chaplain. To Bickel, the psychiatrist half of the man suggested special usefulness, but the enigma of the chaplain offered only mysticism and open-end arguments.

I never know which mask Flattery's wearing, Bickel thought. He wished then there could have been a way to avoid having a chaplain on the Tin Egg. But there had been no way; the world's religious millions paid an enormous amount of taxes. The psychiatrists, in training Flattery and his backups, had approached the job sincerely. They had had little choice. It had been a long time since psychiatrists denied they served a witch-doctor function . . . and the step from witch doctor to divine was a short one.

Timberlake came up beside Bickel, studied the gauge which showed the timed pulse in the navigational analogue banks.

"That acts like a Doppler reference pulse from the time log," he said. "You been checking our position?"

"No," Bickel said, and as he spoke, the answer to this variant pulse clicked home in his mind. He *had* set up a telltale warning net in the computer to alert him when ship damage reached a critical point. Damage to the navigational system could be most critical—especially internal damage. But unlike destruction of hardware, that internal damage would only betray itself by position errors. His telltale circuitry had alerted one of the ship computer's master programs. A running Doppler reference check was being made on their position.

Bickel shifted to the computer board, ran a series trial

on the navigational loops, read the induced resonance off the pulsing gauges. It checked.

He explained what was happening.

"The computer acts...almost...human," Flattery said.

Bickel and Timberlake exchanged a knowing smile. *Almost human, indeed!* The damn thing merely was doing what it was designed to do.

"We'd better take the computer schematics and the design specs and have a real skull session on what the lack of an OMC may be doing to it," Timberlake said.

Bickel nodded. He was thankful then that Timberlake was, in many respects, as good an electronics man as anyone on the ship—the necessary foundation for his specialty. There was always that *almost* qualification on his abilities, though. Life-systems work trapped men into a "generalist" corner. They knew plenty of biophysics, but they were not doctors. They were adept in electronics, but fell short of that smooth juggling of variables which marked the creative engineer.

"You ready for a break, John?" Flattery asked.

"Anytime. How's Prue?"

"*Doctor* Weygand is asleep now," Flattery said. "She needs a few more hours' recuperation."

Why is he so formal? Bickel wondered. *Raj must know I shared classes with her. She was always Prue then. Why should she suddenly be Doctor Weygand?*

"I'll take the board on the count," Flattery said, and they began the change of watch.

Timberlake, sensing Bickel's questions, realized that Flattery's emphasis on *Doctor* Weygand had not been aimed at the electronics engineer.

Raj was saying something to me, Timberlake thought. *He was telling me that Doctor Weygand may have had medical reasons for her strange behavior. Raj is telling me to keep my mouth shut.*

And Timberlake found himself resenting the fact that Flattery had found the warning necessary.

Bickel closed off his link to the controls, slipped off his couch, and began exercising the stiffness out of his muscles. Remembering the classes he had shared with Prue Weygand—computer math, servo-sensor repair, ship function—he recalled the woman. She was a disturbing female-plus creature, sensitive and with her feelings all too apparent. Bickel realized then that a photograph of Prue Weygand in repose would show a rather unassuming woman with regular features and a good, but not sensational figure. She was the kind who attracted male stares, though. She radiated some vital, sparking thing—especially when she walked.

Is that why I chose her? Bickel wondered. He broke off his exercises to consider the question. The Prue kind of woman presented a source of trouble in an otherwise all-male crew—unless they all went on anti-S. But they couldn't afford to dull their faculties that way.

I chose her because, in a ship of quintuple backup, she appears unique, Bickel reassured himself. *She is trained in ecology, medicine, and computer math. She is going to be damned useful to us.*

But doubts remained.

Bickel forced them out of his mind by looking around Com-central, focusing his attention on the ship. The ship-cum-computer-cum-hybernating-colonists—here was one set of resources that Bickel felt they could fit into a logical pigeonhole, assess and weigh and use as they needed.

He sensed the ship stretching out from him in its sixteen concentric shells, a great ovoid bulk almost a mile across its long axis. Beyond the water barrier and baffles that shielded the core lay miles of corridors and tubeways, self-sealing compartments. Through it all stretched the organized clutter of materiel needed to make life possible for humans in an alien environment.

In the hyb tanks they had two thousand adult humans, a thousand human embryos, and more than six thousand animal embryos—a "full ecological spectrum."

Bickel turned, looked at his own computer board. His plan involved dangerous risk to the computer, but the risk was necessary. The others might fight him, but they would have to come around.

He looked at Flattery busy on the big board, Timberlake taking a relaxing massage on his action couch. He looked back at the computer board. The Tin Egg's computer was basically a multisystem system with internal ruby laser "real time" clocks to log its own "experiences." It incorporated more than 800,000 specialized routines (installed by a prodigious spending of manpower). Bickel weighed the computer's untried potential: its trinanosecond thoughtput and multischeduling facilities allowed it to interleave thousands of programs simultaneously. It could monitor sequencing, cuing, and input through a core memory with enormous reserves of trapping functions, branching operations, and alarm systems networks.

With an OMC tied in as supervisory program—as supreme decision-maker—the computer and the ship it controlled had been a living creature of metal. But three *brains* had failed in that delicately powerful linkage. And Bickel-the-pragmatist trusted only that which worked. Without an OMC, the ship computer remained an inert mass of machinery whose output-on-demand followed a fixed design and could be accepted or rejected only after a human decision.

"How long until Prue will be with us?" Bickel asked.

"About three hours," Timberlake said.

"I want her opinion on the postmortem," Bickel said. "I'm not satisfied with what we found in the first two brains."

Timberlake shut down his couch massage, directed a probing stare at Flattery.

The psychiatrist-chaplain only smiled, reminding himself that Bickel was logic-prone with a disregard of everything except the main line of reasoning that made him sound boorish at times.

"Moonbase'll ask some questions for which we have no answers," Bickel said. "We can't afford to sound fumbling." He looked at Timberlake. "They're going to take us apart, one by one—life systems to..."

"Life systems were perfect!" Timberlake snapped.

"We'd better be able to prove it," Bickel said.

"I went through the entire console when Brain One failed," Timberlake said. "Check it yourself."

"I did. A couple of things bothered me. Brain One preferred to be called Myrtle. Why? I find nothing in the memory core to explain that—except that *Brain One* was removed from a genetic monster that probably was female."

"Myrtle's personal life system tested within .0002 of homeostatic center on the Anders Base," Timberlake said.

"Don't let that identity preference seduce you," Flattery said. "It was for our benefit—so we could anthropomorphize the ship-OMC."

"Yeah," Bickel said. "That's the reason they each gave, but is it the right one?"

"Those *brains* were as perfect as any ever born," Flattery said, and he wondered why he allowed Bickel's attitude to irritate him. "Okay, they were raised from infancy as part of the total ship-sensor-servo system. So what? They didn't know any other life or want—"

"You said a couple of things were bothering you," Timberlake interrupted. "What's the other one?"

"Your life-systems report," Bickel said, "entry 9107 on Myrtle. It says: 'None of the systems appear then to have been at fault.' Why'd you use that word *appear*, Tim? You have some doubts you couldn't enter in the report?"

"Not a damn one!" Timberlake said. "Those systems were perfect!"

"Then why didn't you just say so?"

"He was only being cautious," Flattery said. "If you have checked the records, you'll find my medical report confirms his findings in every respect."

"Except one," Bickel said.

"And *what* is that?" Timberlake asked. He glared at Bickel, his face flushed. A muscle worked along his jaw.

Bickel ignored the signs of anger, said: "Nothing explains the internal burn damage that Raj found in those brains. 'Internal burn damage,' you say, 'especially along the overlarge axon collaterals of the afferent side.' What the devil do you mean *overlarge*? Overlarge compared to what?"

"A main channel leading into the brain's higher centers was about four times the size of anything I had ever seen," Flattery said. "I don't know why, but I can guess it was compensatory growth. These OMCs had to handle many more incoming data bits from more sensors than the normal human ever encounters. You'll note that the frontal lobes were larger, too, but the..."

"The design specs on the OMC process explain all that," Bickel said. "Compensatory growth, yeah, but I don't find one word about large axon collaterals. Not one word."

"These *brains* had been in the system longer than any others ever examined," Timberlake said. "The literature reports only on four previously that died of natural causes and we—"

"*Natural* causes?" Bickel asked. "What's a natural cause fatal to an OMC?"

"You know what happened as well as I do," Flattery said. "Accidents—irritant matter in the food bath, a radiation shield left down for—"

"Human error, not OMC error!" Bickel snapped. "Not *natural*. And here is another thing: Myrtle lapsed into catatonia or whatever you want to call it just ten days, fourteen hours, eight minutes, and eleven seconds from Moonbase. We threw Little Joe into service and he lasted six days, nine hours, one second. So we turned the ship over to Harvey—our last chance—and Harvey took fifteen hours even. Kaput!"

"Greater and greater stress and they broke down faster and faster," Flattery said. "But you'll notice that the last words from each betrayed a type of deterioration akin to schizo—"

"Akin!" Bickel sneered. "That's what you see all through these damn reports: 'Something similar to...' 'A condition that reminds one of...' 'Akin to...'" He glared from Flattery to Timberlake. "The truth is we don't know what the hell goes on in an OMC's gray matter."

A clicking-buzzing erupted from the master board above Flattery.

Bickel waited while Flattery fought out a manual temperature adjustment in an inner hold. Presently, Flattery wiped perspiration from his forehead, studied his gauges to be certain the balance was holding.

"Man, that board is murder," Timberlake muttered. "I don't wonder those OMCs caved in."

Flattery risked a glance away from the board. "You know better than that, Tim. This part of the job was child's play for a functioning OMC. They could handle most ship homeostasis problems by something akin to reflex action."

"Akin," Bickel said.

"All right!" Flattery barked, and pretended to be busy with the board to hide his confusion at allowing Bickel to get to him that way.

A long silence settled over Com-central, broken when Flattery regained his composure and said, "I was about to say that the end tapes on each brain show statements similar to schizophrenic writing. It makes a pretense of meaning...and sometimes stumbles onto a colorful phrase, but the essential..."

He broke off as the master board grew three diagonal stripes of flashing yellow. Flattery's hands darted to the controls as Bickel shouted, "Grav shift!" and dove for his couch.

Cocoons snapped closed around them and they felt the creeping, jerking weight shifts, the runaway fluctuation of the field-centering system—the unexplained gravity variance that had killed Maida.

CHAPTER 5

The thing about computers—it's like training a dog. You have to be smarter than the dog. If you make a computer smarter than you are, that has to be accident, synergy, or divine intervention.

—Interview with
John Bickel (original)
at La /Paz

BICKEL WATCHED FLATTERY's hands fight the gravity system back into balance. It had taken several bruising minutes, but the tugging and jerking had begun to ease. The system centered slowly. Flattery waited it out. Presently, he made a fine adjustment in the controls.

"Where were we?" Timberlake asked.

"We were raking through our data, seeking anything useful," Bickel said. "It's a clumsy way to operate, but necessary."

"Guilt-sharing," Flattery said.

"What?" Bickel was outraged.

"Never mind," Flattery said. "Back to square one: You will recall that OMC/Myrtle said: 'I have no incarnation.' That may have been the only accurate thing in her jabbering. After all, except for gray matter, she had no flesh. But then, remember, after a long silence she said: 'I'm counting my fingers.' She had no fingers, no conscious memory of fingers. And that final question: 'Why are you all so dead?' The best guess is that any meaning in these statements and questions was purely accidental."

"I think she was referring to us, to the crew," Bickel said. "It's nuts, yes, but it was a direct question over the vocoders and we were the only possible audience."

"Unless she was referring to the colonists in the hyb tanks," Flattery said. "They might appear dead under some—"

"Myrtle had direct contact with the hyb-tank sensors," Timberlake pointed out. "She'd have known if they were alive."

Bickel nodded. "What do you make of Little Joe roaring out over every vocoder in the ship: 'I'm awake! God help me, I'm awake!'"

"A cry for help, perhaps," Flattery said. "Most insane raving is a cry for help in one form or another."

"That leaves Harvey," Bickel said. "Harvey screamed: 'You're forcing me to be unhealthy.' And when we—"

"What could we do?" Timberlake asked, and Bickel heard the note of hysteria in his voice. "There was nothing wrong with any of their life systems. I know there wasn't!"

"Easy does it, Tim," Flattery said. "That was just another nonsense statement."

"We all knew what it meant, though," Bickel said. "I did not see anybody showing surprise when Harvey said: 'I've lost it!' and signed off . . . permanently. And there we were with three dead *brains* and no spares."

The callous way Bickel put it sent a shudder through Timberlake, and he could not explain it. He had never been deeply attached to the OMCs. There had always been something faintly accusing about the "ship creatures." Raja Lon Flattery had assured him this was strictly subjective, something from his own attitudes. Raj had always been so positive that the OMC-ship-computer entities were perfectly reconciled to their way of life, happy with their own compensations.

What compensations? Timberlake wondered. *Expectancy of long life? But what is three or four thousand years of living if each year is hell?*

Timberlake realized then that none of the pat answers from his training classes really touched the basic issue of OMC happiness.

What if it really is a hellish way to live? he wondered. *It must be. They are harnessed like engines to all this metal and glass and plastic and time stretches out ahead of them...forever. Maybe death was preferable.*

CHAPTER 6

Every symbol has hidden premises behind it.
Every word carries unspoken assumptions
buried in the history of the language and the
conditioning experiences of the speakers. If
you snatch those buried meanings out of your
words, you spill a whole stream of new
understanding into your awareness.

—Raja Lon Flattery
The Book of Ship

ALMOST HALF OF Prudence Weygand's recuperation time
had passed and it had been marked by recurrent
uncomfortable silences in Com-central.

Flattery did not like those silences. He felt that every
one of them carried his companions farther away—
perhaps beyond control. And he had to maintain that
delicate contact, that means of control.

One of those silences gripped them now. It seemed to
reach into them from the space beyond the ship's hull.
Flattery knew he had to say something but he felt
oppressed by the silence. He cleared his throat before
speaking.

"I wish to say something about anger. I've seen several

shows of anger since our emergency—my own anger included."

The formal tone, the set of his face—all signaled that Flattery was speaking officially as their chaplain. "Anger could destroy us," he said. "The Proverbs warn us: 'He that is soon angry dealeth foolishly: and a man of wicked devices is hated. He that is slow to wrath is of great understanding: but he that is hasty of spirit exalteth folly.' Let us practice the soft answer and not stir up wrath."

Bickel took a deep breath. Flattery was right, he knew, but Bickel resented the way the man retreated into religion to make his point. How much simpler just to say they were clouding their reason with excess emotion. That was the thing he resented about religion, Bickel thought— the way it appealed to emotion rather than intelligence.

"We've been floundering around, trying to do too much," Bickel said. "That master board is a jury-rigged monstrosity. We need a consistent, organized plan to meet our problems. When Moonbase answers, I want to be able to say we have—"

Sharp, heavy G force pressed him against the side of his couch cocoon. It struck without klaxon warning or alarm light. Cocoon safety locks sealed home. Now, red alarm lights flashed with the yellow in long webs across the master board.

Flattery slammed the gravity disconnect with the heel of his left hand. G force ebbed. Yellow alarm lights winked off as their pressure switches released. A line of red alarm lights remained.

"Damage to hull three, section six/fourteen," Flattery said. He began activating remote sensors to inspect the area.

Without conscious thought or discussion, Bickel took over ship command: "Tim, take the G repeaters. Leave gravity disconnected while you trace the relays and get the system back in balance."

Timberlake pulled his board close to obey.

Bickel swung the AAT board to his side, keyed for ship systems/computer control, began feeding coded demands into the core recorders. What had the ship encountered that might explain that brutal deflection? What had the automatic sensors recorded?

The responders began kicking out tape almost immediately—much too fast.

"Data error," Flattery said, reading the output over Bickel's shoulder.

In abrupt fury, Bickel pulled the master override stop from his core switch, jammed a set of jumper jacks across the AAT controls, opened the core system for standard reference comparison.

"You are into the core!" Flattery said, his voice sharp with fear. "You have no guide fuse or master reference. You could louse up the command routines."

"Unhook that!" Timberlake shouted, lifting his head from the cocoon clamps to glare across at Bickel.

"Shut up, both of you. Sure, the core is delicate, but something in there is already loused up—bad enough to kill us."

"You think you have time to check some eight hundred thousand routines?" Timberlake demanded. "Don't talk nuts!"

"There are specific injunctions against what you are doing," Flattery said, fighting to keep his voice reasonable. "And you know why."

"Don't try to tell me my job," Bickel said.

While he spoke, Bickel rolled over core memory responders, direct contact, doing it gently to avoid current backlash.

"You make one mistake," Timberlake said, "and it would take six or seven thousand technicians with a second master system and several thousand imprint relays to repair the damage. Are you ready to—"

"Stop distracting me!"

"What are you looking for?" Flattery asked, interested in spite of his fear. He had realized that Bickel, conditioned to deep inhibitions against turning back, was incapable of doing anything to deprive them of one of their basic tools.

"I'm checking availability of peripherals from the core memory," Bickel said. "There's got to be a bypass or pileup somewhere. It'll show in the acquisition and phase-control loops of the input." He nodded toward a diagnostic meter on his board. "And here we are!" The meter's needle slammed against its pin, fell back to zero, stayed there.

Slowly, Bickel ordered a master diagnostic routine into direct contact, put the core standard back on fused auxiliary, began rolling the troublesome core-memory section. Working with only occasional references to the core standard, he forced the routine through the data-reference channels as modified by new sensor input.

Error branchings began clicking from his responders. Bickel translated aloud as the code figures appeared on the screen above his board.

"Core memory/prediction region rendered inactive. Proton mass and scatter relative to ship course/mass/speed did not agree with prediction."

Aside, Bickel said, "We're hitting something other than hydrogen and hitting it in unexpected concentrations—partly because of our speed/mass figure."

"Solar winds," Timberlake whispered. "They said we—"

"Solar winds, hell!" Bickel said. "Look at that." He nodded at a code grouping as it worked its way across the screen.

"Twenty-six protons in the mass," Timberlake said.

"Iron," Bickel said. "Free atoms of iron out here. We're getting a plain old-fashioned magnetic deflection of the grav field."

"We'll have to slow the ship," Timberlake said.

"Nuts!" Bickel was emphatic. "We'll put a fused overload breaker in the G system. I don't see why the devil the designers didn't do that in the first place."

"Perhaps they couldn't conceive of any force large enough to deflect the system," Flattery said.

"No doubt," Bickel's voice was heavy with disgust. "But when I think a simple cage switch with a weight in it could have prevented Maida's death..."

"They depended on the OMC's reflexes, too," Flattery said. "You know that."

"What I know is they thought in straight lines when they should've been thinking in the round," Bickel said.

He unlocked his safety cocoon, shifted his suit to portable, launched himself diagonally across Comcentral to the Tool & Repair hatch. The weightless drifting reminded him they had a time limit on returning to gravity conditions. Too long without gravity and the crew would suffer permanent physical damage.

CHAPTER 7

I considered the being whom I had cast among
mankind and endowed with the will and power
to effect purposes of horror ... A being whom I
myself had formed, and endued with life, had
met me at midnight among the precipices of an
inaccessible mountain.

—Mary Shelley's
Frankenstein

BICKEL GRABBED A hatch handle to steady himself and
swung out the repair traveler. He opened a panel to get at
the gravity system, identified the cables, and bent to his
work. He went about it silently, angrily, with swift,
decisive movements, and all the time he thought about
their dilemma.

Iron. Free ions of iron out here?

Possible, but was there a simpler answer to the
anomaly, something that would produce an illusory
report on their instruments?

Was it possible that some part of the ship's compu-
ter/reporting system had been concealed from them,
shielded away from their prying? He knew it not only was
possible but probable. Why would Moonbase do that?

The complete answer escaped him, but he knew he would have to continue probing for it.

Presently, he had an improvised cage switch clamped into the main power cable into the gravity generator. He made the connections to the breaker, tested the circuits with a false load, replaced the cover plate.

"It'll have to be reset manually each time," he said. He put a foot against the bulkhead, propelled himself back to his couch, locked in, glanced at Timberlake. "System balanced?"

"Near as you can tell from here," Timberlake said. "Give it a try, Raj."

Flattery checked to see that both Timberlake and Bickel were sealed in their cocoons, closed the gravity switch. The sound of the generators building up grew to a faint hiss that subsided as the system stabilized. Flattery felt the pressure against his shoulder blades, reached up to the board, slowly refined Timberlake's settings.

"Tim," Bickel said, "I want the schematics for the OMC chamber—every sensor tie coded for function—and laid out in layers from gross to fine. I'll need the same thing for servo control, a complete—"

"Why?" Timberlake asked.

"Are you thinking of tying in a colonist's brain?" Flattery demanded, trying to hide his feelings of outrage at the idea.

"A mature human brain probably wouldn't survive such a transfer," Timberlake said. And he felt shame at how much the thought had appealed to him. Every inhibition of his training cried out against such a move. But if the OMC system were restored, none of them here ever again would have to undergo the nerve-crushing responsibility of that Com-central master board. He looked up at the live green arrow denoting that Flattery had the controls, felt himself go clammy with fear at the thought of that arrow swinging back to his position.

"What the hell!" Bickel snapped. "Where'd you two get that idea? Not from anything I said." He lifted his head from the cocoon clamps, looked from Timberlake to Flattery. "We don't know what happened to our three *perfect* brains. Why the devil'd I want to tie in an untested one?" He sank back. "It's impossible anyway. A man should have some say in what's done to him. How could we poll everyone in the hyb tanks? We can't wake them all."

"You thinking of dismantling the OMC controls and converting us to a closed ecological system?" Flattery asked. "If you are, you should—"

He broke off as the high-pitched hummm-buzzz-hummmm of the AAT receiver filled the room, alerting them that a message was being processed.

Bickel followed the play of lights across his board as the message was gulped by the receivers, fed through the comparison blocks, refined to a single playback (with probable accuracy quotient logged beside each character), and finally was slowed to make it intelligible for human ears.

Sure as hell took 'em long enough, Bickel thought. He read the time log, subtracted the distance lag. *Almost seven hours*. He thought then of the first ships using single-channel radio, punching their messages across the solar system with only a few watts—but the error-uncertainty factor built up with distance and cumulative adverse interference. The Tin Egg's system had been engineered for computer-monitored automatic reports over stellar distances to tell watchers as yet unborn back on Earth how things fared with their star probe.

The message-ready chime sounded. Bickel keyed the vocoder. The voice of Morgan Hempstead, United Moonbase director, rolled out of the speakers, recognizable and still with its iced iron overtones preserved by the AAT's comparators.

"To UMB ship *Earthling* from Project Control. This is Morgan Hempstead. We hope you understand our distress and concern. Every decision from this point must have a prime motive of preserving the lives of yourselves and the colonists."

So much for the record, Flattery thought. *There are seven nations and four races represented in the hyb tanks—but all just as expendable as the ones who went before us.*

"We have several prime questions," Hempstead said.

I've a few questions of my own, Bickel thought.

"Why was Project Control not alerted when the first Organic Mental Core failed?" Hempstead asked.

Bickel mentally logged the question. He knew the answer, but it was nothing he would ever transmit. Hempstead knew it as well as he did. The Tin Egg had momentum as an idea that had survived six failures. Nothing short of another ultimate failure would stop it. Nothing short of desperate emergency could make them risk aborting the mission by calling for help.

"Doppler reference indicates you'll be out of the solar system in approximately three hundred and sixteen days at present stabilized speed," Hempstead said. "Time to Tau Ceti: four hundred-plus years."

As he listened, Bickel pictured the man behind the voice: flintlike face with gray hair and gray-blue eyes—that aura of momentous decision even in his smallest gesture. The psych boys had called him "Big Daddy" behind his back, but they had jumped when he commanded. Now, Bickel focused on the fact that they never again expected to see Hempstead, yet the man still could reach into their midst with his decisions.

"First analysis indicates these possibilities," Hempstead went on. "You could turn back to orbit around UMB until the problem is solved and new Organic Mental Cores installed. That would return us to the old problem of sterile control under less than ideal conditions. It also would remove the ship from the situation of probable cause in the OMC breakdowns, perhaps making solution impossible."

"He always was a long-winded bore," Timberlake said.

"Second possibility," Hempstead said, "would be for you to convert to a closed ecology and continue at present speed, enlisting replacements from your hybernation tanks or breeding and raising your own crew complement. You would, of course, face high probability of genetic damage through the necessity of staying outside your core-shield areas long enough to build quarters for prolonged occupation. However, food would be your major problem unless you adopted a more closely integrated recycling system."

"Closely integrated recycling," Flattery said. "He means cannibalism. It was discussed."

Bickel turned to stare at Flattery. The idea of cannibalism was repellent, but that was not what had caught Bickel's attention. "*It was discussed.*" That simple statement contained volumes of unanswered questions and hidden implications.

"Third possibility," Hempstead was saying, "would be to build the necessary consciousness into your robo-pilot, using the ship computer as a basis. Our computations indicate you have sufficient materials, including neuron packages intended for colony robots in your stores. This is theoretically feasible."

"Theoretically feasible!" Timberlake sneered. "Does he think we've never heard about all the failures in—"

"Shhhh," Flattery hissed.

"Project Council suggests you continue present course and speed," Hempstead said, "as long as you are within the solar system. If a solution has not been reached by then, present opinion is that you will be ordered to turn back." There followed a long silence, then: "... unless you have alternative suggestions."

"*You will be ordered to turn back,*" Flattery thought. He turned to see how those key words sat with Bickel. They were aimed at Bickel, contrived for him, fitted specially to trigger his deepest motives.

Bickel lay in thoughtful silence staring up at the speech microscope display above the vocoder, checking the accuracy of message reception.

"At this time," Hempstead said, "Project Control requires a detailed report on condition of all ship systems with special reference to hybernating colonists. It is recognized that prolonging the voyage increases probability of hybernation failure. We recognize that you must replace crew losses from the tanks. Suggestions on replacements will be made upon request. We share your grief at the unfortunate accidents among you, but the Project must continue."

"Detailed report on all ship systems," Timberlake said. "He's out of his mind."

How cold was Hempstead's commiseration, Flattery thought. The phrasing betrayed the care with which it had been composed. *Just enough grief; not too much.*

The vocoder emitted a filter-dulled crackling, then: "This is Morgan Hempstead closing transmission. Acknowledge and answer our questions immediately. UMB out."

"They left too much unsaid," Bickel said. He sensed the "deletions for reasons of policy" all through the message. The thin political line they walked had been betrayed most in what was not said.

"Build consciousness into our computer," Timberlake growled. "How stupid can they get?" He glanced at Bickel. "You were on one of the original attempts at UMB, John. You get the honor of telling 'Big Daddy' where he can shove that idea."

"That attempt flopped and badly," Bickel agreed. "But it's still the only real course open to us."

Timberlake raged on as though he hadn't heard: "There were people on the UMB fiasco who make us look like a pack of amateurs."

Flattery had heart, though, and he hid a knowing smile by turning away and speaking mildly: "We all read the report, Tim."

"The only part worth reading was their summation." Timberlake pitched his voice in a sneering falsetto: *"'Impossible of achievement at present level of technology.'"*

"That was an excuse, not a summation," Bickel said. And he thought back to UMB's fruitless search for the Artificial Consciousness Factor. There had always been that sterile wall between his part of the group and the station personnel, but the triple-glass walls had never hidden the smell of failure. It had been all around the project from the beginning. They had been lost in tangles of pseudoneuron fiber, in winking lights and the snap of relays, the hiss of tape reels and the bitter ozone smell of burnt insulation from overloaded circuits. They had looked for a mechanical way to do what the least among them could do within his own flesh—be conscious. And they had failed.

Over them all had hung the unspoken fear, the knowledge of what had happened to the one project that reportedly had achieved success—and its own doom—back on the surface of Earth.

Timberlake cleared his throat, lifted a hand out of his couch cocoon, studied his fingernails. "Well, how're we going to answer their damn questions? They must be living in a dream world back there, expecting us to produce a detailed report on ship systems without the help of an OMC."

"But they had to ask for it," Bickel said. "And we'll have to doctor up some kind of report."

Bickel looked at Flattery. "You can cook up a report for Hempstead, Raj. Psychiatrists are experts at deception."

At times, this Bickel is uncommonly aware of subtleties, Flattery thought. *I must warn Prudence.* "All of us renounced deception, John."

"Just like we renounced birth and parents," Bickel said. "It was easy. Somebody did it for us."

Flattery knew he had to speak quickly, before this conversation devolved into self-pity. He kept his attention on a tiny paint flaw in the hard-baked surface of the master board, chose his words carefully: "The ship has to have conscious direction for the long haul, John. It has to. The trip involves too many unknowns that have to be dealt with on conditions of immediacy. So what do we do?"

"You're asking me?" Bickel asked. "You're the psychiatrist."

But I'm not the motivator here, Flattery thought. *I'm not the one who can inject purpose into our efforts.*

"This is going to require more direct methods," he said.

Bickel stared at him.

"Well, what're you going to tell them?" Timberlake asked. "They want to know why we didn't alert them when the first *brain* conked out. Of all the—"

"There's another thing," Bickel said, shifting his attention to Timberlake. "They gave us no code for that particular emergency. Are we to assume they thought it impossible for the OMCs to fail? We are not! We have to assume they had some other motive. They put the threshold high on that one for a specific purpose."

"Ah, for hell sakes," Timberlake protested, "you're finding bogeymen where they don't exist, Bick."

Bickel shook his head from side to side. "No...they were telling us in no uncertain terms that once we blew the whistle we were on our own. We have to find our own long-haul driver for the Tin Egg."

He's circling all around it, Flattery thought. *When will he zero in?*

Bickel wet his lips with his tongue. This borderline conversation, skirting the need for a consciousness to command the ship, disturbed him deeply. He was too honest with himself to ignore this fact.

Timberlake, picking up the threads of a previous conversation, said: "There was no physical reason for those *brains* to fail. The life systems were perfect. It's as though they committed suicide...under some unknown stress."

With an abrupt gesture, Bickel shifted his AAT board into transmit phase: "Okay, we'll stall 'em on their detailed report. They know it'll take time, anyway. As to why we didn't alert them earlier, I've decided to tell 'em flatly it was because they goofed and didn't give us a code for this particular emergency. If they—"

"You'll only get Hempstead angry," Flattery said.

"Hempstead angry will be more help to us than Hempstead cool and devious," Bickel said. "The angry man will make mistakes. He'll let some real help slip through to us."

"What makes you think Big Daddy would try to foul us up?" Timberlake asked.

"He's a political administrator. Even if it's unconscious . . . " Bickel hesitated; an idea had flicked into his mind . . . then eluded him. He went on, in a lower tone: "Even if it's unconscious, he'll put political considerations ahead of anything else. His first efforts will be to keep himself in power. We're in a position to throw out political elements and concentrate on our immediate problem. To do that, we throw monkey wrenches into the political gears and focus just on what we need. The things we need will come through."

Adroit, subtle, and capable of profound cunning, Flattery thought. *This Bickel bears the most careful watching.*

"Things we need," Timberlake said. "Such as what?"

"Such as advice from certain specialists at Moonbase, and as much computer time as they can spare us."

"You can't separate the political from everything else," Flattery objected. "You'll only stir things up and—"

"If you want to see what's in the bottom of the kettle, you have to give it one hell of a stir," Bickel said. "And I want them to define consciousness for us."

He was way ahead of me again, Flattery thought. *I have to stop underestimating him. One slip could ruin everything.*

CHAPTER 8

Of all the *Earthling*'s crew, Raja Lon Flattery has been provided with the most accurate information, suitably weighted, of course. This was necessary because he had to be provided with a secret terminal in his quarters through which he can monitor the mood of ship and crew. A primary fuse has to be connected to the system, and Flattery is that fuse.

—Morgan Hempstead
Lectures at Moonbase

SHE HAD COME into Com-central still feeling weak and disoriented. It was obvious that the shift of dominance had gone faster than expected, and she had forced herself to overcome her body's weaknesses, putting on a mask of well-being and composure that she did not feel.

The ovoid Com-central room should not have confused her—she had put in too many hours of training among these dials and gauges and pipes and keyboard consoles before their departure—but the feeling of unfamiliarity persisted. Then, as awareness increased, she saw the subtle changes in connections and controls and readouts. Bickel's handiwork.

All the changes were necessary to put the ship on manual, she realized, but she could feel the inadequacies of what had been done.

It was only then that she realized the thin edge they walked, and she turned her attention to Flattery who was finishing out his shift on the big board. The signs of strain were obvious in his movements—still exact with a surgeon's sureness, but the control betrayed its thinning energy in the way he relaxed abruptly after each adjustment of the board.

He should be relieved now, she thought, but she knew she was not yet ready to have that green dial point down at her, and she was not sure of the conditions of Bickel and Timberlake.

Timberlake radiated glum silence.

Bickel had greeted her warmly enough, then handed her a load of programming. The task obviously pointed toward construction of an electronic multi-simulation model of their main computer's core memory input/output.

Much of the programming remained to be completed. She lay back on her action couch, examined the test display of one series on the screen beside her. She felt the couch's enfolding cocoon through the vacsuit, wished there were time to let her body recover fully from its dehyb ordeal.

The evidence was all around her, though, that she had to get to work. There was no time for the luxury of slow recuperation.

Okay, you're so proud of your position and title... Prudence Lon Weygand, M.D., she told herself. *You asked for this job. You know what you have to do; get with it...*

The old self-lecture failed to rekindle her energies, and she steeled herself to hide all signs of weakness before speaking.

"Moonbase is taking longer to answer this time than it did before," she said. "And I gave 'em some questions to answer."

"They're too busy trying to decide what our reply *really* means," Bickel said.

"Or they could be figuring out how to tell us we've bitten off more'n we can chew," Timberlake said.

She heard the fear in his voice. "Raj has been on that board over four hours. Isn't it time somebody spelled him, Tim?"

Flattery knew what she was doing, but could not prevent the feeling of tension from gripping his spine. There was always the possibility Timberlake couldn't take this.

Timberlake felt the dryness in his mouth. Naturally, she assumed he was giving orders here. He *was* the life-systems man. She had not volunteered to take the board, either...the bitch. But maybe it was too soon after dehyb. Metabolisms differed. She would know her own capacities, certainly. Besides, she was scheduled to follow Bickel on the board in the normal rotation.

His glance followed the Com-central track, the way the board circled around their positions. Bickel was in number-one spot, then Prue, then Flattery—and he sat here on the end.

It's my watch, Timberlake told himself.

He felt perspiration start in his palms.

Bickel had taken the board in his turn, obviously begrudging every minute away from his damned computations. *He* would not volunteer.

I've got to take that board, Timberlake told himself.

He thought of the more than three thousand lives immediately dependent on him when that green arrow slid over to his position...all the other lives and dreams that had been poured into this project.

Every bit of it pointing a finger at him.

I can't! he thought.

He's taking too long, Flattery thought. "I'll give you the board on the count, Tim. I'm wearing pretty thin."

Before Timberlake could protest, the count had started and his hand went automatically to the big red switch. Board and arrow came to him. Necessities of the job caught him immediately. Almost a third of the shield temperature control needed trimming to bring it into better balance.

We should trace out the OMC linkages for this and install automatics for the gross part of the job, he thought.

Presently, he fell into the routine of the watch.

"Here's our operating procedure," Bickel said. He looked up, caught an exchange of knowing glances between Flattery and Prue, hesitated. *Something going on between those two?* If it was man-woman problems, that could cause trouble.

"You were saying," Prudence said.

Bickel saw she was staring directly at him. He cleared his throat, glanced at his figures and schematics for reassurance. "The computer must be the basis for anything we build, but we can't interfere with core memory and switching controls. That means we have to use an electronic simulation model. Part of the AAT system . . ."

"What about communication with Moonbase?" Prudence asked.

That's a stupid question, he thought, but he hid his irritation. "A switching system will automatically restore AAT function when the reply burst hits our antennas. We'll use an alarm klaxon."

"Oh." She nodded, wondering how far she could go before he realized he was being irritated purposely.

"This will be an operational model," he said. "It'll duplicate real characteristics of the total system, but won't function as completely as the computer-based system. However, it will give us direct observation of functions with conventional equipment. It'll tell us where we have to go unconventional. The environment, the signals, and the system parameters can be observed and changed as development progresses. And we'll only need a one-way, fused link with the computer to permit it to record all our results."

This much was predictable, Flattery thought. *But where does he go from here?*

"We'll generate an environment in scaled time and

apply its own effect signals to the system under analysis," Prudence said. "Good. What then?"

"Based on my experience with the UMB experiments," Bickel answered, "I can tell you which avenues aren't worth exploring and which avenues *may* give us an artificial consciousness. *May* do it. From here on in, it's cut and try."

"Are we going to have to fight the time lag and possibility of transmission errors while we let Moonbase analyze our progress?" Flattery asked.

Bickel glanced at his computations and schematics, looked back at Prudence. "Do we have a mathematician aboard competent enough to break down the embodied transducers of our results?"

Prudence looked across Bickel at the displays and stacks of schematics. She had followed enough of what he was doing there to combine that with the programming he had handed her, but it was the same old self-reflexive circle every time they faced this problem—where did the round of consciousness begin?

"Maybe I can handle the math," she said. "And that's all—just maybe."

"Then which *avenue* do we explore first?" Flattery asked.

"The field-theory approach," Bickel said.

"Oh, great!" Timberlake growled. "We're going to assume that the whole is greater than the sum of its parts."

"Okay," Bickel said. "But just because we can't see a thing or define it, that doesn't mean it isn't there and shouldn't be added into the sum. We're going to be juggling one hell of a lot of unknowns. The best approach to that kind of job is the engineering one: if it works, that's the answer."

"Define consciousness for me," Prudence said.

"We'll leave that up to the bigdomes at UMB," Bickel said.

"And our only contact between the simulation model and the main computer will be through the loading channels?" Prudence asked. "What do we do about the supervisory control programs?"

"We're not going to touch the inner communications lines to the computer," Bickel said. "Our auxiliary will go into it through a one-way channel, fused against backlash."

"Then it won't give us total simulation," she pointed out.

"That's right," Bickel agreed. "We'll have an error coefficient to contend with all along the line. If it gets too high, we change our plan of attack. The simulator will be just an auxiliary—kind of dumb in some respects."

"And there's no way for this auxiliary to run wild?" Flattery asked.

"Its supervisory program will always be one of us," Bickel said, fighting to keep irritation from his voice. "One of us will always be in the driver's seat. We'll drive it—like we'd drive an ox pulling a wagon."

"This Ox won't have any ideas of its own, eh?" Flattery persisted.

"Not unless we solve the consciousness problem," Bickel said.

"Ngaaa!"

Flattery's word pounced.

"And when it's conscious, what then?" he asked.

Bickel blinked at him, absorbing this. Presently, he said, "I . . . suppose it'll be like a newborn baby . . . in a sense."

"What baby was ever born with all the information and stored experiences of this ship's master computer?" Flattery demanded.

Bickel's being fed this too fast, Prudence thought. *If he's kept too much off balance he may rebel or start to probe in the wrong places. He mustn't guess.*

"Well . . . the human *is* born with instincts," Bickel said. "And we do train the human baby into . . . humanity."

"I find the moral and religious aspects of this whole idea faintly repugnant," Flattery declared flatly. "I think there's sin here. If not hubris, then something equally evil."

Prudence stared at him. Flattery betrayed signs of real

agitation—a flush in his cheeks, fingers trembling, eyes bright and glaring.

That wasn't in the program, she thought. *Perhaps he's tired.*

"All right," she said. "We construct a field of interacting impulses and that puts us right smack dab into a games-theory problem where countless bits are—"

"Oh, no!" Bickel snapped. "The UMB stab at this thing got all fouled up with games-theory ideas like the 'Command Constant' and 'Mobility Constant' and inner-outer-directed behavior. It took me one hell of a long time to realize they didn't know what they were talking about."

"Easy for you to say," Prudence said, holding her voice to a slow, cold beat. "You forget *I* saw the games machine they produced. The more it was used, the more it changed in—"

"Okay, it changed," Bickel admitted. "The machine absorbed part of its... personality from its opponents. What's that mean? It had *some* of the characteristics of consciousness, sure—but it wasn't conscious."

She turned away, conveying a sneer by the movement alone. *He has to think he can rely on no one but himself.*

Flattery shifted his attention from Bickel to Prudence and back. He found it increasingly difficult to hide his resentment of Bickel.

Psychiatrist, heal thyself, he thought. *Bickel has to take charge. I'm just the safety fuse.*

Flattery glanced at the false plate on his personal repeater board, thinking of the trigger beneath that plate and the mate to it in his quarters concealed by the lines of the sacred graphic on the bulkhead.

"Arbitrary turn-back command," Flattery reminded himself. That was the code signal he must listen for from UMB. That was the signal he must obey—unless he judged the ship had to be destroyed *before* receiving that signal.

A simple push on one of the hidden triggers would activate *the* master program in the ship's computer, open airlocks, set off explosive charges. Death and destruction for crew, ship, all the colonists and their supplies.

Colonists and their supplies! Flattery thought.

He was too good a psychiatrist not to recognize the guilt motives behind the careful provisioning of this ship.

"If you solve the Artificial Consciousness problem, you can plant a human colony somewhere in space. Not at Tau Ceti, of course, but ..."

And he was too good a divine not to penetrate the religious hokum, not to see through to the essential rightness of his role in the project.

Given the known perils, there had to be a safety fuse. There had to be someone willing and able to blow up the ship.

Flattery knew the reasons. They were reality of the most brutal kind.

The first crude attempts at mechanical reproduction of consciousness had been made on an island in Puget Sound. The island no longer existed. *"Rogue consciousness!"* they had screamed. True enough. Something had defied natural laws, slaughtered lab personnel, destroyed sensors, sent slashing beams of pure destruction through the surrounding countryside.

Finally, it had taken the island—God knew where.

Poof!

No island.

No lab personnel.

Nothing but gray water and a cold north wind whipping whitecaps across it and the fish and the seaweed invading the area where land and men and machinery had been.

Just thinking about it made Flattery shiver. He conjured up in his mind the image of the sacred graphic from his quarters, absorbed some of the peace from the field of serenity, the tranquility of the holy faces.

Even Moonbase didn't walk too close to this project now. It was all a sham to educate ship personnel, to frustrate the eager young men and women.

"Each project ship must maintain its coefficient of frustration," went the private admonition. *"Frustration must come from both human and mechanical sources."*

They thought of frustration as a threshold, a factor to heighten awareness.

It made a weird kind of sense.

Thus, there were crew members like Flattery...and Prudence Lon Weygand, and machinery that broke down, robox repair units that had to have a human monitor every second—and programmed emergencies to complicate real emergencies.

CHAPTER 9

The universe is derived from an ultimate principle of spiritual consciousness, the one and only existent from eternity. Accepting this, you become an affirmer of The Void, which is to be understood as the Primordial Nothingness: that is, the raw stuff out of which all is created as well as the background against which every creation can be discerned.

—The Education of
a Chaplain/Psychiatrist
(Moonbase Documents)

IT HAD BEEN a tiring watch and Flattery longed to return to his quarters. He wanted to bathe himself in the field generator there, to examine the *mood* of the computer complex. That was one of his prime duties: to be certain that the computer had settled back into pure mechanism after being deprived of its last Organic Mental Core. There was always the off chance that one of these attempts might achieve success by accident.

But there was no way he could leave early without arousing the wrong kinds of suspicions. Well, there was another duty for the psychiatrist-chaplain to perform. He looked at Bickel.

"You can't monitor every nuance of your machine's behavior," Flattery said. "You can't be certain of every way its circuits may interact."

"Yeah," Bickel said. "Adding all the parts doesn't give you the sum you want—or need. So why wouldn't those numbskulls at UMB build their circuits around Eng multipliers? Answer me that."

Timberlake glanced at Flattery, thought: *Go ahead! Get Bickel started on* that *subject. He's Johnny One-Note on that one!*

"There was some mention back at UMB," Flattery said, "that you were trying to get them to use—"

"Trying?" Bickel snarled. "I practically got down on my knees and begged. They acted like I was a moron, kept saying computers only add—even when they're multiplying it's only series addition. They kept this up until I—"

"You offered no logical circuit changes," Flattery said. "That's the way I heard it."

"Because I didn't get the chance," Bickel said. "Look! The Eng multiplier is solid-state and small enough to fit into any of our miniaturization requirements. It works something like a cathode follower; so the circuit requirements aren't too weird for us to follow. It's essentially a multiplier. Depending on the circuitry, it'll take several potentials of linear, semilinear or even nonlinear circuits and it'll yield a potential which is the product of the inputs. It multiplies them. But what's more important, when you reverse the circuitry, you get a device that taps a circuit—divides it, mind you—at a point which varies with the load. It works like a nerve cell!"

"The UMB team must've had good reason not to take you up on this," Prudence said. "If they—"

"They said I hadn't proved this was an analogue of organic function," Bickel sneered. "Hadn't proved it! Kee-rist! They wouldn't even spare me computer time to work out test circuitry. Everything was tied up trying to define consciousness."

"You buy their definition, don't you?" Flattery asked.

"If I did, I wouldn't've asked them to define it again," Bickel snorted. "I've had about all the label juggling I can stomach. Consciousness is *pure awareness*, they said. Then what about the objects of consciousness? I ask. Disregard them, they say. It's pure awareness. What's awareness without an object to focus on? I ask. Not important, they say. It's *pure awareness*. Then they turn right around and say this pure awareness is a pattern of three primary forces. What are these three primary forces? An 'I' entity plus the organism of this entity plus everything external which could act as a stimulus. Plus objects! But that's not it, they say. This merely means pure awareness juggles three factors and it's a senseless complication to try to multiply them two and two when you could add them and follow the circuits in a much more direct fashion."

"You're oversimplifying the argument," Prudence said.

"All right, I'm oversimplifying! But those are the essentials."

"And you had a ready answer, of course," she said.

"I've already told you I couldn't beg, borrow, or steal any computer time."

"But you insist you can prove your—"

"Look," Bickel said, "they told me I couldn't prove an organic analogue. But I know I can."

"You just *know* it," she said. "You can't find words to quite—"

"When you've worked with as many thoughtput instrumentation and computer designs as I have," he said, "you get a feeling for function. There are times when you can just look at the design of a circuit and you know immediately how it's supposed to function. You don't need the manufacturer's specifications."

"Do I understand you correctly?" Flattery asked. "You're referring to God as a manufacturer? If that's—"

"Go ahead!" Bickel snapped. "Look at the design of the human cerebellum. Don't try to pick a fight with me over who designed it. Just look at it. You're a doctor. What's it suggest to you?"

"What does it suggest to *you*?" Flattery countered.

"That some potential effect is mediated there," Bickel said. "This is a balancing system...very like the vestibular reflex that keeps us from falling on our asses when we walk."

"But the cerebellum also is a terminus," Prudence said.

"Cerebral output to the cerebellum doesn't even stop when you're asleep," Flattery said. "How can you—"

"So the cerebellum soaks up energy like an infinite sponge," Bickel said. "Energy is always pouring into it—emotional, sensory, motor, and mental energy. Why do we blandly assume the cerebellum engages in no activity? You can't find that anywhere else in nature or in devices made by man—where a system as complicated as this just sits there and does nothing."

"You're arguing that the cerebellum is the seat of consciousness?" Flattery asked.

"And you haven't defined consciousness," Prudence said. She kept her attention fixed on Bickel, hiding her excitement. His argument wasn't new, but she sensed he had a clearer understanding of where he was going with it then ever before.

"Seat of consciousness? No! I'm arguing that the cerebellum could mediate consciousness, integrate it, balance it...and that consciousness is a field phenomenon growing out of three or more lines of energy. We are more than our ideas."

"Prue's right," Flattery said. "You're not defining it." He glanced at Prudence, aware of her excitement and resenting it. Knowing the source of his resentment gave little solace.

"But I can come at it through the back door," Bickel said.

"What it's *not*," Prudence said.

"Right!" Bickel said. "It's not introspection, not sensing, feeling, or thinking. These are all physiological functions. Machines can do all these things and still not be conscious. What we're hunting is a third-order phenomenon—a relationship, not a thing. It's not synonymous with awareness. It's neither subjective nor objective. It's a relationship."

"We're more than our ideas," Prudence said.

"There's the answer to the UMB's glorified adding machines," Bickel said. "It's what I kept telling them... about this undefined human consciousness. When you add the inputs as a series in time you don't always get an answer corresponding to the outputs. And since it isn't addition, it has to be a more sophisticated mathematical problem."

Timberlake, listening to Bickel, could feel the fitness intuitively. Bickel was going in the right direction, even though the *landscape* around them was fuzzy. *We're more than our ideas.*

Prudence leaned back, weighing Bickel's words. He had to be given free rein, that was the directive. But he also had to feel he was being obstructed. Sensing that she had let herself get too close to the problem, she forced anger into her voice: "Damn it to hell, you still haven't defined it!"

"We may never define it," Bickel said. "But that doesn't mean we can't reproduce it."

"You want to start mocking up a prototype to test your theories?" Flattery asked.

"Using our communications AAT system as a basis," Bickel said.

"The AAT is linked directly to the computer core," Flattery said. "It's part of the translation master program. If you make a mistake, you destroy the heart of the computer. I'm not sure we should—"

"It'll be securely fused," Bickel said. "No chance of a backlash getting through to—"

"Without the computer, our automatics cease functioning," Timberlake said. "Maybe we'd better reconsider. If—"

"Come off of that, Tim!" Bickel protested. "You could set up this safety system as well as I could. There's not a chance of anything getting through to the—"

"I keep thinking of the UMB's so-called thinking machines," Timberlake said. "We can't see all their *behavior*. If we miss one linkage we could upset a vital master program."

"We're just not going to miss any linkages. The schematics are all available. This isn't flying blind. The AAT is the only thing we could really foul up, and at this distance from Moonbase it's of dubious value."

Does he want to cut us off from the UMB? Flattery wondered. *They suggested he might try it. We can't let him do that.*

"If you demolished the AAT system," Flattery said, "how long would it take to restore communications?"

"Fifteen to twenty hours," Bickel said. "We could have a jury rig doing the job by then."

Flattery looked questioningly at Timberlake.

"That's about right," Timberlake agreed.

"We use the AAT as a basis for our simulator," Bickel said. "We'll raid colony stores for reels of neuron fiber, Eng multipliers, and the other basic components. What we have to get is a system that simulates human nerve-net function."

"But will it be conscious?" Flattery asked.

"All we can do is cut and try," Bickel said. "Our computer and even the AAT work on analogue additive principles. We're going to build a system that's strictly infinite-multiplying. Our system will produce message units that are products of many multipliers."

"You make it sound so simple," Prudence said. "Connect net A to net B at points D and D prime and you get the Consciousness Factor—CF for short."

Bickel's lips thinned. "You have a better plan?"

Did I push too hard? she wondered. And she spoke quickly, "Oh, I'm with you, Bickel. You obviously know all the answers."

"I *don't* know all the answers," Bickel growled, "but I'm not going to sit out here moaning about fate... and I'm not turning back."

What if we have to turn back? Flattery wondered. *What do we do about Bickel's inhibition then?*

"Are you going to wait for Moonbase to answer?" Flattery asked.

Bickel glanced at Prudence. "I'd prefer starting at once, but that means I'd miss my shift on the board ... and since I'll need Tim—"

"We can handle it," Flattery said. "Everything seems to be running smoothly."

Prudence looked up at the big board and the inactive repeaters over her couch, wondering at her sudden feeling of chill. *I'm afraid to take that board*, she thought.

Those thousands of lives down in the hyb tanks ... all depending on right-the-first-time reactions. *Did the UMB big-domes really know what they were doing when they sent us out here? Was this the only way? Should we dehyb more people to help us? But that would overload several systems ... including the Bickel system.*

CHAPTER 10

The Chase has fascinated humankind from the
beginning, and with good reason. What many
failed to understand, however, was that there
could be the excitement of the chase even
where the only thing you were chasing was an
idea, a concept, a theory. As awareness
developed, it became apparent that this was
the most important chase of all, the one upon
whose outcome all of humankind survives or
fails.

—Raja Lon Flattery
The Book of Ship

THE CREAKING OF their action couches, the click-click of
relays—all of the subtle and familiar sounds of Com-
central worried at the edges of Prudence's awareness.

For the past half-hour, Bickel had been fussing
through the schematics, plotting his way into the
computer, sharing parts of his plan with the others. She
had come to dislike the sound of the schematics being
shuffled.

There were tensions here that she did not fully

61

understand, but her own role remained clear—mediate and goad . . . mediate and goad.

The common stench of Com-central carried an acridity which she identified as fear.

We have a chance at glory, she told herself. *Very few people ever have that opportunity.*

It was an empty pep talk, forever confronted by that inescapable fact:

I am not people.

For the first time since coming out of the hyb tank, she felt the old familiar pain-of-wonder, asking herself what it might have been like to have been born into a normal family in the normal way, to have grown up in the noisy, intimate *belonging* of the unchosen.

"You are the cream, the select few," Morgan Hempstead and his cohorts had kept reminding them. But they all knew where the cream had originated. Normal biopsy tissue from a living human volunteer had been suspended in an axolotl tank, the genetic imprint triggered and the flesh allowed to grow. It produced an identical twin—an expendable twin.

Select few! she thought. *Something precious was taken from us and the compensations were inadequate.*

She tuned the small screen at the corner of her board to one of the tail eyes, looked back toward the center of the solar system, toward the planet that had spawned them.

A stabbing pang of homesickness tightened her breast, made breathing difficult for a moment.

They had been molded and motivated, twisted, trained and inhibited—wound up like mechanical toys and sent scooting off into the darkness with their laser "whistle" tooting to let UMB know where they were.

And where are we? she asked herself as she blanked the screen.

"Prue, you'd better take the big board," Flattery said. "You'd normally follow John."

Sight of the big board's dials and gauges filled her with an abrupt anger and fear. She felt the immediacy of the emotions in a dry throat, heat in her cheeks.

"I . . . haven't had enough time off the board . . . to recuperate," Flattery said, speaking hesitantly. "Or I'd—"

"It's all right," she said. "I'll take it."

She took a deep breath, leaned back, signed to Timberlake to begin the count.

The appeal to her nursing instinct did it, Flattery thought. *She was ready to funk out. She had to take the board now or she might never be able to face it.*

Flattery glanced at Timberlake, saw the relief so apparent on the man's face as he switched the green arrow to Prudence.

Timberlake, dominated by intuition, was terrified by the responsibility of Com-central. Prudence, deep in sensation, shared that fear.

And I, because I feel their fear, overcome my own repugnance, Flattery thought.

Only Bickel, logical and with penetrating intelligence seemed immune to these pressures. It was a flaw in Bickel's character, Flattery thought, but he knew their lives could depend on that flaw.

"Get the manifest and ship-loading plans, Tim," Bickel said. "I'll give you a list of what we need from colony stores. We can set up in the computer maintenance shop next door for easy—"

"Don't stay outside the shield area too long," Prudence said. "You'd better key your dosimeters to repeaters in here; we'll keep an eye on you that way."

"Right," Bickel said.

He slipped off his couch, looked back at Prudence, studying her profile, the intent way she watched the big board. He shifted his attention to Flattery, who lay back with eyes closed, resting for his shift at the controls; then to Timberlake, who was taking copies of the ship-loading plans from the computer memory-bank printers.

None of them has really focused on what has to be done here, Bickel thought. *They haven't faced the fact that the simulator eventually has to be tied directly to the computer. We'll just be building a set of frontal lobes—if we're successful. And our "Ox" can have but one source of experience upon which to come alive and conscious—the computer and its memory banks.*

When they did face this fact, Bickel saw, he was going to have a fight on his hands. Too much of the ship was almost totally dependent on the master programs. Juggling those programs involved a kind of all-or-nothing danger. It was a flaw in the Tin Egg's design, Bickel felt. He could see no logical reason for it. Why should everything on the ship depend on conscious control or intervention—even down to the robox repair units?

Prudence sensed Bickel's attention on her, saw his face reflected in a gauge's plastic cover. His questionings, doubts, and determination were all there for her to read just as surely as she read the dial beneath the plastic reflector. She had set him up—she had done that part of her job as well as could be expected, she thought. She focused now on the total console, *feeling* the sensory pulses of the ship reaching outward to the hull skin and beyond.

Job routine was beginning to smooth off the harsh edges of her fear. She took a deep breath, keyed a forward exterior sensor to the overhead screen, studied the star-spangled view of what lay ahead of the Tin Egg.

That's our prize, she thought, looking at the stars. *First, we clean out the Augean stables—then we get to be first ... out there. The candy and the stick. That's the candy, a virgin world of our own (and we have our tanks full of colonists to prove Earth's good faith) and I ... I am the stick.*

The screenview appeared suddenly repulsive to her, and she blanked it, returned her attention to the big board and its pressures.

It's the uncertainty that gets to us, she thought. *There's too much unknown out here—something has to go wrong. But we don't know what it'll be ... or when it'll hit. We only know the blow when it falls can be totally destructive, leaving not a trace. It has been before—six times.*

She heard Bickel and Timberlake leave, the hiss of the hatch expanders sealing behind them; she turned and looked at Flattery. He had a small blue smudge-stain on his cheek just below his left eye. The stain appeared suddenly as an enormous flaw in an otherwise perfect creature. It terrified her, and she turned back to the big board to hide her emotion.

"Why . . . why did the other six fail?" she asked.

"You must have faith," Flattery said. "One ship will make it . . . one day. Perhaps it'll be our ship."

"It seems such a . . . wasteful way," she murmured.

"Very little's wasted. Solar energy's cheap at Moon-base. Raw materials are plentiful."

"But we're . . . alive!" she protested.

"There are plenty more where we came from. They'll be almost precisely like us . . . and all of them God's children. His eye is ever on us. We should—"

"Oh, stop that! I know why we have a chaplain—to feed us that pap when we need it. I don't need it and I never will."

"How proud we are," Flattery said.

"You know what you can do with your metaphysical crap. There is no God, only—"

"Shut up!" he barked. "I speak as your chaplain. I'm surprised at your stupidity, the temerity that permits you to utter such blasphemy *out here*."

"Oh, yes," she sneered. "I forgot. You're also our wily Indian scout sniffing the unknown terrain in front of us. You're the hedge on our bets, the 'what-if' factor, the—"

"You have no idea how much unknown we face," he said.

"Right out of *Hamlet*," she mocked him, and allowed her voice to go heavy with portentousness: "'There are more things in heaven and earth, Horatio, than are dreamt of in your philosophy.'"

He felt an abrupt pang of fear for her. "I'll pray for you, Prudence." And he cursed inwardly at the sound of his own voice. He had come through as a fatuous ass. *But I will pray for her*, he thought.

Prudence turned back to the big board, reminding herself: *A stick is to beat people with . . . to goad them beyond themselves. Raj can't just be a chaplain; he has to be a super-chaplain.*

Flattery took a deep, quavering breath. Her blasphemy had touched his most profound doubts. And he thought how little anyone suspected what lay beneath their veneer of science, deep in that Pandora's box where *anything* was possible.

Anything? he asked himself.

That was the bind, of course. They were penetrating the frontiers of *Anything*...and *Anything* had always before been the prerogative of God.

CHAPTER 11

> Symbolic behavior of some order has to be a
> requisite of consciousness. And it must be
> noted that symbols abstract—they *reduce* a
> message to selected form.

> —Morgan Hempstead
> Lectures at Moonbase

"SPREAD OUT THAT software on the bench, Tim," Bickel
directed. "Start by putting the pertinent parts of the
loading plan on top what we need'll be in robot stores. I'll
be with you in a minute."

Timberlake looked at Bickel's back. Control had
passed so obviously into the man's hands. No one
questioned it . . . now. He shrugged, began laying out the
manifests and loading plans.

Bickel glanced around the room.

The computer maintenance shop was designed in such
a way that Com-central nested partly into the curve of one
wall. The shop presented one flat wall opposite Com-
central, a wall about four and a half meters high and ten
meters long—its face covered with plugboards, comparators, simultaneous multiplexers, buffer-system monitors,
diagnostic instruments—dials and telltales.

Behind that wall's hardware and shields lay the first banks of master-program routing that led down to core memory sections and the vast library of routines that marked out the limits of the equipment.

"We'll have to block-sort the system to find all the audio and visual links and the AAT bands," Bickel said. "It's going to be a bootstrap operation all the way and the only information going back into the system will have to come from us. That means one of us will have to monitor the readout at all times. We'll have to sort out the garbage as we go and keep a running check on every control sequence we use. Let's start with a gate-circuit system right here." Bickel indicated an optical character reader on the wall directly in front of him.

It was all clear to him—this entrance into the problem. If only he could keep this gate of his own awareness open—one step at a time.

But there remained the weight of those six previous failures . . . reasons unknown: more than eighteen thousand *people* lost.

They don't think of us as real people, Bickel told himself. *We're expendable components, easily replaced. What happened with the other six ships?*

He wiped perspiration from his hands.

The conference hookups with station personnel had served only to frustrate him. He remembered sitting at his pickup desk staring into the vid-eye screen across his ink-stained blotter, watching the movement of faces in the screen divisions—faces he knew only in an untouchable, secondhand way.

The memory was dominated by Hempstead's voice issuing from that harsh wide mouth with its even rows of teeth:

"Any theory introduced to explain the loss of those ships must remain a theory at present. In the final analysis, we must admit we simply do not know what happened. We can only guess."

Guesses:

System failure.

Mechanical failure.

Human failure.

And subdivisions within subdivisions to break down the rows of guesses.

But never a word of suspicion about the Organic Mental Cores. Not one hint or theory or guess. The *brains* were perfect.

"Why?" Bickel muttered, staring at the gauges of the computer panel.

The stacked schematics on the bench rustled as Timberlake looked up. "What?"

"Why didn't they suspect OMC failure?" Bickel asked.

"Stupid mistake."

"That's too pat," Bickel protested. "There's something...some overriding reason we weren't given all the facts." He approached the computer panel, wiped away a small smudged fingerprint.

"What're you getting at?" Timberlake asked.

"Think how easy it was to keep a secret from us. Everything we did or said or breathed or ate was under their absolute control. We're the orbiting orphans, remember? Sterile isolation. The story of our lives: sterile isolation—physical...and mental."

"That's not reasonable," Timberlake said. "There're good reasons for sterile isolation, big advantages in a germ-free ship. But if you keep information from people who need it...well, that's not óptimum."

"Don't you ever get tired of being manipulated?" Bickel asked.

"Ahhhh, they wouldn't."

"Wouldn't they?"

"But..."

"What do we really know about Tau Ceti Project?" Bickel asked. "Only what we've been told. Automatic probes were sent out. They say they found this one habitable planet circling Tau Ceti. So UMB began sending ships."

"Well, why not?" Timberlake asked.

"Lots of reasons why not."

"You're too damn suspicious."

"Sure I am. They tell us that because of the dangers,

they send only duplicate-humans... Doppelgangers."

"It makes sense," Timberlake said.

"You don't see anything suspicious in this setup?"

"Hell, no!"

"I see." Bickel turned away from the glistening face of the computer panel, scowled at Timberlake. "Then let's try another tack. Don't you find it at all difficult to focus on this problem of consciousness?"

"On what?"

"We have to make an artificial consciousness," Bickel said. "That's our main chance. Project knows it... so do we. Do you find it difficult to face this problem?"

"What problem?"

"You don't think it'll be much of a problem manufacturing an artificial consciousness?"

"Well..."

"Your life depends on solving it," Bickel said.

"I guess so."

"You guess so! D'you have an alternative plan?"

"We could turn back."

Bickel fought down a surge of anger. "None of you see it!"

"See what?"

"The Tin Egg's almost totally dependent on computer function. The AAT system uses computer translation banks. All our ship sensors are sorted through the computer for priority of presentation on Com-central's screens. Every living soul in the hyb tanks has an individual life-system program—through the computer. The drive is computer-governed. The crew life systems, the shields, the fail-safe circuits, hull integrity, the radiation reflectors..."

"Because everything was supposed to be left under the control of an OMC."

Bickel crossed the shop in one low-gravity step, slapped a hand onto the papers on the bench. The movement sent several papers fluttering to the deck, but he ignored them. "And all the *brains* on six—no, seven! ships failed! I can feel it right in my guts. The OMCs failed... and we weren't given one word of warning."

Timberlake started to speak, thought better of it. He bent, collected the schematics from the deck, replaced them on the bench. Something about the force of Bickel's words, some product of vehemence prevented argument.

He's right, Timberlake thought.

Timberlake looked up at Bickel, noting the perspiration on the man's forehead, the frown lines at the corners of his eyes. "We still could turn back," Timberlake said.

"I don't think we can. This is a one-way trip."

"Why not? If we headed back..."

"And had a computer malfunction?"

"We'd still be headed home."

"You call diving into the sun home?"

Timberlake wet his lips with his tongue.

"They used to teach kids to swim by tossing them into a lake," Bickel said. "Well, we've been tossed into the lake. We'd better start swimming, or sure as hell we're going to sink."

"Project wouldn't do that to us," Timberlake whispered.

"Oh, wouldn't they?"

"But...six ships...more than eighteen thousand people..."

"People? What people? The only losses I know about are 'Gangers, fairly easy to replace if you have a cheap energy source."

"We're people," Timberlake said, "not just Doppelgangers."

"To *us* we're people," Bickel said. "Now, I've a real honey of a question for you—considering all those previous ship failures and the numerous possibilities of malfunction: Why didn't Project give us a code for talking about failure of OMCs, ours...or any others?"

"These suspicions are...crazy," Timberlake said.

"Yeah," Bickel said. "We're really on our way to Tau Ceti. Our lives are totally dependent on an all-or-nothing computer system—quite by the merest oversight. We've aimed ships like ours all over the sky—at Dubhe, at Schedar, at Hamal, at—"

"There was always the off chance those other six ships

made it. You know that. They disappeared, sure, but—"

"Ahhhh, now we get down to the meat. Maybe they weren't failures, eh? Maybe they—"

"It wouldn't make sense to send two seeding ships to the same destination," Timberlake pointed out. "Not if you weren't sure what was happening to—"

"You really believe that, Tim?"

"Well..."

"I have a better suggestion, Tim. If some crazy bastard tossed you into a lake when you couldn't swim, and you learned to swim like that"—Bickel snapped his fingers—"and you found then you could just keep on going, wouldn't you swim like hell to get away from the crazy bastard?"

CHAPTER 12

DEMAND: Define God.
OMC: The whole is greater than the sum of its parts.
DEMAND: How can God contain the universe?
OMC: Study the hologram. The individual is both laser and target.

> —Fragment from Message Capsule #4
> thought to have originated with
> Flattery (#4B) model

IN COM-CENTRAL, the sounds were those the umbilicus crew had come to accept as normal—the creak of action couches in their gimbals, the click of an occasional relay as it called attention to a telltale on the big board.

"Has Bickel unburdened himself at all about the artificial consciousness project back at UMB?" Prudence asked.

She removed her attention momentarily from the master console, glanced at Flattery, her sole companion on the lonely watch. Flattery appeared a bit pale, his mouth drawn downward in a frown. She returned her attention to the console, noting on the time log that her shipwatch had a little more than an hour yet to run. The strain was beginning to drag at her energy reserves. Flattery was taking a hell of a long time to answer, she thought... but he was famous for the ponderous reply.

"He's said a little," Flattery said, and he glanced at the hatch to the computer maintenance shop where Bickel and Timberlake were working. "Prue, shouldn't we be listening in on them, making sure they—"

"Not yet," she said.

"They wouldn't have to know we were listening."

"You underestimate Bickel," she said. "That's about the worst mistake you can make. He's fully capable of throwing a trace meter onto the communications—as I have—just on the off chance something interesting'll turn up... like finding us listening."

"D'you think he's started... building?"

"Mostly preparation at this stage," she said. "They're collecting material. You can pretty well follow their movements by watching the power drain here on the board, the shifts in temperature sensors and the dosimeter repeaters and the drain on the robox cargo handlers."

"They've been out into the cargo sections?"

"One of them has... probably Tim."

"You know what Bickel said about the UMB attempt?" Flattery asked. He paused to scratch an itch under his chin. "Said the biggest failure was in attention—the experts wandering away, doing everything but keeping their attention on the main line."

"That's a little too warm for comfort," she said.

"He may suspect," Flattery said, "but he can't be certain."

"There you go underestimating him again."

"Well, at least he's going to need our help," Flattery said, "and we'll be able to tell what's going on from *how* he needs us."

"Are you sure he needs us?"

"He'll have to use you for his deeper math analysis," Flattery said. "And me... well, he's going to be plowing through the von Neumann problem before he gets much beyond the first steps. He may not've faced that yet, but

he'll have to when he realizes he has to get deterministic
results from unreliable hardware."

She turned to stare at him, noting the faraway look in
his eyes. "How's that again?"

"He has to build with nonliving matter."

"So what?" She returned her attention to the board.
"Nature makes do with the same stuff. Living systems
aren't living below the molecular level."

"And *you* underestimate...life," Flattery said. "The
basic elements Bickel has to use are from our robot
stores—reels of quasibiological neurons and solid-state
devices, nerex wire and things like that—all of it nonliving
at a stage far above the molecular."

"But their fine structure's as relevant to their function
as any living matter's is."

"Perhaps you're beginning to see the essential hubris in
even approaching this problem," Flattery said.

"Oh, come off that, *Chaplain*. We're not back in the
eighteenth century making Vaucanson's wonderful
duck."

"We're tackling something much more complex than
primitive automata, but our intention's the same as
Vaucanson's."

"That's absolutely not true," Prudence said. "If we
succeeded and took our machine back to Vaucanson's
time and showed it to him, he'd just marvel at our
mechanical ability."

"You miss the mark. Poor Vaucanson would run for
the nearest priest and volunteer for the lynch mob to do
away with us. You see, *he* never intended to make
anything that was really alive."

"It's only a matter of degree, not basic difference," she
protested.

"He was like Aladdin rubbing the lamp compared to
us," Flattery said. "And even if his intentions *were* the
same as ours, he wasn't aware of it."

"You're talking in circles."

"Am I, really? This is the thing that writers and
philosophers have skirted for centuries with their eyes

half averted. This is the monster out of folklore, Prue
This is Frankenstein's poor monster and the sorcerer's
apprentice. The very idea of building a conscious robot
can be faced only if we recognize the implicit danger—
that we may be building a Golem that'll destroy us."

"In your off hours you tell ghost stories."

"Laughter's as good a way as any of facing this fear,"
he said.

"You're really serious!" she accused.

"Never more serious. Why d'you suppose Project's so
happy to send us far out into space to do our work?"

She tried to swallow in a dry throat, realized she *was*
afraid. Flattery had touched a nerve. He had produced a
powerful truth from somewhere. She forced herself to
face this as a fact when she felt an urge to call the
computer shop and beg Bickel and Tim to stop whatever
they were doing. The urge sent a chill along her spine.

"Where do we draw the line between what's living and
what's inanimate?" Flattery asked. He studied her, seeing
the fatigue shadows under her eyes, the trembling of a
nerve at her temple. "Will our . . . creature be alive?"

She cleared her throat. "Wouldn't it be more to the
point to ask if our creature will be able to reproduce itself?
If there's any danger . . . any real danger to—"

"Then, indeed, we may be on forbidden ground." And
he wondered why this thought always brought such an
empty feeling in the pit of his stomach.

"Oh, for God's sake, Raj!" Prudence was vehement.
"Have you completely forgotten that you're a scientist?"

"For God's sake, I can never forget it," he said quietly.

"Stop that!" She realized her voice unconsciously had
assumed the peremptory tone of her dormitory mother
back in the UMB crèche. Dormitory mother! A gray
haired image whose touch was never more than the
padded flexor of a robot which she directed from some
remote sanctuary in Project Central. Such a sad woman
she'd been, so cynical and . . . remote.

"Religion makes demands that can't be denied unless
you're willing to pay a terrible price," Flattery said.

"Religion's just a fact like any other," Prue countered.

We investigate primitive religions. Why can't we investigate our own? Didn't God make us curious? Aren't we as scientists supposed to put ourselves beyond the reach of prejudice?"

"Only a fool imagines he's beyond the reach of his prejudices."

"Well, I prefer to be a Calvinist, I'm willing to be damned for the greater glory of God."

"You mustn't say such things," he snapped. He put a hand to his head, thinking: *I mustn't let her goad me this way.*

"You can't show me anything I mustn't say," she said. "You claim scientists can equate God with ideas of mathematical infinity. We manipulate mathematical infinity; why can't we manipulate God?"

"What silly pretensions," he said. "Mathematical infinity. Zero over zero, eh? Or infinity minus infinity? Or infinity times zero?"

"God times zero," she said. "Why not?"

"You're the mathematician!" he said, his voice pouncing. "You know better'n anyone that these are indeterminate forms, mathematical nonsense."

"God minus infinity. Mathematical nonsense."

He glared at her. His throat felt dry and burning. She'd tricked him into this corner. It was blasphemy! And he was more vulnerable than she was ... guiltier.

"You're supposed to be doing this to me, aren't you," he accused. "You're supposed to push me and test me, give me no peace. I know."

How little he knows ... or even suspects, she thought. *Infinity doesn't follow the conditions of number or quantity. If there's a God, I don't see why He should follow those conditions, either. As for testing you: horseradish! All you need's an occasional kick in the philosophy.*

"Stick to my preaching and let you play with the math, is that it?"

"There's no blasphemy in developing a new kind of calculus or any other new tool to deal with our universe," she said.

"*Our* universe?" Flattery asked.

"As much of it as we can take," she said. "That's the whole idea of a colony ship, isn't it?"

"Is it?" he asked.

She adjusted the course-constant repeater, said, "I'll stick to math. How about a calculus that goes beyond the limits of X over Y as they tend toward infinity? That should be possible."

"Creating a new kind of calculus and building this living, sentient creature aren't the same," he said.

"Without the calculus we may never achieve the creature."

She keeps trying to corner me, he thought. *Why.* "The issue's whether we're intruding on God's domain of creation."

"You Holy Joes are all alike. You want to glorify God but you'd limit the means."

Flattery stared at the curved gray metal of the bulkhead above him, seeing the tiny imperfections in the crackle pattern of its finish. He felt he was being maneuvered. She was stalking him the way a man might stalk game. Was it his soul she was after? He sensed he was in profound danger, that the idea of consciousness as something they could create might inflict itself on his soul as an incurable wound.

He put a hand to his mouth. *I cannot permit her to bait me and tempt me.*

"Raj," she whispered and there was terror in her voice.

He whirled toward her, seeing the streaks of light across the big board like red knife slashes.

"We're almost at red-line temperature in Sector C-8 of the hyb tanks," she said. "Everything I do seems to make the system oscillate."

Flattery's hands flashed out to the life-systems repeater switches, brought his own monitors alive. He scanned the instruments, commanded, "Call Tim."

"Nothing I do seems to work!" she panted.

He glanced at her, saw she was fighting the board, not working with it.

"Call Tim!" he said.

She hit the command circuit switch with the heel of her left hand, shouted, "Tim to Com-central! Emergency!"

Again, Flattery scanned his instruments. There appeared to be three points of temperature shift outside the hyb tanks with corresponding variation inside. As Prue tried to compensate for one fluctuation, the others fell farther toward the red.

He had to force himself to keep his hands off the controls. If tank temperature went into the red without dehyb precautions, there'd be deaths among the helpless occupants. Despite Prue's desperate efforts, death was approaching three sectors of the C-8 tank—some four hundred human lives in there.

The hatch from the computer shop banged open. Timberlake leaped through with Bickel right behind.

"Hyb tanks," Prudence gasped. "Temperature."

Timberlake threw himself across Com-central into his action couch. His vacsuit rasped against the cocoon lips as he turned, grasped the traveler controls. "Give me the red switch," he snapped. "To hell with the count! I'm taking it."

And he took it, the big board swinging across much too fast.

"C-8," she said, sinking back and wiping perspiration from her forehead.

"I've got it," he said. He scanned the dials and gauges, his fingers playing over the console.

Bickel slipped into his own couch, tripped his repeaters. "It's in the hull shielding," he said.

"First two layers," Timberlake said.

Prudence put a hand to her throat, tried not to look at Bickel. *He mustn't suspect our attention's on him,* she thought. Then: *Wouldn't it be monstrous irony to lose our colonists and burden ourselves with guilt before the need for it?*

"That's doing it," Bickel said.

She looked across the board above Timberlake, saw the warning telltales winking out, the dials swinging back into normal range.

"Faulty feedback for a patch of our shell reflectors

focused on C-8," Timberlake said. "The system started to oscillate and that threw the overload switches, left us wide open."

"Another *design* failure," Bickel sneered.

And such a simple problem, Bickel thought. The hull curve acted like a lens to focus energy within the ship... unless reflector and shell shielding systems compensated.

Prudence traced the line of the remaining telltales. "C-8's on a line with that robot stores section you raided. Is that all it takes to throw the ship off balance?"

"Gives you a wonderful feeling of confidence in the Tin Egg's design, doesn't it," Bickel said.

They didn't warn me! she thought. *They cheated. Calculated emergencies, they said, just enough to keep a fine edge on your reaction abilities. Reaction abilities!*

"You overcompensated, Prue," Timberlake said. "Make minimal adjustments to avoid oscillation while you hunt for the source of your trouble. You had sensor telltales flaring right out through the ship to pinpoint where you needed shielding reinforcement."

I panicked, she thought. "I guess I let myself get too tired." Even as she spoke she sensed how lame the excuse sounded.

I was too intent doing the job on Flattery, she thought. *I had him headed for a nice corner where he'd have to fight his way out... and I missed the ship trouble until it was almost ready to wreck us.*

It occurred to her then to wonder if one of the crew had *her* as a "special project" to keep her abilities toned up... on edge.

"Prue, you've got to remember that when the overload switches go, the computer automatics are out of the circuit," Bickel said. "This thing was designed to be brought back into line by a conscious intelligence—one of us or an OMC."

"Oh, shut up!" she flared. "I made a mistake. I know it. I won't do it again."

"No damage was done," Timberlake said.

"I don't need you to defend me!" she snapped. And she

thought: *No damage! Nothing was harmed except one of the crew—me!* She pressed her hands together to still their trembling. *We're sitting ducks for any real emergency. We can't turn back without the risk of a runaway dive into Sol or becoming another of her wandering comets. We can't go on unless we solve the unsolvable.*

"Take it easy, Prue," Flattery soothed. "We probably put you on the big board too soon after getting you out of hyb."

Thanks for the excuse! she thought.

Flattery glanced around the room, seeing the poised silence of Bickel and Timberlake—both of them scorched by Prue's anger. Bickel slid out of his couch, secured a set of test leads in the clip at his left shoulder. A multimeter could be seen protruding from his breast pocket. Timberlake was refining the hull temperature adjustments, putting the system back into the computer circuits.

Flattery returned his attention to Prudence. *She shouldn't have panicked,* he thought. *Not the type. She has a woman's wide perspective and confidence in her intuition. She should be better at the big board than any of us. Is she under greater strain? Does she know something I don't?*

CHAPTER 13

We understand synergy to mean the fortuitous
working together of a set of components which
we have assembled in our attempt to achieve
artificial consciousness. Working together, the
components produce more than . . .

—Prudence Lon Weygand (#3)
Incomplete segment
from message capsule

IT REQUIRED ALMOST twenty minutes for Prudence to
regain her composure. By that time, Timberlake had run a
check-list survey on every hyb-tank complex. He did it
with a compulsive determination that none of them
misunderstood. His function as life-systems engineer had
been ignited.

Flattery let the thing run its course and a bit longer.
Bickel was fretting to get back to his work, but
Timberlake needed this role reinforcement. And Pru-
dence needed recovery time.

Bickel finally had enough waiting.

"Can we get back to work?" he demanded.

"I can take the board now, Tim," Flattery said.

Timberlake studied his instruments. "Okay. On the
count."

They shifted the board, and Timberlake sat up, a sharp ache across his back telling him how tense he had been.

"Let's get back to the shop," Bickel said.

"How far along are you?" Prudence asked.

"Barely beginning," Bickel said. "Let's get cracking."

"Is a man just a machine's way of making another machine?" she asked.

"Just like Sam Butler's hen," Timberlake said. "Philosophy I."

"Philosophy some other time, huh?" Bickel suggested.

"Just a minute," she said. "By attempting to reproduce an artificial consciousness, we're monkeying with variation of variability. Now, there's a field that all good little divines"—she nodded toward Flattery—"and most scientists have agreed by a compact of silence is the exclusive territory of God in Heaven and God's handiwork on earth—the genes."

"Yeah," Bickel said. "That's great. Let's solve it some other time."

"You still don't get it, none of you," she said.

Bickel glared at her. "Don't I? Okay, Prue. Let's strip off the fancy verbiage. We're damned if we solve this problem and dead if we don't. Is that what you were trying to say?"

"Bravo!" she said, and turned to look at Flattery.

Flattery scowled at his board, pointedly ignoring her.

"You see, Raj?" she asked.

She can't possibly know my instructions, Flattery thought. *She might guess, but she can't know. And certainly she couldn't stop me if I had to blow us all to Kingdom Come.*

"Yes, I see," Flattery said. "Don't underestimate John Lon Bickel."

At the sound of his name, Bickel's head came up. He stared at Flattery's profile, seeing the way the man's sensitive fingers moved like spider legs across the big board.

"You're so very clever, Raj," she said. "And so damn stupid!"

"That's enough of that!" Bickel snapped, turning to

glare at Prudence. "We'd better clear a little air, here. We're on our own, Prue. You've no idea how much on our own we are. We have to depend on each other because we sure as hell can't depend on the Tin Egg! We can't afford to snap and bite at each other."

Oh, can't we now, she thought.

"We're trapped on a ship that contains only one top-drawer mechanism," Bickel said. "We've only one thing that functions smoothly and beautifully the way it should—our computer. Everything else works as though it'd been designed and built by six left-handed apes."

"Bickel thinks this was all deliberate," Timberlake said.

Prudence caught herself in an involuntary glance at Flattery, forced her attention away from Bickel and onto Timberlake. *This is far too early for Bickel to suspect*, she thought.

Timberlake avoided her eyes. He looked like a small boy who'd been caught stealing jam.

Flattery broke the silence. "Deliberate?" he asked.

"Yeah," Timberlake said. "He thinks the other six ships had the same kind of failure—something rotten with the OMCs."

Bickel's far more alert and suspicious than anyone suspected, Prudence thought. *Raj or I will have to side with him; there's no other way to keep control of the situation.*

"Why...the OMCs?" Flattery asked.

"Let's not tiptoe around it," Bickel said. "The thing's obvious. What feature of these ships is never mentioned in the stress analyses? What feature do we assume is proof against failure?"

"Surely not the OMCs," Flattery said. He tried to hold his voice to a bantering level, failed, and thought: *God help us. Bickel's seen through the sham far too soon.*

"Certainly the OMCs," Bickel said. "And they gave us three of the damn things! One in service and two for backup. Never a hint that an OMC could fail, yet we had three on the Tin Egg!"

"Why?" Prudence asked.

"To make damn sure we got beyond the point of no return before we got the cold-turkey treatment," Bickel said.

I guess I'm elected, Prudence thought. She said: "More of Project's goddamn maneuvering! Sure. It'd be right in character."

Flattery shot a startled look at her, returned his attention to the big board before Bickel noticed.

"Cold turkey," Bickel said. "This ship's one elaborate simulation device with a single purpose—and my guess is the others were the same."

"Why?" Flattery demanded. "Why would they do such a thing?"

"Can't you see it?" Bickel asked. "Don't you recognize the purpose? It casts its shadow over everything around us. It's the only thing that makes any sense out of this charade. The secrecy, the mystery, the maneuvering—everything's calculated to put us on a greased slide into a very special ocean. It's not just cold turkey, it's sink or swim. And the only way we can swim is to develop an artificial consciousness."

"Then why such an elaborate sham?" Flattery asked. "Why all the colonists, for example?"

"Why *not* the colonists?" Bickel countered. "Ready replacements for any members of the crew slaughtered on the way. Another arrow in the quiver—just in case we do get over the hump to a habitable planet where we can plant the seed of humankind. And . . . maybe there's another reason."

"What?" Prudence demanded.

"I can't say just yet," Bickel said. "It's just a hunch . . . and there's something a hell of a lot more important we have to consider—the destructive potential of this project."

"You'd better explain that," Flattery said, but he could feel in the dryness of his throat and mouth that Bickel already had seen through to the horror element of Project Consciousness.

"Let's not kid ourselves," Bickel said. "If we really solve this, the whatever-you-call-it we develop could be a kind of ultimate threat to humankind—a rogue, Franken-stein's monster, cold intelligence without warm emotions, an angry horror." He shrugged. "Once there was an island in Puget Sound; you all know about it. What happened? Did they solve it?"

"So we install inhibitions, fail-safe features," Prudence said.

"How?" Bickel asked. "Can we develop this conscious-ness without giving it free will? Maybe that was the original problem with our Creator—giving us conscious-ness without permitting us to turn against...what? God?"

Consciousness, the gift of the serpent, Flattery thought. He wet his lips with his tongue. "So?"

"So this ship has an ultimate fail-safe device to protect Earth and the rest of humanity," Bickel said. "The only sure one I can think of, given all the variables, is a human being—one of us." He looked at each of them. "One of us set to pull the pin and blow us all to hell if we go sour."

"Oh, come now!" Flattery said.

"It could be you," Bickel said. "Probably is...but maybe you're too obvious."

Prudence put a hand to her breast, thought: *Holy Jesus! I never once considered that. But Bickel's right...and it's Raj, of course. He's the only one that fits. What do I do now?*

Timberlake stirred out of a deep silence. He had heard the argument and the only thing that surprised him was how easy it was to accept Bickel's summation. Why was Bickel right? He *was* right, of course. But why did they accept it when the thing really wasn't that obvious? Was it awe of Bickel—clearly the strongest mind among them? Or was it that they already knew the facts—unconsciously?

"I tell you something," Timberlake said. "Bickel's right and we know it. So one of us is set to pull the pin. I don't want to know who."

"No argument," Bickel said. "Whoever it is...if this thing goes sour, I'd be the last person in the...Tin Egg to stop him."

CHAPTER 14

The Zen master tells us that an omnipresent
idea can be hidden by its own omnipresence—
the forest lost among the trees. In our normal
daily behavior we are most estranged, most in
the grip of an illusory idea of the self. Every
enchanting inclination of pride and its ego, of
convention and its master—social training—
conspires to maintain the illusion. The seman-
ticist calls it the inertia of old premises. And
this is what holds our analyses of consciousness within fixed limits.

SHE WROTE "Prudence Lon Weygand" at the foot of
the log tape, started it rolling through the autorecorder,
made the synchronous shift to Flattery's tape as he took
over the board. The counter said it was her thirty-fifth
change of shift.

Flattery squirmed in his couch, settling himself for the
four-hour watch. Reflections on the dial faces were
hypnotic. He shook his head to bring himself to full
alertness, heard the hiss of fabric as Prudence got out of
her couch. She stood there a moment stretching, did a
dozen deep-knee bends.

How easily they accept the possibility that I'm the executioner, Flattery thought. He noted how wide awake and alert Prudence appeared. This four-hours-on, four-hours-off routine could be endured as long as no serious problems arose, but it played hob with the metabolic cycle. Prudence should be headed for food and rest, but she obviously was wide awake.

She glanced at Flattery, saw he was settled in for the watch, checked the repair log. Nothing was flagged urgent. That made it a bit more than twenty-five hours with nothing more than minor adjustments on the big board. Smooth. Too smooth.

Danger keeps you honed to a fine edge, she thought. *Extended peace makes you dull.*

But she wondered if Project had anticipated the special danger she had found for herself, and she thought: *Am I the stick to beat not only the others, but myself?*

The line of her own research seemed so obvious, though: define the chemical sea in which consciousness swam. The ultimate clue lay, she thought, in the serotonin adrenalin fractions. The thing she sought was an active principle, something between synhexyl and noradrenalin, a flash producer of neurohormones. The end product would be the root-stimulator of human consciousness. Find that chemical analogue and she could give fine detail to the workings of consciousness; provide a point-to-point sequencing which they could follow with machine simulation.

On the course she had chosen, the dangers to her person were enormous. She had no other guinea pig upon whom to test the derivatives her ingenuity produced. The possibility of deadly error was always present. The last substance, a relative of cohoba with an extra nitrogen addition, had ignited her mind, transported her into a weird consciousness. All sounds had become liquids which merged within her to be translated by a centrifuge process of awareness. It had been a terrifying experience, but she refused to stop.

It was only possible to make the tests during the deep rest periods in her own private cubby, and there was

always the possibility some physical response would
betray her. She could not afford that; the others would
unite to prevent the tests, she knew. Such was their
conditioning.

"You'd better get something to eat and try to rest,"
Flattery said.

"I'm not hungry."

"At least try to rest."

"Maybe later. Think I'll wander in and see how Bickel
and Tim're doing." She looked at the big screen overhead.
It was tuned to the peak-corner lenses of the computer
shop.

"We have to have a constant monitor on each other,"
Timberlake had argued. "We can't wait for somebody to
yell help."

The screen showed Bickel alone in the shop, but
another eye had been keyed; it showed Timberlake asleep
in his cubby adjoining the shop.

*Four hours on and four hours off plus this constant
looking over each other's shoulders will have us batty in a
week*, she thought.

Bickel looked up to his own screen-eye, saw Prudence
watching, said: "Satan finds mischief for idle hands."

They mock me, Flattery thought. *They laugh at God,
at the Devil, at me.*

"How about some coffee?" Prudence asked, speaking
to Bickel.

"Coffee later," he said. "No more food of any kind in
here, anyway. We have to keep the cover plates open and
we can't risk contaminating the fine structure. If you're
free, I could use some help."

She took one low-grav step across to the hatch lock, let
herself through, stopped just inside the shop to study
what Tim and Bickel had accomplished since her last free
period.

Where the optical character reader had been, on the
big panel across from the lock, now stretched a
mechanical excrescence—a piled and jutting structure of
plastic blocks: Eng multiplier circuits, each sealed in
plastic insulator. Linking the blocks were loops and

tangles and twists—a black spiderweb of insulated pseudoneuron fiber.

Bickel had heard her entrance. Without turning from his work at one end of that protruding angular construction, he said: "Take that other micro-tie viewer on the bench. I need 21.006 centimeters of the K-A4 neurofiber with random-spaced endbulbs and multisynapses. Connect it as I've indicated on that schematic labeled G-20. It should be the top one in that pile on the right end of the bench."

Bickel sat down on the deck, slid a new block of Eng multipliers into position. He swung a portable micro-tie viewer across the block, leaned into the viewer's forehead rests, began making the connections.

Yes, sir! she thought.

She found the indicated schematic, reeled off the neurofiber, fed it into the viewer, bent to the eyepiece. The enlarged image of the conductor line with its green-coded synapse sections and yellow endbulbs leaped into view. She looked once more at the schematic, began making the required connections.

"What're we doing now, boss?" she asked.

"Installing a system of roulette cycles," Bickel said.

"Why?"

"A machine can reproduce any form of behavior," Bickel said. "We can engineer this device to satisfy any given input-output specifications. It'll behave any way we want under any *specified* circumstances. "Raj set me straight on that."

She kept her tone light. "That was wrong, huh?"

"You bet your sweet life. Specified environment and behavior—that's deterministic. The manufacturer is still in control. What's worse, it requires a completely detailed memory—everything in the machine's past has to be immediate . . . right *there* and *now*! Memory load gets bigger and bigger every second. And it's all present and immediate. And *that* throws you into an infinite-design problem."

She reeled off a required length of side fiber, made the loop indicated in the schematic. "Infinite design. That means an indeterminate form and, by definition, the indeterminate is impossible to construct. So what do we do now?"

"Don't be dull," Bickel said. "We build for a random inhibitory pattern in the net—behavior that follows probability requirements." He leaned back from his viewer, wiped perspiration from his forehead. "A behavior pattern that results from built-in misfunction."

The way this ship was programmed to behave for us, she thought.

"Deterministic behavior from unreliable elements," she said. And she sensed Flattery's hand in this, an argument, a gentle nudge.

"Bickel," she said, "I've been stewing about your suspicions. Even if you're right—about one of us being set to blow us up if we go sour—how can you be sure this fail-safe person is still among us? I mean, three of the original crew are dead."

"Okay," Bickel said. "Let's say we brought you out of hyb and you found our chaplain-psychiatrist had been killed. What were your orders?"

"Orders?"

"Come off that! We all had special orders."

"I'd have insisted we bring another chaplain-psychiatrist out of hyb," she said in a small voice. "What would you have done?"

"I had my orders, same as you."

She looked up at Flattery visible on the overhead screen. He appeared intent on the big board, paying no attention to the conversation coming over the intercom from the shop. That was sham, she knew. Everything said here was going into his brain, being weighed and analyzed.

Bickel's right, she thought. *It's Raj.*

"Pay attention to what you're doing!" Bickel said.

She turned, saw him watching her.

"You foul up the ties on that loop and I'll put you back in hyb," he said.

"Don't make threats you can't carry out," she said. But she turned back to the micro-tie viewer, finished off an inter-ringed series of loops, tested to be sure they weren't mutually oscillating, traced the output sheaf, and attached a plug for an Eng multiplier connection.

"Let me have that G-20 assembly as soon as you're finished," Bickel said. He yawned, put his knuckles to his eyes.

Prudence checked her assembly against the schematic, saw it matched, lifted it gently out of the viewer and took it to Bickel. He was overdue for a rest and still driving himself, she saw.

"Here," she said, presenting the assembly. "When you get this tied in, why don't you take a break."

"We're almost ready to put this on an initial program," Bickel said. He took the assembly, began connecting it to the newly installed Eng multiplier block, running one sheaf back to a plugboard connection on the computer panel.

Prudence stepped back, studied the mechanical growth that jutted from the wall. As though she saw it for the first time, the construction abruptly took on a new meaning for her.

"That's more than a setup for analysis," she said.

"That's right."

Bickel stood up, wiped his hands on the sides of his vacsuit, swung his own micro-manipulator and viewer to one side.

"This, in addition to giving us our analysis of built-in misfunction, this little 'Ox' we're driving will provide a three-way energy interchange."

"You're tied into the computer," she accused, pointing to the connections in the plugboard.

"Every line in that board has a diode in it. Pulses can come from the computer to our test setup, but anything going into the computer has to be coded by one of us and inserted over there." Bickel pointed to the input heads lined up at the right corner of the wall.

"Three-way interchange?" she asked.

"We're going to test my field-theory approach. I have a source program ready to insert. If our Ox doesn't work, it'll just produce an unconditional transfer of the material at the readout. If the field is produced, it'll act as a filter, and we'll get truncation. It'll pass only the significant digits."

"What about the roulette cycles?"

"The zero suppress will be intermittent," he said, "but we'll still get only the significant digits at the readout."

Prudence nodded, looking at Bickel with a new understanding of what he was doing. "All sense data are intermittent into the human consciousness."

It was an explosive thought: *Wave forms! Everything which consciousness could identify had to move in some organized way. It had to move against a background which set off...which outlined!...the organization. Therefore: intermittence. And Bickel had seen right through to this necessity.*

She found the realization somehow deeply sexual, and awareness of this filled her with disquiet. There was no way she could include anti-S on her present testing regimen. She wondered if her body might finally betray her.

Forcing herself to a calmness which she did not feel, she said: "What we see and identify has to be discrete and significant, it has to dance against some other background."

"Now you have it," Bickel said. "But we assume that the one who views the data is continuous—a *flow* of consciousness. Somewhere inside us, the discrete becomes amorphous. Consciousness weeds out the insignificant, focuses only on the significant."

"That's judgment," she said, "and it's where physicalist theory falls flat on its face. If this is an introspection device, then it won't be conscious. Introspection confuses consciousness with thinking. But sensing, feeling and thinking are physiological processes . . . and consciousness—"

"Is something else," Bickel said. "It's a relationship, a field, a selective interchange. It drops the insignificant digits. It's a weeder. Now, we see if we have a device that can weed on the basis of intermittent data, some of which is erroneous."

"Erroneous data—significant results," she whispered. "What?"

But she ignored Bickel to turn and look at the overhead screen where Flattery was revealed calmly monitoring the big board. Something Flattery had said came now into her mind as though it had been amplified to full volume:

"There's nothing concerning ourselves about which we can be truly objective except our physical responses—the reflections of behavior. We exist in a forest of illusion where the very concept of consciousness merges with illusion."

She turned to look at Bickel where he worked, seeing the stretch of his muscles under the vacsuit fabric as he bent to finish the assembly. And she thought: *To be conscious, you must surmount illusion. Bickel saw that where I didn't.*

A moment of illumination filled her mind and she saw the man at his work as more than flesh and sinew and nerves—more than the physical chemistry with blanks to be filled in. Bickel was both a minuscule and vulnerable creature, but beyond that, he contained powers that could stretch across any universe. Something of this momentary understanding struck her as almost religious . . . holy. She savored it, realizing this was a private and personal thing she could never completely communicate to another creature.

Bickel finished the final tie of the G-20 assembly, stood up, and rubbed the small of his back. His hands trembled as he relaxed after the fierce concentration of the work he had just completed.

"Let's give it a run," he said. "Prue, you monitor the diagnostic board." He gestured to the panel of dials and gauges waiting like so many glistening eyes at his left. "I'll give each net of the roulette cycles a one-fifth-second burst from the shot generator." He moved around to the right of the piled blocks of the test setup, stepping over the leads with elaborate care. He flipped the row of switches to start the source program through the inputs.

"Mark," he said.

"Mark," she said as her dial needles snapped over to register the pulse.

"Give me the mean synapse threshold, mean endbulb threshold, and action time on each net." Bickel depressed three switches simultaneously. "Interchange activated."

He waited, feeling the suspense grow, a tightness in his stomach.

"Interchange now showing entrance pulse," she said.

"Net one," he said, introducing the timed burst from the shot generator.

"There's a jam-up at the fifth-layer nodes," she said. She concentrated on the gauges for the fifth layer as though her thoughts could activate them, but they remained at zero. "No impulses are getting through," she said.

"I'll try sweeping the roulette cycles," Bickel said. He twisted a dial.

"Nothing," she said.

Bickel kicked off his row of switches, moved the jacks to the left. "Here, let's try a trigonometrically oscillating potential in the loops. Give me the new readings for each layer of the nets. Mark one."

"You're getting a nonlinear reaction across *all* the nets now," she said. "It's close to zero linearity."

"That can't be!" Bickel said. "These things are still open circuits no matter what we call them." He depressed another switch. "Read the other nets."

Prudence suppressed a sense of frustration, swept her gaze across the dials.

"Nonlinear," she said.

Bickel stepped back, glared at the input panel. "This is nuts! What we have here is essentially a transducer. The outputs should match!"

Again, Prudence read her dials. "Your products are still zero."

"Any heat?" Bickel asked.

"Nothing significant," she said.

Bickel pursed his lips, thinking. "Somehow, we've produced a unitary orthogonal system for each net and the total assembly," he said. "And that's a contradiction. It could mean we have more than one system in each of these separate nets."

"You have an unknown that's swallowing energy," Prudence said, her excitement kindling. "Isn't that our definition of—"

"It isn't conscious," Bickel said. "Whatever the unknown system is, it can't be conscious . . . not yet. This setup is too simple, doesn't have enough source data . . ."

"Then it's some error in the hookup," Prudence said.

Bickel's shoulders sagged. He took a deep, tired breath. "Yeah. Has to be."

"Where's your record of assembly and circuit tests?" Prudence asked.

"I isolated an auxiliary storage tank," Bickel said. He gestured vaguely to his left. "It's the red-flagged one. Everything's in there . . . including all this." He waved at the diagnostic panel.

"You get something to eat and take a rest break," she said. "I'll start tracing circuits."

"We got a jam-up on the direct test," Bickel said. "It wasn't an open-circuit reaction. And the net-interchange test produces zero at the output without flagging the point of loss. The thing's a goddamn sponge!"

"It'll be some simple error," she said. "Wake Tim and send him in while you're at it. He's had more than his four hours off."

"I *am* tired," Bickel admitted. He thought back, asking himself how long it had been since he had rested. Three full watches anyway.

I let myself get too tired, he thought. *I know better. This is exacting work. Going too long without a break is the surest way to make mistakes.*

"It'll be some simple thing," he said, but he knew as he said it that this was wrong. Sleep. He needed sleep.

Bickel headed toward quarters, pawing at the problem in his mind, rolling it over. The setup produced a contradictory reaction. Nothing simple was going to produce that complex a contradiction.

Behind him, Prudence activated the readouts at the

red-flagged portion of the panel, started getting the feel of the setup. Sometimes with these computer problems, she knew, you could move intuitively into the area of difficulty, save yourself hours of hunting. Certain parts of a setup would *feel* wrong.

Presently, Timberlake joined her, yawning. "Bick told me. Trouble."

"Odd trouble."

"So I gathered." He cleared his throat. "Exactly what happened?"

She told him about the tests, the jam-up at the fifth-layer nodes and the subsequent disagreement between input and output.

"Zero linearity?" he asked.

"Almost."

"And no heat?"

"Nothing showed on the sensors."

Timberlake looked at the readout, the panel on both sides. "This is the storage tank we isolated. Have you examined the whole procedure?"

"I was just getting acquainted with the setup when you came in."

"That thing should've worked," Timberlake said. "It was a clean, straightforward construction all the way. I could've sworn it was going to give us that integrated readout, remove the nonsignificant digits, and we could just go on from..."

He paused, then said, "Unexpected feedback would...might cause the thing to react the way it did."

"I don't follow you."

"An oscillation. A flyback pulse that we didn't take into account."

"That might jam up the direct test," she said, "but it wouldn't account for the other reaction. If you were into the computer, of course...but that's one-way...isn't it?"

"Gated all the way. Our setup could receive selected data from the computer, but nothing went back in. No...I was thinking of this storage bank here." He nodded toward the panel in front of Prudence.

She turned toward the panel, puzzled. "But this is just

a...a complicated recorder. All it does is keep track of our work, step by step. It *is* isolated from the rest of the computer, isn't it?"

"What if it isn't isolated from the rest of the computer?" Timberlake asked.

"But Bickel assured me..."

"Yeah," Timberlake said, "and he probably believed it. I checked the work, too. If the schematics are correct, it's isolated. But what if the schematics are off?"

"Why would they be?"

"I don't know, but what if they are?"

Timberlake moved down the panel to the left, searching. He stopped at a translator output head. "Easy enough to find out. I'll just sort to find out if any of that test setup got into the master banks."

"If it *did* get in, there's no telling what it loused up," she said.

"Not necessarily," Timberlake said. He began cutting a program tape, referring to the computer banks themselves for the necessary data. Presently, he said, "That should do it."

Within seconds the load-and-go signal flashed at the readout in front of Timberlake. He switched it for an on-line printout and began reading the automatic translation.

"That was awfully fast," Prudence said.

Timberlake ignored her, scanning the tape as it chattered from the printer.

"For Chrissakes!" he said.

"What is it?" she asked, suppressing an irrational surge of fear.

"Get Bickel," Timberlake said. "This damn thing is giving us the truncated readout right here."

"What?"

"The answer we expected to get back at that setup if it worked," Timberlake said. "We're getting it here right now!"

"That's impossible," she said.

"Sure it is," Timberlake said. "You helped program this thing; look for yourself."

He whirled, brushed past her and headed for quarters.

Prudence bent over the printout, scanned the selected bits, recognizing some of the math she had worked into the program for Bickel.

With a breath-stopping sense of awe, she realized that the printout was devoid of insignificant digits. It had been weeded down to essentials.

CHAPTER 15

Computers are just systems with a great amount of unconsciousness: everything held in immediate memory and subject to programs which the operator initiates. The operator, therefore, is the consciousness of the computer.

—Raja Lon Flattery
The Book of Ship

IT WAS AT least five minutes before Timberlake returned with Bickel. While she waited, Prudence ran through the experiment a second and a third time. Both tests produced the truncated readout.

She felt a constricting sensation in her chest. Every sound in the room pressed in on her—each tiny metallic click, the low humming of a timer, the faint breathing of a ventilator. She felt that this thing in front of her was something profoundly dangerous. It required her to act with delicate care. Something new had come awake on the *Earthling*.

The hatch slammed open behind her. Bickel pushed her aside, bent over the terminal. "Let me see!" His fingers flew over the keys. He scanned the readout. "My God, it is!"

Timberlake moved up behind him, peered over Bickel's shoulder.

"How?" Timberlake asked.

"Tim," Bickel directed, "take the panel off that storage bank. Check it with everything we have. There has to be a line from it into the main computer somehow...a line that doesn't show on the master plan."

"But why would this thing start feeding us the right answer now?" Prudence demanded.

"That?" Bickel dismissed it with a wave of the hand. "The program went in with a key showing what was expected. Every part of the program was worked out on the main computer. We never cleared our work. It's still in there...acting as a filter. It filtered out everything except the answer that was keyed for optimum. Hell, anybody can make a computer act like that kind of filter. It doesn't mean a thing."

"Not so fast," she said, excited by a sudden inspiration. "What do you really have over there in that test setup?" She looked at the construction which Bickel so irreverently referred to as "The Ox." It still stood there like a surrealistic extrusion from the flat expanse of panel.

"You call it a transducer...of sorts," she said. "What's that really mean? The thing you have there is composed of blocks of nerve-net simulators arranged to integrate three lines of energy. The operational term is nerve-net simulators."

She gets too excited and she talks too much, Bickel thought. He knew this was partly his fatigue thinking for him, but he felt keyed up, buoyed by the quick discovery of what had gone wrong. He wanted to cut the link with the computer and rerun the test.

Timberlake already was removing the panel to get at the storage bank. The panel cover grated on the deck as he pushed it aside.

"Yeah, nerve-net simulators," Bickel said. He kept his attention on Timberlake, admiring the direct, purposeful way the man went at it. Timberlake was good at this work.

Prudence misread Bickel's answer, said: "And what's a nerve-net but an imbedding space? It catches energy . . . the way a spiderweb might catch ink you threw at it. The net makes a record in four dimensions of the energy you throw at it."

"Nice analogy," Bickel said. "You finding anything, Tim?"

"Not yet," Timberlake said. He was on his back now, his head, arms, and shoulders into the crawl space beneath the first wiring layer of the panel-to-storage system.

Noting where Timberlake had concentrated his attention, Bickel said: "I think you're right, Tim. It's most likely to be down there with the primary sheafs."

Prudence, concentrating on following her own train of thought, said: "So we have a multiple imbedding space, an energy catcher in four dimensions. The test program passes through this space as flux impulses in four dimensions and filters past the inhibitory roulette cycles in—"

"How's that again?" Bickel interrupted.

She looked up to find him staring at her.

"How's what again?" she asked.

"That about flux impulses."

"I said the test program passes through the imbedding space as flux impulses in four dimensions and filters past the inhibitory roulette . . ."

"By God, you're right," Bickel said. "The roulette cycles would be a filter. I never thought of it that way. You'd get a pileup of nodal pulses at random points in the net layers. Your test program would have to find its own path through that, canceling out at some points, but passing on wherever it had a higher potential."

"And this filter screens the program through a system of random errors," Prudence said. "So you have to be wrong about the way it produced your truncated answers. The program that got through to the computer couldn't have been anything at all like what you previously punched into the banks. Yet it produced the right answers."

"Let's play this over slowly," Bickel said. "We have circuitry here—the Ox plus computer—that should connect point-events in spacetime. Right?"

"Right. That's your imbedding space in four dimensions."

"So we sent energy pulses through it. And those—"

"Yoh!" Timberlake called, his voice echoing with a hollow resonance from the crawl space.

Bickel looked down, saw that only Timberlake's feet protruded into the shop now.

"Found it," Timberlake said. "It's a fifty-line sheaf, single plug. Shall I pull it?"

"Where does it lead?" Bickel asked.

"According to the color code it leads right down into the accessory storage banks," Timberlake said. His feet disappeared into the crawl space. "All these banks are linked that way! Why the hell doesn't it appear on the schematics?"

Bickel got down on his hands and knees at the mouth of the crawl hole. "Is there any kind of buffer or gating system in those lines?"

A hand light wavered back and forth in the crawl space. "Yeah, by God!" Timberlake said. "How'd you know?"

"Had to be," Bickel said. "That's a computer fail-safe system . . . and something else. Don't mess with it."

"Why . . . what do you mean?" Prudence asked.

"It's a recording system," Bickel said. And he had his answer to an earlier question. *Would Moonbase install hidden elements in the ship-plus-computer system?* Yes, and here was one of those hidden elements.

"Recording?" Prudence was puzzled.

"Yes!" He was angry. "Everything the computer does, everything we do—all recorded."

"Why?"

"So they can recover it and analyze it even if we're not around to help."

"But why wouldn't they tell us about—"

"They didn't want us questioning the purpose of this . . . this *voyage* until it was too late for us to change course."

She was defensive. "We could still go back to—"

"Don't be dense, Prue. A one-way trip. They don't want us back. We could be very dangerous. The only useful thing we have to offer is information . . . discovery."

Bickel rocked back on his heels, fighting a lost, sinking sensation.

Those bastards! he thought. *They knew we'd find this the first time we went looking into the computer's innards. They've tied our hands.*

Timberlake came scooting out of the crawl space, stood up. "There's a cover plate down there with a red-letter warning: 'Extreme Danger! To be opened by Moonbase personnel only!' Does that make sense to you?"

"I wish it didn't," Bickel said. He peered into the hole.

Timberlake was as puzzled as Prudence had been. "But a recorder and fail-safe system with such—"

"That has 'don't touch' written all over it," Bickel said. "I guarantee you—mess with it and something really destructive happens. Don't change a damn thing." He stood up, removed the blocking plugs they had installed to isolate their test system. His movements were wooden and poorly coordinated.

Isolate! He pushed past Prudence who still appeared puzzled. *Did any of the others understand what was really happening here?* The test leads clattered as he threw them onto the bench.

All he'd done with his *experiment* was change the potential at one point and insure that they would not have the addresses on any of the test information they had just sent into the total computer system.

Timberlake followed him to the bench. "But what about those results, the truncated—"

"Use your head!" Bickel whirled on him. "This computer has a random-access system as far as we're concerned—enormous blocks of information filed in it bit by bit in such a way that only the total computer can reproduce it for us. That's why we have so many special-function routines and subroutines and sub-subroutines ad infinitum. The addresses of *those* we know."

"But the fail-safe, the warning..."

"That's a special kind of message to us," Bickel said.

Prudence knew she had to head him away from this conjecture. She spoke quickly:

"The Organic Cores must've known where their information was."

"And they're dead," Bickel said. "Get the message?"

"Wait a minute!" Timberlake said. "Are you trying to tell us..."

"The computer is what keeps us alive," Bickel said. "That's all that keeps us alive. We win or lose with that computer."

Timberlake turned to stare at the open access panel. "But we..." He broke off.

Prudence, seeing what Timberlake had just realized, felt her mouth go dry. Some of the information in this monster would be filed many times, depending on the power with which it had been inserted. Some information was filed just once and could be lost through the kick of a proton. And that *total* system controlled their destiny.

"This computer's storage banks amount to one enormous internally balanced system," Bickel said.

Prudence nodded. It was like a superb human memory in some respects—even worked something like a human memory—but it was a *fine* instrument with all the delicate weaknesses implied by that term.

"Jeeeeesus," Timberlake whispered. "And we shot an unknown program through it."

"Worse than that," Bickel said. "Because of that unrecorded tie-in to the computer..." He swallowed, wondering if they already appreciated the extent of this disaster. Turning, he indicated the piled cubes and rectangles, the sheafs of quasibiological nerve fiber that constituted his "Ox."

The others turned in the direction he pointed.

"That setup is, in effect, an extension of the computer," Bickel said.

"The error factor!" Prudence said. She put a hand to her mouth.

"We've introduced an error factor into the computer," Bickel said. "And that means, first, that we've introduced the probability—no, the certainty, of an unknown number of subspaces within the computer's space time. The program we've just thrown into the computer . . . to land, we know not where, will produce unknown topological linkages, new networks all through the system."

"In the memory storage banks, primarily," Timberlake said.

"And in the transducer nets," Bickel said.

"But this storage unit here produced the circuit-analysis information when I asked for it," Prudence said.

"Certainly," Bickel said. "But your demand amounted to a program for a subroutine. Where the information came from God alone knows. Just in the first stage, there are fifty lines leading out of this unit. And those lines filter through a buffer system, remember. The bits go out of here, charge through that buffer system, and are split up fifty ways, according to their differences in potential. That's just the first stage. At the next stage, your division is fifty times fifty. And then fifty times fifty times fifty. And so on."

It was like trying to work with a memory whose only certain property was that everything stored in it was stored according to a scatter pattern and could only be recovered if you knew the pattern.

Guaranteed selective amnesia. But that . . . was kind of human.

"This bank here was just like a knitting machine," Prudence said. "It took the threads of the record from this test setup and knitted them out through the storage banks of the entire system . . . smearing that record across an unknown number of retainer cells."

"An unknown number of times," Bickel said. "Remember that. And we only have one address for the entire record of that test, the address of a subroutine program. If that's lost the whole record's lost . . . unless we manage to match enough pieces of it in another program to pull it out of the system again."

"But isn't that pretty much the way human memory works?" Prudence asked. "And here's another thing: It produced the right answer at the translator. The *right* answer."

Bickel looked at her, turning that fact over in his mind. *She was right, by God! And not for the reason he had so glibly spouted.*

The thing had produced the right answers in spite of errors and misprogramming. The processing procedure stank. It was heuristic and should not under any circumstances have yielded the desired output.

But it had. Why?

Bickel experienced a mental sensation as though his mind lurched. It was so much like a physical sensation he wondered that the others didn't notice.

The beautiful clarity with which he understood what had happened in the computer washed through him like a stimulant.

Didn't the others see it?

He looked at Prudence, at Timberlake, realized this had all occurred in a fraction of a second.

"For motion produceth nothing but motion."

The words rang through his mind, producing awe at the way apparently disconnected bits—a line of poetry here, a technical phrase there—could link with a simple turn of mathematics to produce a right answer in his mind.

Just the way it had happened in the computer.

Prudence, correctly interpreting Bickel's expression, spoke quietly, "You're onto something, John."

He nodded. "Prudence, you're our mathematician. What's *pi?*"

She stared at him, puzzled.

"I'm serious," Bickel said.

"The ratio of the circumference of a circle to its diameter," she said. "A rational approximation would be approximately twenty-two over seven. A closer approximation would be three hundred and fifty-five over a hundred and thirteen."

"For most applications, that approximation of *pi* would give us significant results?" Bickel asked.

"You don't have to ask that. You know it would."

"Okay, now tell me why you didn't answer my question by saying *pi* is a sweet concoction of starchy crust enclosing a filling often of fruit?"

She saw his seriousness in the way he stared at her, waiting. This bore on the problem in some way. She looked at Timberlake and he interpreted her motion as an appeal for help.

"It's obvious," Timberlake said. "You set up a category first by saying, 'You're our mathematician.' Then you asked: 'What's *pi*?' You didn't say: 'What's *a* pie?'"

"Yeah," Bickel said. "You had two screening references through which to filter the question and come up with the right answer. Then, because you sensed this was a rhetorical question in some way, you didn't try to explain first that there's no rational number for *pi*; you just gave me the rational approximations."

"Well, I knew I didn't have to explain *that* to you," Prudence said.

"That was category 'common information,'" Bickel said. "All you had to do was produce the *significant* answer."

"Holy cow!" Timberlake exploded, seeing where Bickel was leading them.

"Holy Ox, you mean," Bickel said.

Prudence whirled, pointed wildly toward the computer panel. "But it wasn't conscious! It couldn't have been!"

"It wasn't conscious," Bickel agreed. "But first crack out of the box, we've produced a significant result. And it was no accident. What can we say about the results of this test? First, we can say that the computer had sufficient information to produce an accurate answer despite errors in the system. Second, we can say that we've introduced a new kind of sense data into the system previously called a computer. We can go on calling this a computer, but it's a step up from 'computer' now. It has *learned* how to use a new kind of sense data."

Prudence started to speak, stopped.

"Screen everything I've said here through field theory," Bickel said. He grinned at them. "Then remember that we matched *three* energy sources in the Ox. The integrator there set them up to go out identically. The buffer potential of this storage unit here scattered those pulses through the system. They were divided and re-divided ... but wherever they matched they reinforced each other."

"In itself, the original program pulse was a kind of comparator," Timberlake said. "The computer could compare for accuracy on the basis of signal strength."

"And the computer already *knew* how to compare the AAT signals for accuracy by screening them through a code-matching grid," Bickel said. "Signal strength was merely another kind of grid."

"If you're not too busy congratulating yourself," Prudence said, "consider how some of those rematched signals must've grown in strength. The probability is that some elements of the computer have been shocked out of—"

"We're still running," Bickel said, but he spoke defensively, realizing that Prudence was right. There were overload fuses throughout the filter to protect components, but stray signals overriding barrier potentials could have played hob with some of the master programs. He looked at the overhead screen which showed Flattery manning the Com-central board.

Flattery appeared relaxed, but watchful, his gaze traversing the big board.

Damn her! he thought.

One instant everything had been rosy, full of elation that the Ox had come a short step up the ladder—not into consciousness . . . but toward it. And all she could think to do was throw cold water on them.

Bickel met Flattery's gaze in the screen. "Have you been listening, Raj?"

"I've been listening," Flattery said.

"Have we gone sour, yet?" Bickel asked.

"You really think I'm this hypothetical human fail-safe device?" Flattery asked, holding his tone to a nice balance between mockery and injured innocence.

He almost goes too far, Prudence thought. *If he isn't underestimating Bickel, he's pressing the limits. One course is as dangerous as the other.*

"You're the logical candidate," Bickel said, "but I was asking for your comments on progress."

Flattery suppressed an abrupt feeling of jealousy. Bickel, in spite of the obvious flaw—and that was a gaping thing—balanced so beautifully. Or . . . he appeared to balance, which was much the same thing as far as this operation was concerned.

"Ahhh, progress," Flattery said. "If I understand your original test correctly, the pulse-time distances didn't check out with the space distances. They weren't proportional."

"That's essentially it." Bickel wondered why Flattery's tone made him feel so defensive. "They averaged out to almost a zero product."

"The artificial nerve nets produce something vaguely equivalent to psychological space." Flattery paused, scanned the Com-central board, returned his attention to the screen and Bickel. "You can say that the test pulses are more or less like sense data feeding into psychological space—a region somewhat equivalent to what Prudence calls imbedding space. I like her cobweb-and-ink analogy. But there's a big difference between physical space and psychological space."

He let it hang there a long time, forcing Bickel to admit a dependency upon someone else's expertise.

"If you're going to explain it, then get at it," Bickel said. There was anger in his voice. He didn't enjoy depending on Flattery.

"Okay." Flattery kept his tone even and friendly.

"You can time a signal across physical space, repeat it and get matched results. Any difference will have a positive relationship to a change in distance. But psychological space . . . now, that's something else again. The time there could depend on mood. What's mood, John? Is it a comparison between this and previous experiences of a similar kind? Your pulse-time in psychological space will meet many more variables than it does in physical space."

"Are you saying we haven't analyzed our results correctly?" Timberlake asked. He glared up at the screen, feeling that he and Prudence and Bickel were arrayed somehow against Flattery.

"You're trying to arrive at some proportional comparison between the sense world and the physical world," Flattery said. "But you can't use the same rules of measurement. Each neuron in your net will introduce an element of random conduction time and you get more randomness from the similar variation in synaptic delay time. The difference between the sense world and the physical world is the difference between time distance and space distance. And the most casual examination of your setup indicates you'll have random time distances."

"Zero by probability," Bickel said. "That won't wash."

"That shot-effect test," Flattery said, his voice bored, "fired off impulses which weren't time-regulated. You got a variety of delay times there and in your system. That could average out statistically—by probability mechanics."

"Over the entire net?" Bickel demanded.

"Why not? The bigger the net, the more likely this is to be true. And your net here took in the entire computer."

"But we got the right answer from the translator," Bickel said, his voice pouncing. "Try probability on that!"

"I wouldn't think of it," Flattery said. "No more than I'd think of coming to definite conclusions on the basis of one test run."

Bickel glared at him. "Okay, we'll run it again!"

"No, you won't," Flattery said. "Not without figuring how to isolate your Ox from the computer . . . and before you think of taking any storage units out of the system, ask yourself which one it'll be. Will it be a unit protecting the life of someone in the hyb tanks? How about a unit controlling the drive?"

"We can't tell one from the other without a complete block-sort of the entire system," Bickel protested.

"Exactly. That shouldn't take more than eight or nine years—with the manpower available to us."

Flattery's argument was unassailable, Bickel knew. This didn't ease the anger that surged through him at the sight of the man's coldly superior attitude. Still, Bickel felt they had approached some unspoken, elusive, and vital fact that all of them should recognize. They had approached it and wandered away.

"Then we'll transmit the problem back to Moonbase and let them run it for us," Bickel said.

"Forgetting your analysis of why we were sent out here to solve it," Flattery said.

"Ahh, you're admitting we were sent out here to sink or swim."

"I'm admitting nothing, but I'd suggest you come in and man the AAT. A message has been reeling in from Moonbase for the past minute."

CHAPTER 16

The high data-rate sense perception and identification abilities of the human system mostly bypass verbal/analytic awareness. We are generally conscious of a cognitive recognition after the fact. In this way, what we understand as consciousness has to be identified as a reflexive monitoring ability with quite limited application. To produce consciousness (artificial or otherwise) we are stepping *down*, not up.

—John Lon Bickel (#5)
Message Capsule datum

MORGAN HEMPSTEAD's burst-depersonalized voice filled the control room as Bickel started the playback of the new message from Moonbase.

"Calling UMB ship *Earthling*. This is Project calling UMB ship *Earthling*."

A long, rolling silence followed and they grew aware of the hissing of the tape as it sped across its sorting heads.

To Prudence, that hiss was something primordial and perilous. It was a noise from the slime of evolution and she felt that some dangerous part of her own brain came awake at hearing it.

That's foolish, she told herself. *I'm reacting to my last injection.*

That had to be it: the chemical experiments on her own flesh were creating imbalances. She was using a series of variations on tetrahydrocannabinol now, shifting the CH_3 forms and adding oxygen.

That was just the hissing of tapes, she reminded herself. But her head wanted to move from side to side. Something within her was fascinated by that sound.

Bickel glanced around the room—Flattery at the big board yet, composed and so serenely sure of himself; Prudence in her action couch and with her eyes intent on the vocal translator at the AAT; Timberlake in his couch, eyes closed, breathing deeply. One might almost think he was asleep, but for the pulse at his temple. Bickel recognized that mannerism of Timberlake's. It meant the man was chewing over a heavy problem.

"Hit it," Hempstead said.

"That must be an error," Bickel said. "The AAT goofed on that one."

"We do worse ourselves sometimes," Flattery said.

"On the question of defining consciousness," Hempstead said. "Reference is made to nerve barrier and threshold data your computer. Best dive to date."

"Best *definition* to date," Flattery said. "That's what he must've said."

"New Organic Mental Core," Hempstead said. "Medical personnel are directed to abandon all such repeats in their waste of order."

"There's something wrong with the AAT," Prudence said.

"Not with the AAT," Bickel said. "With the translator circuits from the computer."

"That goddamn wild program we flushed through the system like a high colonic," Timberlake growled. He opened his eyes and stared accusingly at Bickel.

"Abandon all such attempts," Hempstead said.

"Repeat: abandon all such attempts. This is a direct order."

"That sounds like him rightly enough," Prudence said.

"Under no circumstances are you to attempt to make inanimate components," Hempstead said.

"Try that one on your violin," Timberlake said.

"Analyze course and reaction data related to mass changes," Hempstead said. "Unknown area derived mathematically."

"Hash!" Timberlake snarled. "Garbage!"

"Project over and out," Hempstead said. "Acknowledge year compliance."

Timberlake sat up, swung his feet to the deck. "Go ahead, Bick," he said. "Acknowledge *year* compliance."

Flattery glanced at Timberlake, returned his attention to the board. Timberlake obviously was making a bid to regain his authority. That could have been predicted. Their first setback would bring him charging out—from fear for all those lives dependent on the life systems, if not for any other reason. Flattery had watched the way Timberlake studied the life-systems repeaters—nothing wrong there . . . yet. But a threat to any part of the ship was a threat to all.

"Was he asking us to install a new brain?" Prudence asked.

"Where could we get one?" Timberlake asked.

"We've already been through that," she said, looking at each of them in turn.

And for the first time since taking her position with the umbilicus crew, Prudence allowed herself to wonder what it *really* would be like to become that fleshless embodiment, the mentality which was central to a driving behemoth such as this ship.

She shivered.

They taunt me with blasphemy, Flattery thought.

"Are you cold, Prudence?" he asked.

He watches me all the time, she thought. The medical part of her faced the feminine part then. "I'm quite comfortable," she said.

But she wasn't comfortable. Moods of depression and elation shot through her without warning and had to be concealed. Strange psychic aches tortured her mind— fantasies of godlike power competed with the urge for physical abasement.

She suspected she was close to finding the selective stimulator of consciousness. Some of the combinations she was now using on herself provided enormous amounts of oxygen to the brain in abrupt bursts. There seemed to be a threshold effect involving the blood-brain barrier. The experiments produced residual effects, though. One of their by-products had forced her to complete abandonment of anti-S and its body-chemistry-balance substitutes. Lately, she'd had to mask and suppress acute withdrawal symptoms. And she had found herself unable to deny the profound, compulsive hungers for foods heavy in B-complex vitamins.

She also found herself plagued by sexual dream fantasies involving all of her companions.

Bickel turned from the AAT with a length of printer tape, said: "Garbage."

"What else?" Timberlake snapped.

Flattery started to speak, froze in the act while he studied the track graph on his board. He hadn't imagined it; the graph was climbing. "We've been gaining speed for several minutes. Slow . . . but steady."

"Drive problems now!" Timberlake snarled.

Flattery activated the drive readout, scanned it. "No, no emission. G/R level shows the normal radiation drop."

"Mass register?" Bickel asked.

Flattery's hands flicked over the keyboard. He scanned his gauges. "Out of register! Mass reference is out of register!"

"What are your readings?" Bickel asked.

"They vary through ten *argos*," Flattery muttered. "They don't graph back . . . no series-constant in the curve of change. Mass is out of register with speed."

"What'd Hempstead say?" Bickel demanded, looking

back at the printout tape. "'Analyze course and reaction data related to mass changes.' If he—"

"That could be garbage!" Timberlake snapped.

"Still that gradual speed increase," Flattery said. "A slow increment for about four minutes now."

The ship is programmed for emergencies, Prudence thought. *That's what they said. But which are emergencies from that program...and which are emergencies from an unknown source?*

Flattery took a comparator readout. "In the past minute and eight seconds, our speed has gone up .011002 against the fixed reference."

Bickel began shifting plugs on his computer board. His fingers danced over the keys. He checked the telltales, looked to the visual readout screen.

"Mass interference," he said.

Timberlake coughed. "Is that thing saying our speed has raised our mass to a point where something is...colliding with us?"

"We don't know," Bickel said.

"And with that computer, the answer could be garbage," Timberlake said.

"But the problem isn't garbage," Flattery said. "I'm getting direct reports."

"Speed and mass are our major variables," Bickel said. "Mass reference is cockeyed. Something outside their *rated* spectrum is colliding with our sensors. That'd throw the—"

"Prepare for retro-firing," Flattery said.

"Wouldn't it be wiser to turn ship?" Timberlake asked. He kicked the manual cocoon switch and the action couch snapped securely around him.

"Raj's right," Bickel said. "Use minimum change. Something's happening for which we have no experience."

"I am starting retro with micro-emission," Flattery said. "Prue, monitor the track graph. Tim, watch our mass reference. I am recording for later analysis."

"If there is a later," Timberlake muttered.

Flattery ignored him. "John, monitor hull temperature and Doppler comparison."

"Right." Bickel cleared his throat, thinking how crude was this quartered division of functions when compared with a properly working ship-control robobrain. The umbilicus crew was a pack of limping cripples by comparison...and in a situation where they needed to run and dodge and balance with the ability of an athlete.

"Starting retro," Flattery said.

He moved the micro-controls one notch.

Action couches made a slight adjustment to the change. It registered as a creeping movement of their repeater consoles against the conduits, pipes, and instruments of the fixed walls.

"Track graph report," Flattery said.

"Speed is dropping unevenly," Prudence answered. "Fits and jerks."

Bickel, watching the edge of his repeater where it aligned with the edge of a wall plate, could see the bucking movement of the ship as a series of tiny jerks. His hands on the console keys sensed a tremor in the ship.

"Tell me when the graph levels off," Flattery said. "Mass reference report."

"Uneven," Timberlake said. "Graph average is dropping, but the direct register is going up and down...it's .008, .0095... .0069..."

"Let me know if it levels," Flattery said.

Without being asked, Bickel said, "There's a micro-increase in temperature along the first quadrant, stern. Compensation system is taking care of it adequately. Doppler reference shows an actual speed decrease of .00904 plus."

"Mark," Flattery said.

"S over C confirms," Prudence said.

Flattery advanced the micro-control another notch, feeling perspiration along his back and neck collecting too fast for his suit to compensate.

"Track," he said.

"Graph is now dipping below the fixed reference," Prudence said. "Still dropping unevenly."

"Ion reading," Flattery said.

"One over four point two eight double ought one," Timberlake answered. "Agreement with emission rate is positive. Retro normal."

"Rate of down-graph is now even on the track," Prudence said.

"Mass reference is level and .000001001 out of agreement," Timberlake said.

"Hull temperature?" Flattery asked.

"Holding." Bickel allowed himself a deep breath. Changes in hull temperature where they should not occur, changes in their speed without a positive explanation—these were more alarming than a physical breakdown that they could touch with their hands and repair.

Flattery heard the sigh and thought: *The Tin Egg had a close call. But close to what? Does Bickel know? Did he tell us everything he got from the computer? Even so, how can we trust computer information now?*

But Flattery recalled another part of Hempstead's possibly garbled message: *"Unknown area derived mathematically."*

What if that were pretty close to Hempstead's actual words? Flattery asked himself. An unknown of some kind derived mathematically. The ship *had* encountered a mass/speed problem.

Bickel said, "Raj, drop the speed another two points and hold. We'll want regular checks on mass/speed variations from here on out."

"Complying," Flattery said. "Report in order." He turned to the micro-controls, dropped them two more notches.

"Track graph declines on an even slope," Prudence said.

"Mass reference agrees," Timberlake said. "Ion emission normal."

"Temperature holding normal," Bickel reported. "Doppler comparison is positive-zero."

Bickel looked at those two thin black needles of the Doppler comparator. They were what put the bite in this emergency. They provided positive checks on speed through Doppler reference to fixed astronomical bodies. The Doppler comparison and change in speed had agreed one-for-one.

Bickel felt he knew only one area of probability to explain what had happened, but the area involved a theory that had always been treated as a kind of mathematical game. You first had to assume the universe contained two groups of matter, each moving faster than the speed of light in relation to the other. Then the Cavendish extrapolation on gravitational theory produced negative transformations. Wide holes were opened in the Newtonian theory that two bodies *always* attract each other with a force proportional to the square of the distance between them.

It was that word *always* and the implication that *all* matter exerted gravitational attraction, Bickel thought.

"I do not understand what happened," Flattery said, "but I have the distinct feeling we were close to the brink."

"The brink of what?" Prudence demanded. Fear was plain in her voice.

"We were close to running wild out of the solar system," Bickel said. "Out of control, unable to maneuver. Quite likely, we were close to being hurtled into another dimension."

"Without a prayer of escape," Timberlake said.

"The negative transformations in grav theory," Prudence whispered.

"What?" Timberlake barked.

"The implicit energy exchange for enormous mass shifts near the speed of light," Prudence answered him. "The negative forms in the equations don't all cancel out until you build hypothetical transformations beyond the speed of light. There is a region of mass/speed change wherein two bodies theoretically repel each other rather than attract."

"Now," Bickel said, "how do we tell Hempstead and his boys about this without blowing the whole show?"

"We've already blown the whole show," Timberlake growled. "The computer—"

"Isn't necessarily wrecked," Bickel said. "Our life systems still work. Ship servos and sensors appear to be in order. I get consistent replies to demands for information."

"Consistent doesn't mean correct," Timberlake said.

"Was Hempstead telling us to cease and desist?" Flattery asked. "If he was..."

"We don't know," Bickel said. "As long as we don't know, we don't have to obey."

Or disobey, Flattery thought. "How *is* it the computer seems to function on information demand, but not for AAT translation?"

"That could mean only one band to debug," Prudence said. "If it does..." She broke off staring at Bickel.

Bickel had his eyes closed. Perspiration beaded his forehead. The circuitry was as clear in his mind as though projected there from outside himself. He had never completely disconnected the Ox from the AAT system which they had used for the Ox's interpretive routines.

An empty sensation expanded through his chest as he realized every signal from outside into the AAT had gone through the Ox into the computer—there to be lost, there to mix up the AAT translator loops.

"You didn't disconnect the plugboard from the Ox," Timberlake whispered.

"But my computer readout comes through my AAT board," Bickel said. He could hear the desperation in his own voice. "Every program demand I put on the computer went through those same Ox circuits!"

"You were using subroutines with known addresses," Prudence pointed out.

"And everything you asked for has been scattered through the entire system and lost," Timberlake said.

"Has it?" Bickel asked. He opened his eyes. There was only one logical way to be certain, of course. It would not do any more damage than already had been done...if there *was* damage.

We didn't think of Bickel cutting us off from UMB this way, Flattery thought. *Destroying the translator loops!*

Without the translator system to decode the multire-petitive laser-burst messages, the umbilicus crew might just as well use hand signals for its messages to and from Moonbase. Bickel could build a radio transmitter, of course. It would take only a few watts to punch a message across these distances, but no preparations had been made at UMB for such a communications method. And the number of eavesdroppers would be enormous.

Carefully, because he had to be certain the first time, Bickel switched five patches in his AAT board, triple-checked them.

"What're you doing?" Timberlake demanded.

"Be quiet," Prudence ordered, as she recognized what Bickel intended.

"But he's already—"

"A diagnostic routine," Bickel said. "We'll use a simul-synchronous B-register search with a repeat on our original test of the Ox circuitry. If harm has already been done, this will just go right through the same channels. It can't do any more harm."

"And the B-register search could tell us where our data went," Timberlake said. "Yeah."

"Are you sure?" Flattery asked.

"The technique is right," Prudence said.

Working quietly, triple-checking, Bickel patched together the necessary program. He took a deep breath, sent the first elements of the diagnostic routine through the inputs, setting the balance of the test for off-line operation. He had to keep a constant check on this, key each step himself.

Presently, he began to get DDA output. He put it on conditional transfer with printout at each step in the control sequence.

He felt breathing at his shoulder, looked up to see that Prudence had abandoned her action couch, knelt beside him to stare up at the readout.

"The data has been shifted, not lost," she whispered.

"That's how it looks," Bickel said.

"It might as well be lost!" Timberlake barked.

"No," Bickel refuted him. "The computer's fully operative as long as we route everything through the Ox."

"Why didn't the AAT work?" Timberlake demanded.

"Come off that, Tim," Bickel said. "You helped me build that test setup."

"The incoming messages were going through the AAT circuits twice," Timberlake said. "Sure."

"The bits canceled themselves out all along the line," Bickel said. "We probably didn't get a fifth of the message."

"It did seem short," Prudence said.

"That message is the only thing we've really lost," Bickel said. "I'll ask for a repeat on—"

"Wait!" Flattery said.

"Yes?" Bickel looked at him.

"What do you tell UMB happened to the original message!" Flattery asked. He glanced away from the big board, met Bickel's gaze. "And what if they *were* telling us to cease and desist?"

"You know something," Timberlake said, "the beginning and end of Hempstead's message didn't seem to be garbled at all."

"Standard call and signoff," Bickel said. "They could be recognized and translated from the smallest fractional bits."

"But the message load was lightest at the beginning," Timberlake said. "And that could be part of the explanation there. You'd get minimum cancellation. We might be able to salvage more of the message . . . especially in the first parts before the load jammed it up."

This is exceedingly cautious for Timberlake, Flattery thought. *Is he coming around to Bickel's viewpoint?*

Bickel found himself moving hesitantly, not knowing why, but unable to escape the logic in Timberlake's argument. He slid out the message print, shuttled it to the replay rack. If only the print had been the first step in the reception, instead of intermediate, he thought. He removed his feedback patches, sent the print directly into the Ox and then into AAT, routed the readout through the Optical Character Print system and into the screen above them.

Hempstead's original call appeared there, and they all looked up at it.

That had *to be accurate*, Bickel thought.

There came that original long delay, then: "CHOOSE BY LOT FROM THE COLONISTS IN HYBERNATION A SUITABLE BRAIN TO REPLACE YOUR ORGANIC MENTAL CORE PERIOD MEDICAL PERSONNEL ARE DIRECTED TO TAKE A HUMAN BRAIN COMMA INSTALL IT AS TEMPORARY ORGANIC MENTAL CORE COMMA AND RETURN SHIP TO BIDGEYBIDGEYBIDGEY SOMETIMES WITH THE HIT IT PERIOD PERIOD PERIOD PERIOD PERIOD ON THE QUESTION OF DEFINING CONSCIOUSNESS COMMA YOU HAVE THIS DATA SEVERAL TIMES IN YOUR COMPUTER COMMA AND YOU CAN REFER THERE PERIOD REFERENCE IS MADE TO DATA ITEM ANINSZERO FOR NERVE BARRIER AND THRESHOLD DATA ITEM YOUR COMPUTER PERIOD BEST DIVE YET PERIOD NEW ORGANIC MENTAL CORE PERIOD MEDICAL PERSONNEL ARE DIRECTED TO ABANDON ALL SUCH REPEATS IN THEIR WASTE OF ORDER PERIOD"

Bickel broke the sequence. "Do you want any more of it?"

"It's getting increasingly unreliable," Flattery said. "I see no need."

"Those callous, dirty sons-of-bitches!" Timberlake snarled.

CHAPTER 17

"Remember that I am thy creature; I ought to be thy Adam, but I am rather the fallen angel, whom thou drivest from joy for no misdeed ....Like Adam, I was apparently united by no link to any other being in existence.... Satan had his companions, fellow devils to admire and encourage him, but I am solitary and abhorred."

—Frankenstein's Monster speaks

FOR A LONG time after Timberlake's outburst they sat silently in the cocooned isolation of their action couches, absorbing their predicament. Only Flattery at the big board appeared animate. It was his couch which creaked with his movements. Switches clicked as he depressed them. The underlying stink of their enclosed quarters, by introspection, lifted across their awareness thresholds.

Take the brain from a colonist? Prudence thought. Had Hempstead really told them to commit such an atrocity? She believed it.

Bickel appeared almost asleep, but his hands clenched and unclenched.

Prudence looked at Timberlake, seeing how dark his face was, the way he instinctively bared his teeth. *Those fools back at UMB*, she thought. *Didn't they realize they'd be stamping on the rawest inhibition of our life-systems engineer? Kill a helpless colonist in the hyb tanks!*

No, she thought. *What UMB asked was worse than killing.*

Flattery, noting the effect of the message on Timberlake, felt the jangle of conscience . . . and personal fear. Where his own niche on the ship was concerned, Flattery maintained few illusions. He was both Judas goat and sacrificial goat, classic functions of religious extremity. He was giver of life and executioner—and lest he feel godlike in these powers, he was the ultimate victim of whatever would be the *Earthling*'s destiny.

"As a bird that wandereth from her nest, so is a man that wandereth from his place," he quoted to himself.

Aloud he said, "What they command, we cannot do that."

"You'd better not suggest it," Timberlake said.

"Then we'd better assess whatever it is we've built there in the computer shop, and go on from that point," Flattery said. "What have we built, John?"

"Damned if I know," Bickel said.

"Well, it doesn't seem to be a consciousness, anyway," Prudence said.

"Goddammit!" Bickel snapped. "There you go again! Consciousness! Conscious! It isn't flobblegobble! That's what you might as well say. You don't know how to define consciousness. You don't know what it is. But you go around throwing sentences together as though they had meaning and—"

"That's it," Timberlake said. "That's what hits me right in the pit of the stomach. We start out to build something and we don't know what it is we're building."

It's time to hit them with it, Flattery thought.

"You're wrong, Tim," Flattery said. "And so're you, John. Prudence does know what consciousness is, just as you do. She's a human being. Humans are the only creatures within our ken who can possibly know what consciousness is. Computers can't do that job; humans must."

"Then let her define it," Bickel said.

"Maybe she can't," Flattery said. "But she possesses it."

"A while back you were saying we might not have to define it," Prudence said, and she stared accusingly at Bickel.

"It's just damn poor engineering," Bickel said. "Copy the original and hope you get the same results. We can't be sure we're copying everything in the human model. What're we leaving out?"

He's frustrated and striking out, she thought. *Now's the time to push, while Raj has him set up for me.* "Okay, engineer, where do *you* think you're going with your field-theory idea?"

Bickel stared at her, realizing abruptly that she was deliberately pushing him. *All right, I'll play her game,* he thought. *Am I supposed to be angry? No . . . that'd be too easy. The best attack comes from an unexpected quarter.*

"Stretch yourself a bit, Prue, and try to follow what I'm saying," he challenged her. "The field-theory approach deals with three forces: first, you have the source of experience, the universe which inflicts itself upon us."

"That has to be deeply involved with the way your nervous system functions," she said. "Don't try to teach me my specialty."

"I wouldn't think of it. And you're right. That's the second element: there has to be *someone* who experiences that universe."

"And third?"

"Third, you have the really tricky one. This is the *relationship* between that someone and all of this neural raw material which we call experience. This relationship, this third-order phenomenon, that's our field."

"The self," she said.

"A field," Bickel countered.

She shrugged. "Huxley's 'spatio-temporal cage' with its 'confused swarm of ideas.'"

"Yeah, Huxley said the conscious self had to derive

from memory, but he was just playing with words because he was frightened by what lay beyond the words."

"And you're not?" Flattery demanded.

"You'd better listen closer," Bickel said. "When you try to say that a conscious self derives only from our memory function, you're identifying the someone who experiences with that which supplies the experience."

"Memory is experience," Prudence agreed.

"We have to focus on this third-order relationship," Bickel said.

"The total field that's greater than the sum of its parts," she said.

She's ready for her shock, Bickel thought. *For that matter, so's Raj.*

"You self-satisfied medicos give me a pain. You say only humans are conscious. From Raj, that's sacrilege. From you, Prue, that's stupidity. You see one corner of the spectrum and immediately say you know what the whole universe of light is like. Never once has either one of you asked: *Am I really conscious?*"

Flattery felt an unexplainable pain across his chest. The console in front of him blurred for a heartbeat. Then he had himself under control.

Back at UMB, they laughed and quoted Edgar Allan Poe, Flattery thought. They had said individual humans might not have Poe's "organ of analysis," but that a whole society could create such an organ out of one of its members. Had they realized what a dangerous monster they were creating? What could you hide from Bickel if he turned his attention to it? That was what Prue meant, of course, when she cautioned against underestimating Bickel. But had the UMB *manipulators* known what a knight they had loosed among the pawns?

Perhaps they realized—at least unconsciously—when they set me to watch over him, Flattery thought.

"You try to resolve the basic question into smaller and smaller parts," Bickel said. "Smaller and smaller labels. But that's just avoiding the issue."

"Are we conscious?" Prudence whispered, rolling the thought over and over in her mind.

And she thought of her experience with the marijuana derivative, THC—tetrahydrocannabinol. She'd sought an anti-ataraxic, a selective stimulator of consciousness—something to hold the darkness at bay in a very special manner. But the instant she'd neared the stimulation experience, darkness had spilled over all the edges of her awareness.

Adrenochrome, she thought.

It was a sudden and explosive thought, as of something that had crouched in her path and leaped out at her.

Adrenochrome... nitrogen to CH_3. If she inverted it and gave it a common CH_3 bond with one of the THC forms... Ahhh, that was very like some of the deadly ones. But in an extremely small dosage... Would it get through the blood-brain barrier? And adrenochrome was one of the hallucinogens. What of that?

"You get your fingernails over the ledge," Bickel was saying, "and you haven't yet raised your eyes to the lip—you can only see the dim reflection of light, but you lie and tell those around and below you that you can see to the horizon."

As though his words unlocked a door, the memory of a dream flooded through Prudence. She had dreamed it... sometime during a long sleep... sometime when...

In hyb!

She had dreamed it in the hybernation tank!

In the dream, there had been others around her, but she had been rejected by them. The *others* built a low wall and taunted her to climb it. But each time she tried, the *others* raised the wall higher.

Higher and higher.

Until she no longer even attempted it.

Finally, the *others* had ignored her, but she had heard them laughing and talking on the other side of the wall.

Remembering that dream, Prudence looked at Bickel and understood the thing he had probably seen from the beginning. The problem of creating an artificial consciousness was the problem of consciousness itself. It was an enormous structure, like a tall cliff (or a wall) that they must climb. It loomed over them, dour and black—with only the taunting hint of light at the top.

"You did that deliberately to make me feel small," she accused.

"Welcome to the club," Bickel said.

"What're you saying?" Timberlake demanded. "Are you trying to say that even if we build an analogue of a human, we still might not achieve this... this consciousness?"

"Let's take another look at what happened to the ship *brains*," Bickel said. "What's the basic command they were supposed to obey?"

"Remain conscious and alert at all times," Timberlake said. "But, hell, if you're saying they succumbed to fatigue, that's nonsense. They were buffered against all—"

"Not fatigue," Bickel said. "I'm just wondering, what if they took that order literally, that order to remain *conscious*?"

"The *degree* of consciousness," Prudence mused.

"Threshold," Flattery said and there was wonder in his voice.

"Yes," Prudence said. "A hyperconscious subject has a low threshold. Impulses pass into his awareness with ease. You're suggesting the OMC *brains* couldn't handle hyperconsciousness."

"Something like that."

"Look," she said, "the assault of nerve impulses on the human... consciousness..." She looked defensively at Bickel. "Well, what else are we going to call it?"

"Okay," Bickel said. "Go on."

She stared at him a moment. "This assault is constant, gigantic. The impulses are always present. They swarm around you. There *has* to be a limiting factor, a threshold. Impulses have to pass a certain threshold before you grow... *aware* of them."

"And that threshold varies from person to person, even minute to minute in the same person," Flattery said.

"But how do nerve impulses get over that wall?" Bickel asked.

Why did he use that word? she wondered.

"Sometimes the impulses grow stronger," Flattery said.

"But that isn't the whole story," Prudence said. "There's activity on the side of the . . . experiencer, too. You focus your attention on something and that lowers your threshold."

"Danger can lower it, too," Flattery said. And he waited to see if Bickel would pick up that cue.

Bickel looked at Flattery, wondering. "We're in danger right now, Raj. Is that something they did to us—deliberately?"

"You think that danger out there isn't real?" Flattery asked, unconsciously hooking a thumb toward the shortest distance between himself and the outer hull.

Bickel held his silence, feeling his tongue go dry. Unreasoning terror pervaded him. It was a towering oblivion that threatened to engulf him.

"John," Prudence asked, "are you all right?"

"Just a touch of ship vertigo," Bickel managed. He forced a smile. "Perhaps . . . maybe I'm tired. I went more than two shifts at that haywire setup in the shop, and I haven't really had a good rest for I don't know how long."

Knowing when to relax the pressure is half the job, Prudence reminded herself. "Get some chow and shuteye. It might help if we let up on this problem a bit."

And she thought: *I can give him that advice but I won't take it myself.*

Those last chemical experiments on her own body were playing hob with her sense of reality. She wondered if she should take Raj into her confidence, but rejected this thought as soon as it occurred. Raj would say she was meddling. He'd force her to stop and she felt that she didn't dare stop now. There was something . . . something . . . something so close. . . .

"What about answering Hempstead?" Bickel asked.

"Let 'em sweat," Timberlake growled.

"They'll figure it was a transmission breakdown if we go too long beyond the delay period," Bickel said. "They'll retransmit the message."

"That gets us the retransmission without committing ourselves," Flattery said.

"Isn't that a rather devious suggestion for our cleric?" Bickel asked.

"That was the psychiatrist speaking," Prudence said. "Go on, get your sleep."

"And I can sit here and twiddle my thumbs," Timberlake said.

Bickel looked at Timberlake, recalling the man's bitter anger over Hempstead's suggestion. For the first time in many hours, Bickel focused his full attention on Timberlake, seeing the pride the man had swallowed in relinquishing command of the ship, seeing Timberlake's primary concern—for the human lives around him.

There was no easing Timberlake's tensions right now, Bickel realized. The lives *were* in danger . . . every life on the Tin Egg from the lowliest chick embryo in the hyb tanks right up to Timberlake himself.

Timberlake sometimes saw through things intuitively, Bickel realized. And Timberlake was an engineer. It might help him if he were kept occupied . . . and this crew could use any available edge.

"Tim," Bickel said, "we have to solve for consciousness the way you solve for a specific effect in a transceiver or a tuner or an amplifier. You might be chewing that over while I get some rest. I need specific answers that can be translated into working schematics."

"But we're stuck with that thing in the shop," Timberlake protested.

"Only as a beginning. We have to use the Ox, yeah, because it's our only entrance into the computer for some of our vital data . . . now. But it's still a place to begin. Nothing's changed, really."

"Except we're two days closer to our deadline and no closer to a solution," Timberlake growled.

Bickel put down a surge of anger. "Suit yourself." He turned away, crossed to the hatch into quarters, let himself through, sealed the hatch behind him.

The sound of the hatch expanders hissed through him like a sigh and he found himself standing in the galley-round wondering if he had enough energy left to eat *and* get into a sleeping cubicle.

"I have to eat," he whispered. "Got to keep my strength up."

He pushed himself across to the quick-bar, sent half a heat charge through a squeeze tube of soup, gulped it. Chicken. He could feel the broth pouring energy back into him, took a tube of hot chocolate after the soup.

He crossed to his padded tank, checked the cubicle's life-systems repeaters. Every gauge was normal. He let himself into the tank, closed its hatch, pulled the pneumo-pin. Slowly, gently, the tank enclosed him, buoyed him. He felt the flow of oxygen-rich air across his face, the air filtered and refiltered so many times that it had lost most of its ship stink.

His muscles began to unwind and, as usual when he prepared for sleep in the cubicle, he wondered at the soothing effect. It was like a return to the womb.

What womb bore the original me? he wondered. *Somewhere, there was a mother . . . and a father. Even if I was grown in a gestation chamber, somewhere flesh and blood conceived me. Who were they? I'll never know. Useless even to think about it.*

He forced his attention instead onto the "cube" around him, the artificial womb with its deep sense of security to insure sound sleep.

Why do we get more and better rest in a "cube"? A quick nap on an action couch is nowhere near as restful. Why? Is it something atavistic, a phylogenetic return to the sea? Or is it something else, something we have yet to recognize?

Bickel focused his awareness on the billowing softness of the enclosure, the rich moist air. Sleep was sending its tendrils through him and he sensed how slow and even his breathing had become.

How rhythmic.

The set rhythms, he thought, holding back sleep. *There's an oscillation factor in our problem. Oscillation is present in hypnotic captivation, in sleep-breathing, in the heartbeat . . . in sex . . .*

And living cells possess north and south magnetic poles, he thought.

He recalled the biologist-designer, Vincent Frame, expounding on that theme in a lecture for Biological Engineering back at UMB.

I am a structure composed of many different cells, Bickel reminded himself. *Coordinated.*

Frame had hammered at this theme, pointing to vital clues in the oscillations and pulses of human activities— *cell energies.*

In that remembered lecture, Frame had been explaining the design of a low-gravity lounge chair.

Rhythms . . . characteristic rhythms of living.

Frame had returned to that concept time and again. *Oscillation.*

Despite his fatigue and the sleep lurking at the edge of his awareness, Bickel felt the urgency of this "hot track" onto which his mind had stumbled. He thumbed his intercom alive, looked up to the tiny monitor screen.

Timberlake's face peered back at him.

"Remember Dr. Frame's lectures. Oscillation. Discuss it later." Bickel released the intercom switch before Timberlake could answer.

As he sank back, Bickel felt sleep come up from some dark place underneath to engulf him.

CHAPTER 18

Is consciousness merely a special form of hallucination?

—Prudence Lon Weygand (#5)
Message Capsule fragment

FLATTERY HAD JUST shifted the Com-central board to Prudence. He looked across at Timberlake, who sat on the edge of his action couch staring at a memo pad of ship paper. The thin paper rustled faintly as Timberlake folded back a page, scribbled something on a clean surface.

The monitor screen beside Timberlake showed that Bickel had sunk into sleep almost immediately after that strange call.

"Tim, did Bick's message make sense to you?" Flattery asked.

"Maybe." Timberlake looked up from his notepad. "Let's assume that consciousness involves an organic receptor of some kind which produces a field structure."

"And this field structure expands and collapses under different stresses," Prudence said.

Timberlake nodded. "And that field structure itself would be the phenomenon we call consciousness."

"Are you two agreeing with him?" Flattery asked.

"For the moment," Timberlake said. "Now, let's follow this assumption. The organic receptor would be subjected to a constant storm of impressions."

"And most researchers think the cerebellum is the focus of that storm of impressions," Prudence said.

"But it's certainly not the seat of consciousness," Flattery objected.

"There may be no *seat* of consciousness," Prudence said. "We're talking about a motile phenomenon. It can move by itself."

"Okay," Timberlake said. "What's the impression input? What does the cerebellum receive?"

"Electrical inputs of some form," Prudence said.

"Yes. . . . but how is that input sorted into its receiver?"

Flattery inhaled a deep breath, caught at last by the feeling of the hunt with the quarry near. Was it possible that this crew would succeed? He grew conscious that Prudence had asked him a question.

"What?"

"Do you understand this concept? We're talking about electroform inputs of nerve-impulse groups and each group would be of extremely short duration."

"But the groups wouldn't be absolutely discrete," Flattery said.

"Of course not," she said. "It's like the ambiguity of light. Sometimes the physicist has to think of light as waves and sometimes as particles."

"Wavicles," Flattery said, his tone musing.

"Right. So sometimes we think of these nerve-impulse groups as discrete units, particles, and sometimes we think of them as a continuous flow . . . waves."

"Track that discrete flow for me," Timberlake said.

She glanced away from the big console, studied Timberlake. There was no avoiding the excitement in him. With that intuitive sense of his, Timberlake had leaped ahead somewhere and the others were supposed to follow.

"The track's pretty well plotted," Flattery said. "Action currents are conducted over the cortico-ponto-cerebellar tract. What're you driving at?"

She saw it then as a diagram in her mind: *(1) cortico-(2) ponto-(3)cerebellar. Three-phase! Were those the essential three of Bickel's field-self?*

Prudence put this thought into words, waited, not knowing quite what to expect from the others.

"Three tracks, not one," Flattery mused. "No . . . that's not it." Then, pouncing: "Holographic!"

"A holographic field," Prudence said. She saw that Flattery, too, had been caught up in Timberlake's excitement. But the board demanded her full attention for a moment and it was only later that she realized she had missed some silent exchange between Flattery and Timberlake—perhaps a knowing look, a nod . . .

Presently, Timberlake said: "I want you to say it. What's the terminal point of all that input?"

"It goes into the silent or nonfunctional areas of the cerebellum," Prudence said.

Flattery felt a need to expand on this. "That's the superior and inferior lobes, the declive, the folium, and the tuber—the major portion of the cerebellum."

"Mediation is across the tract from the cerebral cortex," Prudence said.

"Silent or nonfunctional?" Timberlake asked. "Don't you medical people ever listen to your own words?"

"What do you mean?" Flattery asked. There was an edge of anger in his tone.

"What's the potential, the effect?" Timberlake demanded.

"I don't—"

"Energy arrives! Does it turn a wheel? Does it turn on a light? You can't keep piling energy into any system indefinitely without some kind of output . . . or balancing effect."

"But you said—"

"What's the output, the potential, the balancing effect? The energy goes in. What does it do?"

"Are you suggesting that this . . . this *potential*, that it's consciousness?" Prudence asked.

And she remembered Bickel calling the field system an "infinite sponge."

Flattery cut across this thought. "Didn't Bickel say something about consciousness being like the vestibular reflex of the inner ear?"

"The way we balance," Timberlake said. "The thing that tells us which way is down and which way is up."

"The strangest thing," Prudence said. "I feel as though I'd been a little bit asleep all along, not awake enough to realize what Bickel was driving at."

"But now you're beginning to get it," Timberlake said.

"That storm of sense impressions doesn't stop when you're asleep," Flattery argued. "Are you trying to tell me that *sleep* is a form of consciousness?"

As he spoke, he remembered making the same argument to Bickel, but now he had to be honest with himself and face up to the obvious answer plus everything that the answer implied.

"Yes, of course," Flattery said. "Sleep's a form of consciousness. It just falls near one end of the spectrum."

"And all that unexplained energy?" Timberlake insisted.

"It has to be used for something," Flattery said. "Yes, I see that."

"All right," Timberlake said. "The consciousness-effect—field or whatever—may mediate that energy balance. Perhaps it's a homeostat."

"All biological control mechanisms are homeostats," Prudence said. "So what?"

"It's not enough to say that consciousness juggles the storm of sense impressions," Flattery said. "That still leaves your question unanswered, Tim. What happens to the energy?"

"There must be another effect somewhere in the system," Timberlake said. "There has to be an unexplained flow of energy somewhere—or a flow that's been explained the wrong—"

"Synergy," Prudence said.

Flattery shot a surprised glance at her. The word had been on the tip of his tongue.

"Synergy," Timberlake mused. "Any medical surprises in there?"

Prudence heard the question within the question. The life-systems engineer had a working acquaintance with synergy, but he wanted to know if a medical simplification might help him. Timberlake was sniffing down a hot trail.

"It's the effect produced by our spinal reflexes," she said. "Synergy acts through the cerebellum, an extra effect. It's on the side of the ... ahhh, circuit that leads out from the cortex."

"We're looking for an integrating or balancing effect," Timberlake said.

"That's ... possible," Flattery said.

This wasn't enough for Timberlake. "Simple synaptic integration is enough on the side leading toward the cortex. Does synergy involve output *from* the frontal lobes or the gyrus? Could it account for our missing energy?"

"Why the gyrus?" Flattery asked.

"I keep looking for secondary mediation areas. We don't dare overlook anything. We have to be right the first time or we go down the tube the same way all the other ships did."

"You're going around in circles the same way Bickel does," Flattery objected. "So you narrow down the mediating area to the frontal lobes. So what?"

Timberlake wouldn't be distracted. "Lot's of researchers think the frontal lobes—"

"Fine!" Flattery interrupted. "No end of good people may've suggested that the frontal lobes are the mysterious center of consciousness. But Prue may be closer to it than you are. Motile, remember? There may be no seat of consciousness."

Timberlake blinked. "What good does it do to know *where* it is if you don't know *what* it is?"

Flattery pressed him. "Synergy may not be totally explained, but it's still useful as a concept. However, if you're suggesting that synergy is consciousness..."

"Dead end," Timberlake said. "But Bickel thinks we're after a field-regulating sensor which deals with mental and emotional responses."

So that's what's bothering him! Prudence thought. She

said aloud: "If we're going to reproduce this thing artificially, whatever we build has to have sensory, mental, *and* emotional responses to regulate."

Flattery pressed himself back into his couch. "Ahhhhh. We can give Bickel's Ox its sensory and mental responses—but how do we give it emotions?"

"What about negative feedback?" Timberlake asked. "Emotions always involve a goal. Negative feedback suggests a goal-seeking element in the system."

"Consciousness requires a goal?" Flattery asked.

He realized by the sudden silence greeting his question that they had lifted themselves to a critical point of this analysis. They could all feel it. Bickel's challenging ideas had goaded them to this effort and now all of them were poised, sprinters waiting for the gun.

"A goal," Timberlake whispered. His voice grew louder. "An object on which to focus." He looked at Flattery. "The field relationship?"

Close, but not quite it, Prudence thought.

Flattery said: "Not an entity or a thing or an area of the brain, but a connecting link between such things or entities or areas."

Out of the corner of an eye, Flattery saw Prudence adjust a dial on the big console. He sensed the waiting tensions in her movements.

"A bridge!" Timberlake shouted. "Of course! Of course! A bridge!"

"A bridge built out of language?" Prudence asked.

"But the symbols are loaded with errors, with weaknesses and flaws," Timberlake said. "That's it."

Flattery saw a new quickness and sureness enter Prudence's movements as she digested this.

"Time spanning," she said. "With words...with symbols."

And Flattery thought: *There is a gateway to the imagination you must enter before you are conscious and the keys to the gate are symbols. You can carry ideas through the gate from one time-place to another time-place, but you must carry the ideas in symbols. Do you know, though, what you carry...and who it is that carries?*

"Every symbol has hidden premises behind it," Flattery said. "Every word carries unspoken assumptions."

"And the most critical word in the whole problem is the word *consciousness*," Timberlake said.

"Which assumes," Prudence said, "that there is a self to be conscious."

"A bridge crosses from one place to another place," Timberlake went on. "If it starts breaking down, the engineers get out the original blueprints, the materials orders, and they go to the bridge and examine it. They study the bridge under static conditions and under loads. Then they may replace parts, put in new bracings—"

"Or tear the whole damn thing down and start over," said Prudence. "Didn't either one of you hear me? Our word assumes there's a self to be conscious."

"We heard you," Flattery said. "But there are more important hidden assumptions...than 'Know thyself.' What about 'Know thy limits'?"

"Limits," Timberlake picked up the word. "At one end—sleep or the sleep of death; and at the other end—waking."

"And the question of Western religion," Flattery said, "is: What lies beyond death? But the question of the Zen master is: What lies beyond waking?"

"For Kee-rist's sake!"

The voice was Bickel's and it plunged down onto them from the command-circuit screen overhead.

Flattery looked up with a smug smile to find Bickel glaring down at him from the screen.

"I leave you for a half-hour, and you lure these poor fools down some mystical dead end! Tossing labels around just like those jackasses back at UMB! Zen master! Next you'll trot out Cosmic Consciousness! Of all the impractical—"

"John, we've refined this question down to its essence," Timberlake said. "If you'd—"

"I asked you to give me some circuit suggestions. I've

been listening to you play verbal medicine ball for ten minutes, and what I want to know is this: How will all that yakking build one circuit? Just one circuit!"

"You yourself asked UMB to define consciousness," Prudence protested.

"Because I wanted to keep them occupied and out of our hair." The screen went blank.

Flattery looked over to the console in front of Prudence, saw that the command-circuit key pointed to "on," but the screen remained blank.

That key is on! Flattery told himself. It had to be turned on deliberately. *She did it! To waken Bickel.*

But why was the screen blank?

As though she read his mind, Prudence said: "John's installed an override on the command circuit. Any idea why?"

"Didn't you see where he was?" Timberlake demanded. "He was in the shop—working on that Ox mess!"

Timberlake unlocked his action couch and, in almost the same motion, launched himself at the hatch to the computer maintenance shop. He wrenched at the lock dogs, but they remained immovable.

"He's jammed the lock!" Timberlake's voice rose in fear. "If he wrecks our computer..."

"You noticed...so you may as well watch," taunted Bickel's voice.

They looked up to see a view of the shop on their big screen. Bickel stood with the detritus of the initial Ox installation around him—dangling leads, meters, neuron blocks—all stacked precariously away from the computer wall.

"Bickel, listen to reason," Timberlake pleaded. "You can't just tear into—"

"Shut up or I'll turn you off," Bickel warned.

He knelt with a substitute neuron block, inserted it between the Ox and the computer wall, began making connections.

"Please, John," Prudence begged, "if you'd—"

"You're not going to stop him by talking to him," Flattery said.

"Listen to Raj." Bickel slipped another neuron block into place against the wall, made new connections.

"Rhythm," he said. "I went to sleep on it...and it woke me up—that and your yakking. Rhythm."

Another substitute neuron block went into place beneath the first two.

"Describe what you're doing," Flattery said, and he motioned for Timberlake to come to his side.

"Brain-vision anatomy can be reduced to the mathematical description of a scanning process," Bickel answered. "It follows that any other brain-function anatomy—including consciousness—should submit to the same approach. I can duplicate the alpha-rhythm cycle for a brain-scanning sweep by setting it up in the time-cycle of these neuron blocks. If I trace each rhythm from a human model and duplicate—"

"What's the function of each of these human rhythms?" Flattery demanded.

As he spoke, Flattery scribbled a note on a pad of ship flimsy, pressed it into Timberlake's hand.

Timberlake looked up to the screen, but Bickel still had his back to the video eyes that matched the screen-view.

"We don't know that function for certain, do we?" Flattery asked, and he motioned frantically for Timberlake to read the note.

Timberlake turned his attention onto the paper, read: "BACK WAY, AROUND THE HYB TANKS. BICKEL HASN'T JAMMED THE HATCH FROM QUARTERS. TAKE THE OTHER TUBE AND SURPRISE HIM."

Again, Timberlake looked up to the screen.

The Ox was taking on new shape under Bickel's hands—reaching out to the angle of the shop against the computer wall. It began to assume a feeling of topological improbability in Timberlake's eyes—with jutting triangles of plastic, oblongs of neuron couplers, strips of Eng multipliers...and the color-coded leads interweaving like a crazy spiderweb.

Timberlake felt a hand grab his arm, shake him. He looked at the hand, followed its arm to Flattery's glaring face.

Flattery gestured to the note in Timberlake's other hand.

Again, Timberlake looked at the note, recognizing why he remained rooted to this spot. *Around the hyb tanks?*

No.

It would have to be through the hyb tanks.

Flattery must know that.

Timberlake turned his tortured gaze on Flattery, bringing the terror up to full awareness. *Bickel has infected me with his cynical skepticism. I'm afraid of what I'll find in the hyb tanks if I look too close. I'll find the tanks empty, and nothing but leads back into the computer from the tanks. And the computer will be programmed to simulate the presence of hybernating life in those tanks. The whole thing will turn out to be a monstrous hoax.*

I'll discover I've been life-systems engineer to ... nothing. . . .

Why do I fear that? he wondered. Even this thought set him shivering.

Again, Flattery shook his arm.

Why doesn't *he* go? Timberlake wondered. *He's so anxious!*

The answer was obvious: Flattery wasn't as knowledgeable about computers. He couldn't analyze what Bickel was doing and repair—if that was possible—the damage.

I'm panic-stricken, Timberlake thought.

But he knew he couldn't stay rooted here. He had to take that other passage. And when he got into the hyb tanks, he wouldn't be able to resist the close inspection. He'd look beyond the dials and gauges and repeaters. He'd look into the tanks.

Despite his unexplainable terror, the other possibility remained—that the tanks contained life, and this life shared their danger.

CHAPTER 19

The cell has energies that oscillate and pulse
with the tumult of living. We see reflections of
this root-activity in that coordinated cell
structure which we commonly refer to as a
human being. Have you ever watched a man
tapping his finger nervously on a desktop?
Have you ever timed the periodicity of the
human eyeblink? Breathing has characteristic
rhythms for different conditions of the total
cell structure. You must keep this in mind
when you design devices to be used and
occupied by this human bundle of cells. You
must always remember the pulse and the
needs of the component cells.

—Vincent Frame
Biochemist/Designer

I'll use the shot-effect generator again, Bickel thought.

He leaned into the organized clutter of the Ox, clipped
a lead onto the temporary input, threaded the lead out,
and draped it to one side.

The effect and the way to achieve it were still clear in
his mind. He had awakened suddenly, not knowing how

long he had slept, but feeling refreshed and with this *answer* filling his mind.

He turned to the computer leads, linked the Ox through a buffer that would feed its impulses into a test-memory bank, connected this to the new bank of neuron blocks, and put the system on full interlock.

"Will you at least explain what you're doing, John?" Flattery's voice flowed out of the screen.

Bickel glanced back, saw Prudence at the controls, Flattery sitting on the edge of an action couch—no sign of Timberlake. But this screen's eyes didn't expose all of Com-central. It was probable that Timberlake was trying the hatch. *Well, let him.*

"We have only ourselves to use as models for producing this Consciousness Function," Bickel said. "And everybody keeps saying we can't get *into* ourselves the way an engineer should to duplicate the mechanism. But, friend, there's another approach—thoroughly tested and effective."

Prudence said: "Raj?"

Flattery looked at her.

"I'm getting current drift on the auxiliary power supply."

"It's the shop," Flattery stated flatly. "John's taken a direct line to prevent us from shutting him off." He looked back at Bickel. "Right?"

"Right. It shouldn't cause you any trouble. I've isolated the line. Your main board is still functioning." Bickel turned back to the Ox, began tying in a series of timed neurofibers.

"What's the tested, effective method?" Flattery looked up at the telltales on the Com-central board, following Timberlake's progress by the heat sensors. Timberlake was out in the second zone now, turning in toward the opposite side of the shielding and the hyb tanks.

Why was Tim so reluctant to go? Flattery wondered.

Bickel finished a triple connection along the timed fibers, straightened. "The system you can't tear apart and examine is called a black box. If we can make a *white* box sufficiently similar and general in *potential* to the black box—that is, make it sufficiently complex—then we can force the black box, by its own operation, to transfer its pattern of action to the white box. We cross-link them and subject each to identical shot-effect bursts."

"What's your white box?" Flattery asked, his interest and attention caught in spite of his fears. "That thing?" He nodded toward the crazy-block construction of the Ox.

"Hell, no, this is nowhere near complex enough. But out entire computer system is."

He's gone crazy! Flattery thought. *He can't be suggesting seriously that he'd throw a scrambling shot-effect burst into the computer!*

Again, Flattery glanced up at the telltales. Timberlake was at the edge of the hyb tanks, moving at a maddeningly slow pace.

"Then . . . how does the Ox function in this?" Flattery asked, returning his attention to the screen.

"This is our sorter," Bickel said. "It sorts the rhythms of the system and acts as a crude set of frontal lobes." He linked two parts of his construction by cross-jacks in a patchboard. "There. Now to run a few tests."

"Shouldn't you wait?" Flattery demanded. "Shouldn't we discuss this a bit more? What if you've made a mistake and—"

"No mistake," Bickel said.

Flattery looked to the telltales. Timberlake was in the hyb tanks now, but he wasn't moving—just stopped there.

We set Bickel, our "organ of analysis," at too high a pitch, Flattery thought. *We should've known it could run wild.*

What was keeping Timberlake?

"Straight line test, first," Bickel said, and closed a key on the computer wall. He stared at the diagnostic-circuit dials above him.

Flattery held his breath, turned slowly to look at the big board in front of Prudence. If Bickel's test loused up the central computer system, it'd show up first on the big board.

The flashboard retained its quiet green. The steady ticking of relays through the graph counters and monitors held at an even pace. Everything appeared soothingly ordinary.

"I'm getting individual nerve-net responses on the separate blocks," Bickel said.

Flattery kept his attention on the flashboard. If Bickel ruined the computer, the ship was dead. Most of the Tin Egg's automatic systems depended on the computer's inner lines of communication and supervisory control programs.

"Didn't you hear me?" Bickel demanded. "I'm getting nerve-net response! This thing'll behave like a human nervous system!"

"Raj, he is!"

It was Prudence. Flattery dropped his gaze to where she was pointing. She had shifted a small corner of her own auxiliary board into a repeater system tied to Bickel's diagnostic circuits.

"Beta rhythm," she said, pointing to the scope in the center of the board.

Flattery watched the sine play of the green line on the scope, digesting what Bickel had said, what that scope implied.

Black box—white box.

Perhaps it was possible, theoretically, to use the entire computer as a white box to take the transfer pattern called consciousness. But there remained many unanswered questions—and one was more vital than all the others.

"What do you intend using as a black box?" Flattery asked. "Where'll you get your original pattern?"

"From a conscious human brain. I'm going to take one of our spare hyb tanks and adapt the electroencephalographic feedback system as a man-amplifier."

He's utterly mad, Flattery thought. *The shot-effect shock would kill the human subject.*

Bickel looked out of the screen, stared at Flattery—realizing that the psychiatrist-chaplain had seen the possible deadliness of this proposal.

Who will bell the cat? Bickel thought. He swallowed. *Well, if necessary, I will.*

"How would you protect the subject from the shot-effect bursts?" Prudence asked. "Curare?"

Even as she asked, she wondered how she was protecting herself from her own experiments. The answer was daunting: No better than Bickel would! What had made this crew so prone to all-or-nothing efforts?

"I believe the subject will have to be fully conscious," Bickel said. "Without any medication . . . or narcoinhibitions."

He waited for the explosion from Timberlake. This idea was sure to outrage the conditioning of the life-systems engineer. Where *was* Timberlake?

"Absolutely not!" Flattery exploded. "It'd be murder!"

"Or maybe . . . suicide," Bickel said.

Prudence looked away from the console, met Bickel's eyes. "Be reasonable, John," she pleaded. "You're already endangering the computer with that . . ."

"The ship's still functioning, isn't it?" Bickel countered.

"But if you throw a shot-effect burst through that—" she nodded toward the stacked blocks and interwoven leads of the Ox beside Bickel "—how'll you avoid damage to the computer's core memory?"

"Core memory's a fixed system and buffered. I'll keep the Ox potential below the buffer threshold. Besides . . ." he shrugged, "we've already put shot-effect bursts through the computer without—"

"And scattered information from hell to breakfast!" she snapped.

"We can still find that information if we use the Ox to sort the addresses for us," Bickel said.

Flattery glanced at the sensors in front of Prudence. What was wrong with Timberlake? Was he injured? Unconscious? But the sensors revealed a narrow path of movement from the life-systems engineer . . . all of it within the hyb tank complex.

"If I understand you correctly," Prudence said, "you'll have to add nerve-net simulation channels to the Ox until it and the computer are as complex as a human nervous system. As you build it and test it, we become more and more dependent on that jury-rigged Ox monstrosity for our very lives."

"It has to have a full range of sensory apparatus," Bickel said. "There's no other way."

"There must be!" she said. "Where'd you get such a mad idea?"

"From you."

Shock momentarily stilled her tongue. "That's impossible!"

"You're a female," Bickel pointed out, "capable of biological reproduction of conscious life. In that method, you have a substrate of molecules that are capable of assuming a large number of forms . . . different forms. Those molecules assume a *particular* form in the presence of a molecule that already has that form." He shrugged. "Black box—white box."

"I thought you meant from me personally," she said, looking up at the telltale sensors and seeing the apparently irrational movements of Timberlake.

"Look," Bickel said, unaware of their preoccupation, "the basic behavior of the computer will remain intact. We won't interfere with supervisory programs or command constants. We want to set up a system dealing with probabilities, with mobility constant for the—"

"Games theory!" Flattery sneered. "You can't predict all the behavior of your machine." He looked back at the telltales.

What was Tim doing?

"That's just it!" Bickel said. "If the machine's going to be conscious, we can't predict all of its behavior . . . by the very nature of consciousness, by definition. Consciousness is a game where the permissible moves aren't arbitrarily established in advance. The sole object's to win."

Anything goes? Flattery wondered. He focused suddenly on Bickel, recognizing the essentially blasphemous nature of such a concept. There *had* to be rules!

"The machine gets part of its personality from its creator, part from its opponents," Bickel said.

Something from God, something from the Devil,
Flattery thought. *There had to be essential error in this
path...somewhere. Bickel was behaving far outside the
predictions. Their "organ of analysis" was acting
illogically. He was not making the best possible move
each time.*

"You'll introduce error factors and loss increment into
the entire computer," Prudence cautioned. "That's not
only illogical, it's—" She broke off, studied her board,
made a pressure-balance correction in the atmospheric
recirculation system, and waited to see if the automatics
could hold the new setting.

"You have to make the best possible move at all times,"
Flattery said. "Your suggestion does not appear to—"

"There you've hit it," Bickel agreed. "Best possible
move. Sometimes your best possible move is to make a
dangerously *poor* move that changes the entire theoretical structure of the game. You change the game."

"What about all those lives down in the hyb tanks?"
Prudence asked. "Do they have any choice in
this...game?"

"They already made their choice."

"And while they're helpless, you change the rules,"
Flattery said.

"That was one of the chances they accepted when they
accepted hybernation," Bickel said. "That was their
choice."

Flattery abandoned the argument, pushed himself off
his action couch.

"What're you going to to do?" Prudence asked.

"Check on Tim."

"Where *is* Tim?" Bickel asked.

"Down in the hyb tanks," Flattery said, knowing
Bickel could get the answer himself—once he consulted
the shop's repeaters.

"Deep in the hyb tanks?" Bickel asked.

"Of course!"

"Prue!" Bickel snapped. "Try to raise him on the
command circuit."

She heard the urgency in Bickel's voice, whirled to obey.

There was no response from Timberlake.

"You fools!" Bickel said.

Flattery stopped at the tube hatch, glared up at the screen.

"Who let him go down into the deep tanks?" Bickel demanded. "You blind idiots! Don't you know what he's likely to find down there?"

"What do you mean?"

"This whole damn ship's nothing but a simulation device," Bickel said. "There'll be nothing down there except a few crew replacements. Those tanks have to be empty!"

He's wrong! Flattery thought. *Or is he?*

The thought staggered Flattery. He saw immediately how that might pull the props out from under Timberlake—a man tuned as fine as the rest of them for a specific function.

"He'd still have the crew systems," Prudence said. She stared across the room at Flattery, feeling the loneliness. The Tin Egg with its programmed peril might contain only a few isolated humans launched into nowhere.

They wouldn't, Flattery thought. *But if they'd prepare me to cheat the rest of the crew . . .* His feet felt rooted to the deck. He swallowed in a dry throat. *But it's impossible! They promised me when I discovered the actual Tau Ceti records—if we succeeded we could just send back the message capsule and continue as . . .*

"Raj, are you sick?" Prudence asked. She studied him, seeing the lost, sunken look in his eyes.

"The Tau Ceti planets are uninhabitable, yes," Hempstead had admitted when confronted with the evidence. *"No Eden. But the universe is known to contain billions of inhabitable planets. You realize you can't come back here, of course. The danger to your hosts."*

"The biopsy donors were all criminals," Flattery had said, springing his other suspicion.

"Brilliant people, but misdirected," Hempstead had protested. *"That is one of the reasons you can't come*

back, but nothing's to stop you from going on to explore
and find your own Eden."

Remembering the words, Flattery felt how hollow they
sounded.

Sham and trickery all the way, he thought. *But why?*

CHAPTER 20

In a right-handed person, the so-called rational function operates mainly from the left hemisphere of the cerebral cortex. The 'intuitive' operation, however, lives mainly in the right hemisphere. There is strong evidence for positive feedback between the two hemispheres operating along the corpus callosum. The substance of this interchange remains largely a mystery, but there can be no doubt that it serves an important function in consciousness.

—Morgan Hempstead
Lectures at Moonbase

TIMBERLAKE HAD launched himself down the communications tube with desperate haste, knowing he had to move swiftly or become stalled in terror.

At the tube-distribution lock, he sealed the hatch behind him, snatched a robox-monkey from its rack, tuned the sensors to the track imprinted in the tube wall, slammed its wheels onto the guide marks, and grabbed the handhold controls. Again he encountered that terrifying reluctance to move, and stared up the tube, studying the long, infinity curve of it visible through the transparent safety locks.

I can't go back, he thought.

With a sudden wrench, he twisted the little robox tow unit's drive to full on, let it jerk him ahead along that curving track.

The wind of his passage was a dim hiss. He was like a loose piston driving down that tube. Locks opened automatically to the robox signal, closed behind him. He slowed for the protective jog through the shielding layer, twisted around through the branching outside the hyb tanks, dove back down along the flat angle that returned through the watershield, and stopped in the lock chamber to the tanks.

He racked the robox, stared at the hatch. It was a big yellow oval, its seal warning in heavy blue letters: "THIS HATCH MUST BE CLOSED AND DOGGED BEFORE INNER HATCH WILL OPEN!"

Now that he was faced with it, Timberlake felt a calm submission to fate. He gripped the hatch dogs, broke the seal, seeing the line of frost inside as the hatch swung open. His suit generators hummed upscale, compensating for the drop in temperature as chill air spilled out of the lock.

Timberlake slipped into the lock, closed and sealed the outer hatch, turned around. A rack of heavy-duty generators hung over the inner hatch with a big warning sign above them: "EXTREME DANGER! DEEP SPACE OR L-T SUIT REQUIRED BEFORE ENTERING THE NEXT LOCK. BE SURE YOU HAVE SPARE GENERATOR IN WORKING CONDITION BEFORE OPENING THIS HATCH."

Timberlake looped the straps of a spare generator over his shoulder, gave the thing's turbine drive a short burst to check it. The generator hummed briefly. He swung the rack of them aside, broke open the next hatch, slipped through and dogged it behind him.

Now, a smaller hatch greeted him, and lettered on its face: "ADMISSION ONLY TO LIFE-SYSTEMS ENGINEERS OR MEDICAL PERSONNEL. SUIT SECURITY MUST BE MAINTAINED AT ALL TIMES BEYOND THIS POINT. DO NOT OPEN THIS HATCH UNTIL YOU HAVE ADJUSTED YOUR SUIT FOR THE EXTREME LOW OF HYBERNATION TEMPERATURES."

Timberlake coupled the auxiliary generator to his suit, checked both generators, adjusted them for temperature-security override. The remembered routine occupied his awareness, keeping his mind off the space beyond that hatch. Suit seals slithered under his gloved fingers as he secured them. He dropped the anti-fog viewplate over his faceplate, ran a check tape along the seals.

The moment of final decision had come.

Timberlake forced himself to act slowly and calmly. More than his own life depended on what he did now, he told himself. Stray heat inside there could play havoc with helpless lives. He passed his suit's baffles in front of a heat sensor, studied the gauge.

Zero.

His gloved hands went to the dogs of the inner hatch, broke the seal. The hatch popped slightly, indicating a small difference in pressure—nothing abnormal. He stepped through into the glittering dry chill of the first bank of hyb tanks. This was where Prudence had been. He saw her empty tank on his left, its leads dangling, the cushioned carrier still open inside.

Everything around him was revealed in harsh blue light. He studied the chamber.

It was like a giant barrel—an open space in the center surrounded by the smaller barrels that were the individual hybernation tanks. A grid-floored catwalk led down the open center, with short ladders and handholds branching up to the separate tanks.

Timberlake kicked off down the length of the tank in three low-grav jumps, caught a handhold beside the breaker lock that separated this section from the next one.

He looked back. *No . . . they weren't little barrels,* he thought. The individual tanks stretched away from him— all around—like so many sections of gray culvert pipe waiting to be assembled into something useful . . . like a drain.

There was no point examining the tanks in here, he knew. This was the No. 1 section: high-priority crew replacements. If there was deception, it'd be farther along the line—in one of the deeper sections.

Timberlake opened the safety valve at the breaker lock, swung open the hatch, let himself through, reset the mechanism to isolate the section in the event of partial damage.

He looked around the new section. It was the twin of the other except for the absence of a raided tank.

Timberlake swallowed. His cheeks felt damp and cold. A place between his shoulder blades itched.

Quite abruptly, he found himself remembering Professor Aldiss Warren, the lecturer in biophysics back at UMB. He was a goat-bearded old man with a senile-sounding voice and a mind like a scimitar.

Why do I think of old Warren—now? Timberlake wondered.

As though the question released a hidden awareness, he recalled the old man diverging from a seminar discussion to talk about moral strength.

"You wish to test moral strength?" he'd asked. "Simple. Construct a med-computer with a public callbox attachment. Set it so that anyone submitting to the computer's probes can find out to within a day or so when he'll die ... of natural causes, of course. If you wish to call old age natural. Then you step back and see who uses the thing."

Someone—a female student, had asked, "Wouldn't it take a kind of courage *not* to use this computer?"

"Pah!" old Warren had exploded.

Another student had said, "Hypothetical questions like this always bore the hell out of me."

"Sure," old Warren had answered. "You young toughs haven't faced the fact we could build such a med-computer—right now, today. We've had the ability to build it for more than thirty years. It wouldn't even be very costly—as such things go. But we don't build it. Because very few people—even among those who could build it—have the moral strength to use it."

Timberlake held himself still and silent in the hyb tank, realizing why he had remembered that incident. Coming into this cold-lighted tank was like using old Warren's hypothetical death predictor.

Bickel infected me with the certainty that this ship is not what it seems to be, Timberlake thought. *He took over command, pushed me aside. The only reason for being that was left me*—He looked up and around the tank—*was in here. If this is taken from me, then I'm truly useless . . . except as a kind of computer-shop flunky for Bickel.*

Yes, Bickel. Right away, Bickel. Is there anything else, Bickel?

With a sense of astonishment at how he had unconsciously dramatized the change of relationships within the crew, Timberlake rolled this realization over and over in his mind. There was a kind of pride in the awareness of his inner workings, the quirks his mind possessed, and an understanding that this stemmed in part from his conditioning.

Presently, he launched himself up to an individual tank hanging low on the left center. The tank was like all the others racked in curving rows around it. He activated the inner cold light, caught a handhold, and bent close to the tank's inspection port.

The light flickered, glowed. It illuminated the metered master tubes dropping from the tank's other side, a color-coded sheaf of spaghetti that trailed down left and right to the figure under the light.

A man's craggy profile lay there, waxy skin and faint black beard. He was like a mannequin figure—and Timberlake thought immediately of elaborate human-size dolls racked here to maintain the pretense.

The man's name was there on the tank's identification plate immediately below the place where the spaghetti of life-support connections entered.

"Martin Rhoades." And the code number which identified the specialties conditioned into him. He was an organizer, an executive . . . and another medical person.

If that were a real person.

Timberlake found his thoughts flitting from concept to concept. *Person. Persona. Does a Persona provide a Raison d'être?* That meant "a reason to be."

What's my reason for being?

Timberlake studied the life-systems telltales above the spaghetti sheaf. They registered a faint flame of life within the tank. Timberlake made a tiny adjustment in the oxygen meter, caught the immediate feedback surge on the tank's electroencephalographic coupling.

The oxygen meter reset itself.

This, then, was a hybernating man. That feedback reaction, with its elaborate encephalographic play, could not be programmed for the unexpected. The oxygen shift at this moment in time obviously could not have been anticipated. A human homeostat had detected it, though, and reacted correctly.

Timberlake dropped down to the gridded catwalk, checked a tank opposite, and another farther down the line.

He went through them at random, pausing only to check that each held a living human.

Names leaped out at him from the I.D. tags:

"Tossa Lon Nikki."

"Artemus Lon St. John."

"Peter Lon Vardack."

"Legata Lon Hamill."

One of them he recognized—black hair, olive skin with its waxy undertone, chiseled features—Frank Lipera, a fellow student in human engineering.

Presently, Timberlake went on to the next section . . . and the next. He found he recognized many of the occupants. This filled him with a feeling of loneliness. He felt that he might be the keeper of a museum, guarding old relics for a brief human life span, sequestering beneath these blue cold lights a share of man's culture and knowledge.

He came at last to a corner of section seven, another recognizable face from his UMB past—blond and Germanic, pale wax skin. Timberlake read the name etched above the inspection port: "PEABODY, Alan—K-7a."

Yes, it was Al Peabody, Timberlake agreed. Yet, in a way it wasn't Al. . . . It was as though the companion of Timberlake's gym classes, his opponent in handball and moon tennis, had gone away somewhere to wait.

But Peabody, Alan—K-7a proved to be a viable human with individual homeostatic reactions. He could be awakened to speak and act and think. He could be awakened to consciousness.

And consciousness is a thing beyond speaking and acting and thinking, Timberlake thought.

He loosed the handhold, dropped lightly back to the catwalk, feeling no particular need to check further. He knew with an inner certainty that all the tanks held hybernating humans. Bickel might be correct about the Tin Egg being an elaborate simulation, but in here the simulation went too far to be anything other than what it seemed. The hyb tanks had not been larded with obvious deception.

I was supposed to come through here, surprise Bickel and stop him, Timberlake thought. *Stop him from what?*

Some tiny, unregistered perception worked on the edge of Timberlake's awareness, assuring him that whatever Bickel was doing right now in the shop held no immediate danger to these helpless sleepers.

Whatever Bickel's doing, he must be doing it right now, Timberlake thought. *I've been gone... almost an hour.*

He looked up at the rows of tanks.

Yet, every tank I checked was functioning at peak efficiency, as though the entire system were tuned to a critical optimum.

Timberlake nodded to himself. You might almost think a mental core still rode monitor on the ship's vital parts. He felt that he could almost hear the tremendously slowed oscillations of life around him.

The spot between his shoulder blades had ceased to itch, but he felt painfully tired now, slightly dizzy, his body dragging at his muscles.

It occurred to Timberlake then that they could be going at the problem of reproducing consciousness too literally. *Will we have to install mechanisms that permit the Ox to grow tired?* he wondered. *We're too liter-*

al...like peasants asking the genie for three wishes. Maybe we won't like our wishes if we get them.

God, I'm tired.

Something moved near the far bulkhead—a spacesuited figure. For one instant of unreality, Timberlake thought that one of his hybernating charges had revived itself. Then, the moving figure came full into the glare of the cold light and Timberlake recognized Flattery's features behind the anti-fog plate of the helmet bubble.

"Tim!" Flattery called.

His voice boomed from the suit amplifiers, echoed with a metallic ringing through the cold air of the tank.

"Something wrong with your suit receiver?" Flattery asked, stopping in front of Timberlake.

Timberlake looked down at the command set near his chin, saw that its circuit-indicator light was dark.

I left it off, Timberlake thought. *Never even thought of turning it on. Why'd I do that?*

Flattery studied Timberlake carefully. The man's motions when first seen across the tank had indicated nothing seriously wrong. He moved. He seemed aware of his surroundings.

"You feel all right, Tim?" Flattery asked.

"Sure. Sure...I feel all right."

Like three wishes, Timberlake thought. *Like the three S's of our school joke: Security, Sleep, and Sex.*

Something touched his shoulder, and he realized he had heard the inner bulkhead open. He looked around to see Bickel standing there.

"You feel up to some work, Tim?" Bickel asked. "I need your help."

Some carrier inflection of Bickel's voice, a subtly shaded overtone, told Timberlake that Bickel had been worried about him.

But he must know I was sent through here...to try to stop him.

In that instant, Timberlake realized they were very close, the three of them standing here. And the closeness went beyond physical proximity.

"Whatever you're doing, Bick," Timberlake said, "it's having no adverse effect on the hyb tanks. Every sleeper I checked was humming along nicely."

"Every..." Bickel nodded. "You found...ahh..."

"Look for yourself," Timberlake said, realizing Bickel had not dared test his own suspicion that the hyb tanks were a sham. "They're all occupied."

"Excuse me." The politeness sounded odd coming out of Bickel's suit speaker. He jumped to an overhead handhold, swung to a ladder and, oddly, picked the tank of Peabody, Alan—K-7a.

Presently, he worked his way along the K-line of tanks, pausing only to peer into the inspection ports. He dropped back down to the catwalk near its center, returned to them.

"All of them?" he asked, nodding back toward the other sections.

"The only empty tank's the one that held Prue," Timberlake said.

"Prue!" Flattery said. "She's all alone in Com-central." He thumbed the outside switch of his transceiver, changing circuits. They saw his lips move, but his voice was only a faint chatter.

Bickel looked down, saw that he had ignored his command set. He flicked the switch, caught Prudence saying: "...so far. But I don't like the idea of being all alone in here in case there's a real emergency."

Bickel, too, preferred silence, Timberlake thought. *He wanted a moment alone.*

Flattery returned his suit circuits to voice amplifier, looked questioningly at Bickel. "Had we better be getting back?"

Raj seems more relieved than Tim that these tanks are what they seem, Bickel thought. *Why?* "You don't want to check the tanks for yourself?

"I can take your word for it," Flattery said.

"Can you?"

What's he doing? Flattery wondered. *Is he trying to goad me?*

Timberlake heard the derision in Bickel's voice, felt their moment of closeness shatter. Without moving their bodies, they had pulled apart. But Timberlake realized with an odd feeling of elation that he had aligned himself with Bickel.

"This isn't illusion," Flattery said. He waved at the tanks around them.

"And you *are* conscious," Bickel said.

Flattery suppressed a feeling of rage, but felt a sour taste in his mouth. *I will not let myself be goaded,* he thought. "Of course I'm conscious."

"Never apply 'of course' to consciousness," Bickel chided. "Consciousness can project illusions—insubstantial stimulus objects—onto the screen of your awareness." He motioned to the tanks above them. "Go ahead, check. We'll wait."

Flattery felt stubborn now. "I will not." He started to push past Bickel.

"Where're you going?" Bickel asked, catching the arm of Flattery's suit in one gloved hand.

"The shortest way back—through the shop," Flattery said. "If you don't mind!" He shook his arm free.

"Be my guest," Bickel said, and stepped aside.

Timberlake stared at Flattery as the psychiatrist-chaplain wrenched the hatch dogs, opened the hatch and slipped through to the next chamber.

Flattery's fear was something other than worry about me, Timberlake realized. *He's still afraid!*

Bickel took Timberlake's arm, helped him through, followed, and dogged the hatch. Flattery already was at the next hatch, had it open.

Damn poor procedure, Timberlake thought, but he let it go.

Presently, they came to the inner locks and the back passage beneath the primary computer installation and up into the shop. They slipped through, sealed the hatch.

Bickel threw back his helmet. Flattery and Timberlake did the same. Bickel already was loosening his glove seals.

Timberlake stared at Flattery, watching the way the

man studied the jutting boxes and angles, the interwoven leads of the Ox.

"Infinite counting net?" Flattery asked.

"Why not?" Bickel asked. "You have it. You can count beyond the number of your own total nerve supply. The Ox has to do the same."

"You know the danger," Flattery said.

"Some of the danger," Bickel admitted.

"This ship could be one gigantic sensory surface. Its receptors could achieve combinations unknown to us, could contact energy sources unknown to us."

"Is that one of the theories?"

Flattery took a step closer to the Ox.

"Before you do anything destructive," Bickel said, and he nodded toward the patterned confusion clinging to the computer wall with its wire tentacles, "you'd better know I'm already getting conscious-type reactions on a low scale—the system itself activating various sensors. It's like an animal blinking its eyes—a heat sensor here, audio there . . ."

"That could be a random dislodge pattern due to the shot-effect bursts," Flattery said.

"Not when nerve-net activity accompanies each reaction."

Flattery digested this, feeling his conditioned fear-alertness—the reaction for which he was but a trigger—come to full amplitude. His memory focused on the two red keys and the self-destruction program they would ignite through the computer links of the ship.

"Tim, how tired are you?" Bickel asked.

Timberlake looked at Bickel. *How tired am I?* Minutes ago, he had been shot through with fatigue. Now . . . something had keyed him up, filled him with elation.

Conscious-type reactions!

"I'm ready for another full shift."

"This thing's too simple yet to even approach full consciousness," Bickel said. "Most of the ship's sensors bypass the Ox circuits. Robox controls aren't connected and it has no—"

"Just a minute!" Flattery snapped.

They turned, caught by the anger in Flattery's voice.

"You admit this goal-seeking mechanism may operate entirely outside your control," Flattery said, "and you're still willing to give it eyes—and muscles?"

"Raj, before we're finished, this thing has to have complete control of the ship."

"To get us across the Big Empty and safely to Tau Ceti," Flattery said. "You're assuming that's the ship-computer's basic program?"

"I assume nothing. I checked. That's the basic program."

To Tau Ceti! Flattery thought. He felt like both laughing and crying. He didn't know whether to tell them the truth—the fools! But . . . no, that would render them less efficient. Best to play the charade out to its silly conclusion!

He took a deep breath to get himself under control. "Okay, John, but you can't anticipate every goal of your . . . Ox."

"Unless we design all its goals into it," Timberlake answered.

Flattery waved Timberlake to silence. "That defeats your purpose."

"We'd have to foresee every possible danger," Bickel agreed. "And it's precisely because we *can't* foresee every possible danger that we need this conscious awareness guiding the ship, its . . . hands on every control."

Flattery reviewed the argument, trying to find a chink in Bickel's logic. The words merely echoed many of the UMB briefings to which Flattery had been subjected: *"You'll be required to find a survival technique in a profoundly changed environment. Remember, you can't foresee every new danger."*

"Fail-safes won't work, of course," Flattery said.

"Same argument," Bickel said. "Fail-safes work only when your dangers are known and anticipated."

"Can you prevent damage to the computer core?"

"It'll be buffered forty ways from Sunday. I've already started the buffering."

"The ship had an overriding supervisory program," Flattery said, "a command to get us safely to Tau Ceti—you're sure of that?"

"The command's there. They didn't fake it."

"What if it develops that it's fatal to go to Tau Ceti?"

Why is he quibbling? Bickel wondered. *Surely, he knows the answer to that.* "A simple binary decision solves that. We give it a turn-back alternative."

"Ahhhhh," Flattery said. "The best of all possible moves, eh? But we're in the Queen's croquet game. You said it yourself. What if the Queen of Hearts changes the rules? We've no Alice in this wonderland to haul us back to reality."

A deliberately poor move somewhere along the line changing the theoretical structure of the game, Bickel thought. *That's an indicated possibility.*

He shrugged: "Then we get sent to the headsman."

CHAPTER 21

"No distinct ideas occupied my mind; all was confused.... A strange multiplicity of sensations seized me, and I saw, felt, heard and smelt at the same time; and it was, indeed, a long time before I learned to distinguish between the operations of my various senses."

—Frankenstein's Monster speaks

PRUDENCE, AT THE controls less than an hour, already was beginning to feel the edge of fatigue which she knew would have her hanging on only by willpower at the end of her shift. Part of the load on her was the seemingly endless wordplay of those around her—the concept-juggling.

Words were so pointless in their situation. They needed action—determined, constructive action.

Timberlake cleared his throat. He felt a powerful curiosity to inspect and test what Bickel had built—to trace out the circuitry and try to find out why it was not upsetting gross computer function.

"If we run into the Queen of Hearts problem," Timberlake said, "the ship stands a better chance if it's controlled by an imaginative, conscious intelligence."

"*Our* kind of consciousness?" Flattery asked.

There's what's eating him, Bickel thought. *He's obviously the one charged with seeing we don't loose a killer machine in the universe. Homeostasis for a race can be different from the balance needed to keep an individual alive. But we're isolated out here—an entire race in a test tube.*

"We're talking about creating a machine with a specific quality," Flattery said. "It has to operate itself from the inside, by probability. We can't determine everything it's going to do." He raised a hand as Bickel started to speak.

"But we *can* determine some of its emotions. What if it actually cares about us? What if it admires and loves us?"

Bickel stared at him. That was an audacious idea—completely in keeping with Flattery's function as chaplain, colored by his psychiatric training, and protective of the race as a whole.

"Think of consciousness as a behavior pattern," Flattery said. "What has contributed to the development of this pattern? If we go back..."

His voice was drowned in the klaxon blare of the emergency warning.

They all felt the ship lurch and the immediate weightlessness as the caged fail-saft switch disconnected the grav system.

Bickel drifted toward the forward end of the shop, caught a stanchion, swung himself around and kicked off toward the Com-central hatch, where he dislodged his lock. He went through the hatch in the same fluid motion of opening it, hurled himself toward his couch. He locked in, swept his gaze across his repeaters. Tim and Flattery were right behind.

Prudence was making only minimal corrections on the big console, studying the drain gauges.

Bickel saw that the computer was drawing almost eighty percent of its power capacity, began checking for fire and shorts. He heard cocoon triggers snap as Flattery and Timberlake took their places.

"Computer drain," Timberlake said.

"Radiation bleed-off in Stores Four," Prudence said, her voice hoarse. "Steady rise in temperature back of the second hull bulkheads—no; it's beginning to level off."

She programmed for a hull-security check, watched the sensor telltales.

Bickel, looking over her shoulder at the big board, saw the implications of the flickering lights as soon as she did. "We've lost a section of outer shielding."

"And hull," she said.

Bickel lay back, keyed the repeater screen for monitoring the sensors, began an analysis outward into the indicated area. "You watch the board; I'll make the check."

Images flickered on and out in the little screen at the corner of his board as he keyed it to new sensors farther and father out. Halfway through Stores Four, he was staring into the star-sequined darkness of open sapce. The sensor eyes revealed foam coagulant flowing into a wide, oval hole from the hull-security automatics.

Out of the corner of his eye, Bickel saw Flattery running a micro-survey along the edge of the break in the hull. "It's as though it were sliced off with a knife," he said. "Smooth and even."

"Meteorite?" Timberlake asked. He looked up from a check of the hyb tanks.

"There's no fusing at the edge or evidence of friction heat," Flattery said. He took his hands off his board, thinking of the island in Puget Sound—the wild destruction in the surrounding countryside. *Rogue consciousness. Has it started already?*

"What could make that cut through the outer shielding and hull without heating them at least to half-sun?" Bickel asked.

No one answered.

Bickel looked at Flattery, seeing the white, drawn look of the man's mouth, thought: *He knows!*

"Raj, what could do that?"

Flattery shook his head.

Bickel took a reading on the laser-pulsed timelog off

his own repeaters, extracted a position assessment, noted transmission-delay time to UMB, swung his transmitter to his side and keyed it for AAT coding.

"What're you doing?" Flattery asked.

"*This* we'd better report," Bickel said. He began cutting the tape.

"How about some gravity?" Timberlake asked. He looked at Prudence.

"System reads functional," she said. "I'll try it." She thumbed the reset.

The ship's normal quarter gravity pulled at them.

Timberlake unlocked his cocoon, stepped out to the deck.

"Where're you going?" Prudence asked.

"I'm going out and have a look," Timberlake said. "Some force takes a slice off our hull without crisping the area or spreading a shatter pattern? There is no such force. This I've got to see."

"Stay right where you are," Bickel said. "There could be loose cargo out there...anything."

Timberlake thought of lovely Maida crushed by runaway cargo. He swallowed.

"What's to prevent it slicing us neatly right down the middle, next time?" Prudence asked.

"What's our speed, Prue?" Timberlake asked.

"C over one five two seven and holding."

"Did...whatever it was slow us at all?" Flattery asked.

Prudence ran the back check on the comparion log. "No."

Timberlake took a deep, quavering breath. "A virtually zero-impact phenomenon with a force effect of...what? Infinity?" He shook his head. "There's no kinetic equivalent."

Bickel tripped the transmission switch, waited for the interlock, looked at Timberlake. "Did the universe begin with Gamow's 'big bang' or are we in the middle of Hoyle's continuous creation? What if they're both..."

"That's just a mathematical game," Prudence said. "Oh, I know: the union of infinite mass and finite source can be accomplished by postulating zero impact—infinite force, but it's still just a mathematical game, a cancelling-out exercise. It doesn't *prove* anything."

"It proves the original power of Genesis," Flattery whispered.

"Oh, Raj, you're at it again," Prudence remonstrated, "trying to twist mathematics to prove the existence of God."

"God took a swipe at us?" Timberlake asked. "Is that what you're saying, Raj?"

"You know better than to take that attitude—under these circumstances," Flattery retorted. *When they get that message at UMB, they'll know we've achieved the stage of rogue consciousness. There's no other answer.*

"You were going to make a guess, Bick," Timberlake said.

Bickel watched the signal timer creep around its circle. It had a long way to go yet before giving them the *blip* that would tell them the message had enough time to reach its mark.

"Maybe some kind of interface phenomenon that exists only out here in the trans-Saturnian area," Bickel said. "A field effect, maybe, from pressure waves originating in the solar convection zone. The universe contains a hell of a lot of oscillatory motion. Maybe we've hit a new combination."

"Is that what you suggested to UMB?" Flattery asked.

"Yes."

"What if it isn't a mathematical game?" Timberlake asked. "Could we program for a probability curve to predict the limits of such a hypothetical phenomenon?"

Bickel lifted his hands from the AAT keyboard, considered Timberlake's question.

Such a program could be figured in matrix functions, he felt. It was something like their hunt for the Consciousness Factor—trying to trace an exceedingly complex system on the basis of scant data. They could approach it through stacks of linear simultaneous equations, each defining parallel hyperplanes in n-dimensional space.

"What about that, Prue?" he asked.

She saw where Bickel's imagination had led them, and took a trial run in her mind, visualizing the diagonal entries when they appeared as coefficients of the simultaneous equations.

The entire process was over in seconds, but she held herself to silence, savoring the experience. It was a new one. She had set up a programming simulation in her mind, checked it out and filed the results in memory, recalling the bits precisely where she needed them. It was a feat of which she had never thought herself capable. Her own mind . . . a computer.

She told Bickel what had happened, replayed the results for him. Bickel found himself filling in the gaps where she skipped over the process to the answers. Somewhere—probably in the long skull sessions back at UMB—he had absorbed an enormous amount of esoteric math. Necessity and Prue's lead had pushed him over onto a plateau where that knowledge became available.

He felt suddenly robust, inches taller. The mental effort had lifted him to a hyperawareness—relaxed, yet ready, aware of his entire vascomuscular state and emotional tone.

The sensation began to fade. Bickel sensed the ship and its pressures on him—the steady, solid motion of matter bound outward from the sun.

The entire experience had taken less than half a minute.

Bickel felt raging sadness as the sensation faded. He thought he had experienced something infinitely precious, and part of the experience remained with him in memory. It was like a thin thread linking him to the experience, holding out the hope of once more following that thread—but the pressure of the ship and those around him wouldn't permit the indulgence.

He realized abruptly that he carried some enormous weight within him that might shatter that precious thread completely, and this sent a pang of fear through him.

"Do you think such a program's possible?" Timberlake pressed.

"Programming it is out!" Bickel snapped. "We can't

limit the variables." He turned back to the AAT keyboard, began punching out the message with savage motions.

Bickel thought about the alterations he had made to the computer system. *Black box—white box.* The ignition of this thing they were building required a black box and there was only one obvious black box to give itself over to the imprinting process on the computer's white box: a human brain.

I will be the pattern.

Would the computer/thing then be another Bickel?

Prudence stared up at the big console, wondering at Bickel's sudden anger, using the focus on this as an excuse for not thinking about what had happened to the ship. But she couldn't avoid that problem.

The damage had been caused by something outside the ship. There had been a faint lurch transmitted through the Tin Egg, but that had come afterward. The damage telltales already had been flaring out red and yellow. The lurch had been associated with power drain and a shift of switching equipment to the necessities of automatic damage control.

Zero impact—infinite force.

Something outside the ship had sliced through them like a razor through soft butter. No—infinitely sharper.

Something from outside.

She put a hand to her cheek. That pointed to something beyond the dangers programmed into the ship.

They'd encountered something out of the wide, blank unknown. She thought suddenly of sea monsters painted on ancient charts of the earth, of twelve-legged dragons and humanoid figures with fanged mouths in their chests.

She restored a degree of calmness by reminding herself that all these monsters had faded before humanity's monkey-like inquisitiveness.

Still—something had struck the Tin Egg.

She ran another visual survey of her board, noting that automatic damage control had almost completely flooded out Stores Four with foam seal. Section doors were sealed off for two layers around the damage area.

Whatever had hit them, it had taken only a thin slice... this time.

Bickel raised his hand to the transmitter pulse switch, depressed it. The room around him filled with the hum of the instrument as it built up the energy to hurl its multiburst of information back across space. The "snap-click" of the transmission interlock with its dim smell of ozone came almost as an anticlimax.

"They won't make any more of this than we do," Timberlake said.

"UMB has some of the top men in particle physics," Bickel said. "Maybe they can solve it."

"A neutrino phenomenon?" Timberlake asked. "Nuts! They'll claim we misread the evidence."

"Time for my watch," Flattery said. "Prue?"

Flattery's words made her aware in a sudden rush of acceptance how tired she was. Her back ached and the muscles of her forearms trembled. She could remember only once before having been this tired—after almost five hours of surgery.

In many ways, she was making too-heavy demands on her flesh—with long watches, work in the shop, and the tests using her own body as a guinea pig. But the adrenochrome-THC was proving difficult. It wouldn't cross the blood-brain barrier into active contact with neural tissue... unless she dared use a near-fatal dosage. She hadn't yet dared, although the prize appeared dazzling.

If she could only inhibit the lower structures of the brain and release the higher structures to full activity, she could hand Bickel the sequential steps to duplicate as electronic functions.

"Shift the board on the count," she said.

As they shifted the big board, Flattery scanned the instruments preparing to fit himself into the *mood* of the ship. *And the Tin Egg does have her moods.*

Sometimes, he felt as though the ship carried ghosts within it—of the sixteen clones killed by accident during the construction on the Moon, of umbilicus crew members killed by the ship's programmed savagery—or perhaps of the OMCs sacrificed on this altar. An altar to human hubris. . . . Those previous tests—all of the dead crews, colonists . . . and the OMCs. *All ghosts riding with us.*

Did those bodiless brains have souls? Flattery wondered. *For that matter—if we breathe consciousness into this machinery, will our creation have a soul?*

"Have the automatics finished sealing the break?" Bickel asked.

"All sealed," Flattery said. And he asked himself: *When will the rogue consciousness hit us again?*

"What was in Stores Four?" Prudence asked. "What'd we lose?"

"Food concentrates," Bickel answered. "First thing I checked." His tone said, *"You had the watch; you should've checked that."*

"Raj, do you want us to start sharing watch and watch?" Timberlake asked. "After I've had some rest . . ."

"After you've had some rest, you can help me in the shop," Bickel said.

Flattery glanced at Bickel, then at Timberlake, wondering how the life-systems engineer would take that rebuke. Timberlake had his eyes closed. His fatigue was obvious in the pale, flaccid look of his face. He appeared almost asleep . . . except for tight, shallow breathing.

"You want to go right ahead, eh?" Prudence asked. "You don't think we should wait for Hempstead's trained seals to chew this over?"

"Whatever hit us came from outside," Bickel said. "That's *another* problem."

"John's right," Timberlake rasped. He cleared his throat, unsnapped his action couch, sat up. "I'm bushed."

"We've just decided," Prudence said, "just like that . . ." she snapped her fingers, "—that you can go on stirring around in the computer like a wild man?"

"For Christ's sake!" Bickel said. "Haven't any of you realized yet we were supposed to use the computer as the basic element of attack?"

Bickel stared around at them—Flattery busy on the

board, Timberlake half asleep sitting up at his couch, Prudence glaring at him from her couch.

"That's no ordinary computer. It has elements we don't even suspect. It was hooked up with an Organic Mental Core for almost six years during the construction and programming of the ship. It has buffers and leads and cross-ties that its own designers may not even know about!"

"Are you suggesting it's already conscious?" Prudence asked.

"No, I'm only suggesting that we've come a long way using that computer and our Ox frontal-lobe simulator. We've come further than the UMB project did in twenty years! And we should go on with this. We're cutting a straight line through—"

"There are no straight lines in nature," Flattery said.

Bickel sighed. *What now?* he wondered. "If you've got something to say, spit it out."

"Consciousness is a type of behavior," Flattery said.

"Agreed."

"But the roots of our behavior are buried so far away in the past we can't get at them directly."

"Emotion again, eh?" Bickel demanded.

"No," Flattery said.

"Instinct," Prudence said.

Flattery nodded. "The kind of genetic imprint that tells a chicken how to crack out of its shell."

"Emotions or instinct, what's the difference?" Bickel asked. "Emotions are produced by instinct. Are you still saying we can't bring the Ox to consciousness unless it has instincts-cum-emotions?"

"You know what I'm saying," Flattery said.

"It has to love us," Bickel said. He chewed at his upper lip, caught again by the beautiful simplicity of the suggestion. Flattery was right, of course. Here was a loose rein that could satisfy the fail-safe requirements. It controlled without galling.

"It has to have an autonomic system of emotional reactions," Flattery said. "The system has to respond with a set of physical effects of which the Ox is...aware."

Emotion, Bickel thought. *The characteristic that gives us our sense of person, the thing that summates personal judgments. A process in capsule form that can occur out of sequence.*

Here was a break with all machine concepts of time—emotion as process, an audacious way of looking at time.

"There's nothing of ourselves about which we can be objective," Bickel said, "except our own physical responses. Remember? It's what Dr. Ellers was always saying."

Flattery thought back to Ellers, UMB's chief of psych. *"Bickel is 'purpose,' the force that will give direction to your search,"* Ellers had said. *"You have substitutes, of course. Accidents do happen. But you've nothing honed as fine as Bickel. He's a creative discoverer."*

A "creative discoverer"—the failures of all who went before him...all of those clone-brothers, all was preparation for this assault on the problem. *If we succeed we survive, and if we fail...*

And Bickel was thinking: *Emotion. How do we symbolize it and program for it? What does the body do? We're inside, in direct contact with whatever the body's doing. That's the only thing we can really be objective about. What does the body...*

"It has to have a completely interfunctioning body," Bickel said, seeing the whole problem and answer as an abrupt revelation. "It has to have a body that's gone through trauma and crises." He stared at Flattery. "Guilt, too, Raj. It has to have guilt."

"Guilt?" Flattery asked, and wondered why the suggestion made him feel angry and half fearful. He started to object, grew conscious of a rhythmic rasping. He thought at first it was a malfunctioning alarm, realized then it was Timberlake. The life-systems engineer had reclasped himself in his action couch cocoon. He was asleep—snoring.

"Guilt," Bickel said, holding his attention on Flattery.

"How?" Prudence asked.

"In program engineering terms," Bickel said, "we must install trapping functions, inner alarm systems—

monitors that interrupt operations according to the functional needs of the entire system."

"Guilt's an artificial emotion; it has nothing to do with consciousness," Flattery objected.

"Fear and guilt are parent and child. You can't have guilt without fear."

"But you can have fear without guilt," Flattery said.

"Can you?" Bickel asked. And he thought: *It's the Cain-and-Abel syndrome. Where'd the race pick that one up?*

"Not so fast," Prudence said. "Are you suggesting we install a . . . that we make this . . . Ox afraid?"

"Yeah."

"Absolutely not!" Flattery said. He had his couch exerciser going, but shut it off, turned to stare at Bickel.

"Our creature already has a large, fast memory," Bickel said. "It has fixed memory—if you discount our addressing problems, which aren't interfering with function at any rate—and I'll bet this thing has a protected area of memory that's even ready with illusions when they're necessary for self-protection."

"But fear!" Flattery said.

"This is the other side of your coin, Raj. You want it to love us? Okay. Love's a kind of need, eh? I'm willing to give it a need for external program sources—that's us, you understand? I'll leave the necessary gaps in its makeup that only we can fill. It'll have emotions, but that means an unlimited spectrum of emotions, Raj. The spectrum includes fear."

Guilt and fear, Prudence thought. *Raj will have to face it.* She looked at Bickel, seeing the filmed-over, withdrawn look in his eyes.

"Pleasure and pain," Bickel muttered. He focused on Prudence, the sleeping Timberlake, on Flattery—each in turn. *Did they see that the Ox had to be able to reproduce itself, too?*

Prudence felt her pulse quickening, tore her attention away from Bickel. She put a hand to her temple, checked the pulse there, related this to her quickened breathing, to body temperature, to hungers, to stage of fatigue and awareness. The chemical experiments on her body were giving her an acute awareness of her bodily functions, and that awareness told her she needed chemical readjustment.

"Well, Raj?" Bickel said.

I must compose myself, Flattery thought, turning back onto his couch. *I must appear natural and calm.* He kept his eyes away from the false panel on his repeater board. Under that panel lay death and destruction. Bickel was growing exceedingly alert to the tiniest clues. Flattery marked the quiet green of the flashboard, the ticking of relays through the graph counters. Everything about the ship felt soothing and ordinary—all systems functioning.

Yet, deep inside himself, Flattery felt knotted up, like an animal poised at the sound of the hunter.

Pleasure and pain. It could be done, of course: the gradual orientation toward a goal, then denial...interference...removal...frustration...threat of destruction.

"I'm going back to the shop," Bickel said. "The way to do this is pretty clear, isn't it?"

"Perhaps to you," Flattery said.

"There's no stopping," Prudence said, and hoped Flattery heard the implication: *There's no stopping him.*

"Go ahead," Flattery said. "Assemble your blocks of nerve-net simulators. But let us think long and hard before we tie your system into the full computer." He looked at Bickel. "Do you still contemplate this black box—white box experiment?"

Bickel merely stared at him.

"You know the danger," Flattery said.

Bickel felt elation, a breakthrough in some inner factor that had resisted him. The ship—its living organisms, its problems—all were like marionettes and marionette toys. The way out was so clear to him—he'd only hinted at it before—so clear. He could see the necessary schematics stacked in his mind, like transparencies piled one on another.

Four-dimensional construction, he reminded himself. *We have to construct a net in depth that contains complex world-line tracks. It has to absorb nonsynchronous transmissions. It has to abstract discrete patterns out of the impulse oversend. The important thing is structure— not the material. The important thing is topology. That's the key to the whole damn problem!*

"Prue, give me a hand," Bickel said. He glanced at the chronometer beside the Com-central board, looked at Timberlake. *Let him sleep; Prue could help. She did neat electronics work—surgical in its exactness, clean and with minimal leads and tight couplings.*

"We're going to need a coupling area for each group of multiple blocks," Bickel said, looking at Prudence. "I'm going to turn that job over to you while I build up the major block systems."

As though his words had accumulated in her mind, built up a certain pressure until they spilled over into understanding, she saw what Bickel intended. He was going to feed a continuous data load into an enormously expanded Ox-cum-computer linkup. He was going to project into the computer, like a film projected on a screen—a giant spreadout, an almost infinite psycho-space.

The array of required connectives set themselves up in her mind with parallel rows of binary numbers, cross-linked, interwoven. And she saw that she could reframe the problem, overlap it with matrix functions, creating a problem-solution array like a multidimensional chessboard.

In the instant of this revelation, she realized that Bickel could not have framed his approach to this solution without using the same mathematical crowbar to lever away the heavy work.

"You used adjacency matrices," she accused.

He nodded. She had seen that he was intruding into a new mathematical conception—a calculus of qualities by which he could trace neuron impulses and juggle them within the imbedded psychospaces of the Ox-cum-computer.

Prudence had begun to see what he saw, but the others weren't ready yet for anything more than hints. The possibilities were staggering. The implied methods would permit construction of entirely new computers reduced in size and basic complexity by a factor of at least a thousand. But more important was the understanding this gave him of his own psychospaces and their function in abstraction—the aggregate nerve-cell excitation of his own body and the way this was reduced to recognizable values.

Thinking within this framework, Bickel saw, put him on a threshold. A certain pressure here, a certain application of energy there, and he knew he would be projected into a consciousness that he had never before experienced.

The realization inspired fear and awe and at the same time it lured him. He turned, crossed to the hatch into the shop, opened it, looked back at Flattery.

"Raj," he said. "We're not conscious."

"What? Huh?" It was Timberlake rousing out of his sleep, rubbing his eyes, staring straight out at Bickel.

"We're not awake," Bickel said.

CHAPTER 22

Beyond the senses there are objects; beyond
objects there is mind; beyond the mind there is
intellect; beyond the intellect there is the Great
Self.

—*Katha-upanishad*
Excerpt for instruction
of Chaplain/Psychiatrists

"We're not awake."

During Flattery's watch, the words haunted him.

Timberlake had muttered something about, "Damn
joker!" and gone off to finish his sleep in quarters.

But Flattery, dividing his attention between the
console and the overhead screen that showed the shop
with Prudence and Bickel at work there, felt the ship
assume a curious identity in his mind.

He felt as though he and the others were merely cells of
a larger organism—that the telltales, the dials and gauges
and sensors, the omnipresent visual intercom—all these
were senses and nerves and organs of something apart
from himself.

"We are not awake."

We keep skirting that thought, Flattery reflected.

Bickel's voice talking to Prudence in the shop—
"Here's the main trunk to handle negative feedback.
Follow the color code and tie it in across there." "Here's
the damper circuit; we have to watch we don't introduce
reverberating cycles into the random neural paths."

And Prudence, talking half to herself: "The human
skull encloses about fifteen thousand million neurons.
I've extrapolated from our building blocks and the
computer—we're going to wind up with more than twice
that number in this . . . beast."

Their voices were like echoes in Flattery's mind.

Bickel: "Think of a threshold to be overcome. Several
kinds of pressure will overcome that threshold. They're
the pressures involved in entropy—or the pressures of
proliferating variability: call that one life. Entropy on one
side, life on the other. Each drives past the threshold at a
certain pressure level. When one gets through, that turns
on the Consciousness Factor."

Prudence: "Which is it, homeostat or filter?"

Bickel: "Both."

Flattery thought then of the total ship, the great
machine whose continued life required a certain optimum
organization—an *ordering* process. That involved entropy, certainly, because the system of a total ship tended
to settle into a uniform distribution of its energies.

*As far as the ship is concerned, order is more natural
than chaos,* Flattery thought. *But we're playing the ship
as though all its parts were an orchestra and Bickel the
director. Bickel alone has the score to achieve the music
we want.*

Consciousness.

Bickel: "I tell you, Prue, consciousness has to be
something that flows against the current of time. Time in
which it's embedded."

Prudence: "I don't know. When a cell block fires, that
sets up an impulse. The impulse divides and forms a
multi-branched structure with a single stem—in the nerve-
nets, the embedding space. The stem contains that
original firing, of course, and you have transmission

shooting out through four-dimensional space—it includes time."

Bickel: "And consciousness is like a boat breasting that flow."

Prudence: "Against the flow? You have to include time in the diagram, certainly, but the firing and branching are like a complex solid pushed *into* time, like the veins in a four-dimensional leaf."

Bickel: "Think of the ship's AAT system. What's that? The thing takes hundreds of duplicates on a single message—all the duplicates having been transmitted in a single, compressed burst . . . a single firing—and it slows them down, compares them, breaks off the error stems and passes along to you the translated corrected message."

Prudence: "But consciousness doesn't enter the picture until the message reaches its human receiver."

Bickel: "Negative feedback, Prue. Input adjusted to the output. If the system malfunctions, the human operator repairs it, like repairing a dam in a stream so you catch a significant amount of the flow."

Prudence (looking up from a length of neuron fiber she was feeding into a micro-manipulator): "Consciousness—a kind of negative feedback?"

Bickel: "You ever think, Prue, that negative feedback is the most terrifying perfectionist in the universe? It won't permit failure. It's designed to keep the system running between certain limits no matter what the disturbance."

Prudence: "But . . . these Ox circuits . . . you've deliberately introduced errors that aren't—"

Bickel: "Why not? All our conventional ideas about feedback imply a certain uniformity of environment. But we live in a nonuniform universe. That place out there isn't completely predictable. We've got to keep it off balance out there . . . by changing the rules ourselves at random."

Order opposed to chaos, Flattery thought glancing at the overhead screen. Lord! How that block-upon-block extrusion was spreading out from the computer wall! It had proliferated into two major growths with a jungle of vinelike pseudoneuron sheafs between them and around them and over them.

Bickel lay on his back working beneath the structure. Loops of the main bus connections hung down just above his knees.

We are not awake, Flattery thought.

Oh, God! How easy it'd be to give up right now! He was here in the driver's seat, wasn't he? One of the triggers was at hand. Who'd ever know? The ship would die . . . the problem end. Let the bastards at UMB try again . . . with somebody else.

But that was the real problem: they'd try again, all right, but not with somebody else.

The same miserable charade—over and over and over!

Look at Prue down there, he thought. *She's stopped her anti-S injections. She's experimenting with her body chemistry. She'll be posturing and twisting in front of Bickel pretty soon. And the only way he sees her is as an expert with the micro-manipulator. She does good work!*

We are not awake.

Consciousness itself created variety, developed offshoot probabilities. And variety thrived on variety. The very act of playing their own special *music* produced the unpredictable—produced errors.

Where does communication break down?

Bickel (grunting as he squirmed out from beneath the Ox): "The generalized body and the specialized brain, Prue—put 'em together and what've you got? Illusion. That's the buffer, illusion. It's the protective layer that lets virtually incompatible systems get in bed together. Consciousness is a producer of illusions."

Prudence: "Where'd you store the R_4DBd neuron reel?"

Bickel: "Second rack, left end of the bench. Now, you take the illusion of central position."

Prudence: "That's the natural result of a baby's helpless dependence on its environment. A baby *is* the center of the universe. We never lose that memory."

Bickel: "Well, individual sense impressions are something like pebbles dropped in a four-dimensional pond. Consciousness locks onto the waves created by those pebbles, and gives them a spatial and temporal integration so they can be interpreted. Consciousness has to make sense out of things. But its major tool is illusion."

Spatio-temporal integration, Flattery thought.

The identity that was the ship—their Tin Egg—it lacked a certain integrating ability at the moment. Instead of an efficient self-regulating force, the ship was making do with the inadequate feedback system represented by four humans loosely connected to its "nervous system."

That was one way of looking at it.

But there was a point in the ship's future where damage passed beyond their ability to recover. The humans were failing.

Flattery felt then a deep bitterness toward the society that had sent this frail cargo into nowhere. He knew the reasons but reasons had never prevented bitterness.

"Think of society as a human construction, a very sophisticated defense mechanism," Hempstead and his cohorts had said. *"Society's restrictions get bred into the cells themselves by a process of selection. And these restrictions become part of the self-regulating feedback in society's governing systems. There's a serious question whether humans actually can break out of their self-regulated pattern. It takes audacious methods indeed to explore beyond that pattern."*

The law was stated, Flattery knew, thusly: *"Individual human experience is not the overriding control factor in human behavior. The cellular social pattern dominates."*

Flattery deliberately rapped his knuckles against the edge of his action couch to shock himself out of this reverie. He focused on the console, saw he had the usual temperature adjustments to make. The automatics could never quite hold the line.

Bickel: "Watch those lengths in the time-delay circuits. You'll confuse the Ox's psychological present."

Prudence: "Its what?"

Bickel: "Its psychological present—its 'specious present'—what you experience in any given instant; that

short interval you call *now*. Prof. Ferrel—remember old
Prof. Ferrel-barrel?"

Prudence: "Who could forget Hempstead's son-in-
law?"

Bickel: "Yeah, but he wasn't stupid. We were on the
satellite tracker once—him on his side of the sterile wall
and me on ours. And he said: 'Look at that thing move!' It
was a shuttle ship coming in from earth. And he said: 'You
know for a fact it's changing position fast as hell. But you
seem to see all those position changes right now—in the
present. No sharp edges; just a flow. That's the "specious
present," boy. Don't you ever forget it.' And I never did."

Prudence: "Will the . . . Ox really experience time?"

Bickel: "It has to. Our time-delay circuits have to give it
a way of internal measurement. It has to feel its own time.
Otherwise, it'll be a big package of confusion."

Prudence: "The . . . *now*."

Bickel: "You think about it and you realize we don't
interpret the immediate experience of time. We take big
gulps of time. But real time, now, that has to be something
gradual and progressive, a smooth change against a
background of some measurement constant."

Prudence: "So we line up the Ox's physical time and set
it going like some mechanical toy—in one direction."

Bickel: "The more remote parts of its 'specious present'
have to fade the way they do with us. The past has to be
less intense than what's just appearing on its horizon. It
needs a constant 'serial fadeout'; otherwise, it won't be
able to distinguish points near in time from points remote
in time."

Flattery looked up into the screen, saw Bickel hook an
oscilloscope to the Ox, run a pulse check.

Entropy, Flattery thought. *One direction in time.*

He projected a picture in his mind: jets of water—one
labeled entropy and the other that thrusting probabilism
they called Life. Balanced between the two like a ball on a
fountain danced consciousness.

It's so simple, Flattery thought. *But how do you
reproduce it . . . unless you're God?*

Bickel: "Hold on there! Don't hook in that layer without running your stepdown test."

Prudence: "You and your damn caution!"

Bickel: "Life is a very cautious proposition. An error in those stepdown circuits could screw us up royally. Remember this, Ox has to take complicated inputs and filter them down through simpler and simpler integrating systems until it finally displays the results as symbols on which to act. Think of your own sense of vision. How many receptor neurons in your retina?"

Prudence: "About a hundred and twenty million?"

Bickel: "But when the system gets back to the ganglion layer, how many cells there?"

Prudence: "Only about one and a quarter million."

Bickel: "Stepped down, see? The system takes hordes of sense impressions and combines them into fewer and fewer discrete signals. In the end, we get a sense datum called an image. But we interpret that image out of an enormous file of topological comparisons, all of them out of previously translated experience."

Prudence: "And you think our computer has enough...experiences for that kind of comparison?"

Bickel: "It will have when we're through with it."

And Flattery thought: *Black box—white box.*

Prudence: "Aren't you likely to overload the computer, bog it down?"

Bickel: "For Chrissakes, woman! You personally receive all kinds of information constantly. Doesn't your own system sort through all that information, queue it up, program it, and evaluate the data?"

Prudence: "But the Tin Egg's very existence depends on the computer. If we blunder with..."

Bickel: "There's no other way. You should've realized that the instant you saw this whole ship was a set piece."

Prudence (angrily): "What do you mean? Why?"

Bickel: "Because the computer's the only place where that amount of information can be stored. You see, woman, we don't have time to train a completely uneducated infant."

Before she could answer, the transmission horn blared its warning. The AAT stood on manual bypass to keep its circuits from interfering with the work in the shop. The horn's trigger fired both Bickel and Flattery into action. Bickel threw the action switch in the shop. Flattery slapped the AAT master control switch on his console, realizing with a sense of detachment that the UMB message would pour through the Ox circuits before being displayed for them.

CHAPTER 23

I feel the duties of a creator toward this
Artificial Consciousness. It seems to me that
my primary goal must be to render this
creature happy, to provide it whatever joy I
can. Else this entire project seems pointless.
There already are enough unhappy creatures
in this universe.

—Raja Lon Flattery
Private Communion with the Ox

IT TOOK SEVERAL minutes for the incoming message to
search its way through the AAT and the Ox-accretions
which Bickel had added to the system. They were tense
minutes in Com-central. Flattery's gaze swept back and
forth across the telltales of his board. There were big
unknowns about the system now and any input might
elicit strange behavior from dangerous quarters.

Behavior! Flattery thought, catching the word in his
own mind.

There were anthropomorphic assumptions in that
word.

Why should it play by our rules?

In the shop, Bickel felt his own waiting tensions. Was the incoming message going to be more garbage?

Prudence, standing near him, sensed the unwashed musks of his body, all the evidences of his concentration on their mutual problem.

Why not? He wants to live as much as I do.

Bickel swept his gaze across the repeater telltales in the shop, watched the needles kick over and come to rest in the normal range. There came the characteristic sharp AAT hum, felt now in the shop because the Ox was part of the circuitry. The sound raised a tingling sensation along Bickel's sides and arms.

The gauges registered the usual AAT pause. The multiple bursts of the message were being sorted, compared, translated, and fed into the output net.

Bickel glanced at the screen, saw that Flattery had the system on audio.

Morgan Hempstead's voice began rolling from the vocoders:

"This is Project calling UMB ship *Earthling*. This is Project calling. We are unable to give an exact determination of the force that damaged the ship. We suggest an error in transmission or insufficient data. The possibility of an encounter with a neutrino field of theoretical type A-G is suggested by one analysis. Why have you failed to acknowledge our directive on return procedure?"

Bickel watched his gauges. The message was coming in with remarkable clarity, no garbling at all apparent now that it was routed through the Ox circuits.

There came the distinct sound of Hempstead clearing his throat.

It gave Prudence a peculiar feeling to hear this ordinary sound—a man clearing his throat. The inconsequential thing had been transmitted millions of miles to no effect other than to inform them Hempstead had been troubled by a bit of phlegm.

Again, Hempstead's voice rolled from the vocoders: "UMB is being subjected to heavy, repeat heavy political pressures as regards the abort order. You will acknowledge this transmission immediately. The ship is to be returned to orbit around UMB while disposition is made of yourselves and cargo."

"That's an awful word—disposition," Prudence said. She glanced at Bickel. He seemed to be taking it calmly.

Flattery could feel the heavy beating of his heart. He wondered if the next few words would bring that deadly "kill ship" code signal from Hempstead.

Bickel stared at the vocoder with a puzzled frown. How clear Hempstead's voice sounded—even to the throat-clearing which the AAT should have filtered from the message. He shifted his attention to the Ox's surrealistic growth on the computer wall.

Again, Hempstead's voice intruded: "We expect from this transmission a more complete analysis of your damage. The nature and extent of the damage of paramount importance. Acknowledge at once. Project over and out."

Bickel kept his voice low, casual. "Prue, how'd old Big Daddy sound to you?"

"Worried," Prudence said. And she wondered why Bickel, with his inhibitions against return, could take this so calmly.

"If you wanted to convey the emotions in someone's message how would you do it, Prue?" Bickel asked.

She looked at him, puzzled. "I'd label the emotion or imitate the tone of the original. Why?"

"The AAT isn't supposed to be able to do that," Bickel said. He looked up, meeting Flattery's eyes in the screen. "Don't acknowledge that transmission, Raj."

"The AAT's working better than ever?" Prudence asked.

"No," Bickel said. "It's working in a way it shouldn't be able to. The laser-burst message is stripped to bare essentials. The original voice modulations are there, theoretically, and often strong enough to recognize certain mannerisms, but subtleties are supposed to be beyond it. That last message was high fidelity."

"The Ox circuits make the system more sensitive," she said.

"Maybe," Bickel said.

"Was there nerve-net activity accompanying that?" Flattery asked.

"A fish has nerve-net activity," Bickel said. "Nerve-net activitiy doesn't mean the thing's conscious."

"But sensitized the way consciousness is," Flattery said.

Bickel nodded.

"Selective raising and lowering of thresholds," Flattery said. "Threshold control."

Again Bickel nodded.

"What's this?" Prudence asked.

"This thing"—Bickel pointed to the Ox— "has just demonstrated threshold control . . . the way we do when we recognize something." He looked at her. "When you lower your reception threshold you spread the spatio-temporal message and project it across an internal 'recognition aura' for mental comparison. The message is a spatio-temporal configuration which you superimpose on a recognition region. That recognition region can discriminate quite broadly between 'just right,' which is maximum similarity, and a kind of 'blurring off' you could call 'somewhat alike.' Threshold control does the tuning for this kind of comparison."

With precisely controlled motions, Bickel returned to the circuitry he had been working on when the UMB message interrupted him. He picked up a sheaf of fibers, noting the neuron tag on them and slid the sheaf into a micro-manipulator where he finished the connection to a multijack.

In Com-central, Flattery stretched out his left hand, gripped the stanchion beside his action couch until his knuckles went white.

They were disobeying Hempstead in an outright, flagrant way. The chaplain-psychiatrist had precise instructions about such a contingency. *Obey! If others try to stop you, blow the ship.* But he could feel how Bickel was closing in on the solution to the Project's overriding problem. They were near success. That certainly allowed a bit of latitude.

Who can tell me what to to do, O my soul? Who can tell me where my soul might be?

The words of the 139th Psalm slithered through his mind: *"I will praise thee; for I am fearfully and wonderfully made."*

Do we betray God by making something fearful and wonderful? he wondered.

"Our Father which art in Heaven," he whispered.

But I am in the heavens, he thought. *And the heavens expose me still to spiritual risk!*

The sound of Bickel and Prudence working in the shop was almost a carrier wave for his thoughts.

Faith and knowledge, he thought. And he sensed the eternal clash that now had taken his body as its arena— knowledge thrusting at the boundaries of faith. And he felt the constructive emotions his faith was engineered to contain.

I could end this nonsense, he thought. *But we're all in the same bind and violence betrays us.*

"Religion and psychiatry are but two branches of the healing art." He remembered the words clearly. The lecturer in "Uses of Faith," the second-year course preparing him for this role. "Religion and psychiatry share the same stem."

Heal thyself, he thought. Tears started from his eyes. Where were the faith, the hope and the laughter—the love and creativeness he had been enjoined to employ?

Flattery looked up through his tears, saw in the screen both Bickel and Prudence ignoring him, so intent were they on the project.

See how their hands touch, Flattery thought.

He felt guilt at the sight and remembered Brooks' admonition: "Keep clear of concealment; keep clear of the need of concealment."

"What an awful hour when we first meet the necessity of hiding something," he whispered. "Please God, have I forgotten how to pray?"

Flattery ignored the vital console in front of him, closed his eyes, and gripped the stanchion fiercely. "The Lord is my shepherd," he whispered. "I shall not want."

But the words had lost their power over him.

There are no still waters here . . . or green pastures, he thought.

There never had been these things for him—or for any of them out of the axlotl tanks and the UMB's sterile crèches. There had only been the valley of the shadow of death.

"DO NOT BROACH THIS HATCH WITHOUT READING AIR PRESSURE IN THE NEXT PASSAGE."

Every morning on his way to classes—eleven years—he had passed through the hatch with that warning.

"NO TRAVEL BEYOND THIS POINT WITHOUT FULL SPACESUIT."

That omnipresent sign had set the boundaries on their untrammeled activity. It still did.

The suit was like another social inhibition setting its own limits of behavior. It restricted your contact with other humans, reduced you to code tappings and depersonalized vuphones where every person became like a dancing doll on an oscilloscope screen.

The omnipresent enemy was the *outside*—that total absence of the things to support life that emptiness called space. It was evil and they feared it—constantly. A rod and staff might comfort in the presence of space, but what you dreamed about was washed air and a womblike enclosed cell where you could divest yourself of the damnable suit. This was the true source of comfort no matter if it came from the Devil himself.

The only table you could count on in the presence of this enemy was a squeeze bottle slid from its rack. Oil on the head could only fog a faceplate. You had to crop your hair short and keep down the natural oils with detergent.

Goodness and mercy? That was anything which preserved the hope that you could one day walk unsuited beneath an open sky.

I've lost my faith, Flattery thought. *God, why have You taken my faith from me?*

"Blessed are the pure in heart: for they shall see God," he whispered.

You were a fool, Matthew, he thought. *A harlot can't regain her virginity.*

"The whole universe is a matter of chemistry and mechanics, of matter and energy," he whispered.

But only God was supposed to have complete control

of manipulating the matter and energy.

We aren't gods, Flattery thought. *We're blaspheming by trying to make a machine that thinks of itself by itself. That is why I was set to watch over this mission. We blaspheme by trying to put a soul into a machine. I should go down there now and smash the whole thing!*

"Raj!"

It was Bickel's voice booming from the intercom.

Flattery looked up at the screen, his mouth suddenly dry.

"I'm getting independent action on the photosensory loops of the computer's record-and-store circuits," Bickel said. "Prue, check the current drain."

"Normal," she said. "It's no short circuit."

"It . . . isn't conscious," Flattery said, his voice wooden.

"Agreed," Bickel said. "But what the hell is it? The computer's programming itself in every . . ." There came a charged moment of silence then: "Damn!"

"What happened?" Prue demanded.

"It stopped," Bickel said.

"What . . . set it off?" Flattery asked.

"I tied an inhibitor block into one arm of a single nerve-net simulator and sent a test pattern through it. The test evidently set up a resonant pattern that searched right through the Ox and into the computer net via the monitor connections. That's when I started getting the self-programming reaction."

Prudence sighted along her finger, moving it to trace a thick color-coded connection that looped down from the Ox. "The monitor linkage goes only one way into record-and-store. It's buffered right there."

Bickel pulled the connection she indicated.

"What're you doing?" she asked.

"Disconnecting. I'm going to get the pattern of the experiment out of the memory banks and analyze it before proceeding."

Silence.

Flattery stared up at the screen with a deep sense of repugnance which he knew was grounded in his religious training.

It had been drummed into him: "You are not precisely someone. You are a clone."

There had always been too much emphasis on that statement for him to accept it completely. He understood the reasons for this conditioning, though, and accepted them.

But what about this thing that Bickel's making?

UMB had a complete bank of clones sufficient to recreate the *Earthling*'s crew precisely as it had been at the moment of launching. Minor variables might intrude and the Organic Mental Cores could be different. He had never pinned that one down but he knew it was cheaper to take OMCs from damaged humans than to clone them and prepare them for the ship.

In a strange way the OMCs might be more genetically human than the crew.

Flattery knew he was not supposed to feel guilt at the thought of killing the ship—himself included. The message had been clear: "We can recreate all of you here on the Moon. You are infinite. You cannot completely die because your cells will live on and on."

My exact cells? he wondered. *My exact consciousness?*

But wasn't that the central problem of this whole project?

What is consciousness?

Again, he looked at the screen. *If I kill the ship/computer/brain now . . . will I be killing someone?*

CHAPTER 24

Over a long period of time, clones offer us an
extremely valuable tool for determining genetic drift. It is clear that our cloning techniques at
UMB permit us to clone a clone indefinitely.
Ten thousand years from now we could
possess genetic material which is contempo-
rary with this very moment... now! Perhaps
this will be of greater service to humankind
than the understanding of consciousness.

—Morgan Hempstead
Lectures at Moonbase

ROUTINE SENSOR FIRINGS sent telltale lights flickering
across the computer wall. The passage of the lights
produced a weird shift in the shop's illumination. The
curved bulkhead opposite the computer face reflected
yellow, then green, now mauve... red.

The color shift passed across a chart in Timberlake's
hand as he read it and compared the chart's predictions
with the readings in front of him.

The overhead screen showed Prudence on Com-
central about midway through her watch and Flattery
dozing in his action couch.

Strange he wouldn't take off for quarters, Timberlake thought.

Bickel emerged from between the Ox's two branchings just as a wash of green splashed down on him from the wall.

"That last reading's off only .008," Timberlake said.

"Insignificant," Bickel said. "Waveforms?"

Timberlake nodded at the oscilloscope in front of him, feeling a sharp pain shoot through his neck. He felt tired and stiff. Bickel had driven them, working through three shifts. Timberlake rubbed his neck.

Bickel turned from studying the scope. "Remember I told you to remind me about all the oscillations involved in life? Rhythms, vibrations—just one great big series of drumbeats."

"Yeah," Timberlake said. "You about ready for the full-scale run-through?"

Bickel stared at the flickering lights reluctant to move now that the moment of test had come. He knew the source of his reluctance—the secret thing he had done, and fear of its consequences.

One more test ... and then ... what?

Black box—white box.

"You think it's not going to work?" Timberlake asked. He felt impatient with Bickel but sensed this couldn't be pushed.

"The human nervous system—including the region of the brain we assume influences consciousness—has come through one hell of a lot of tests," Bickel said.

"And this thing ..." Timberlake nodded toward the Ox, "is a logically simple analogue of the human brain."

"Logical simplicity has damn little bearing on our problem. We're engineering something, all right, but not by the old bridge-building rules."

He's stalling, Timberlake thought. *Why?* "Then what're we doing?"

"It doesn't take much, just a word sometimes to upset the logical applecart," Bickel said. "The brain's had to meet a lot of requirements that had nothing whatsoever to do with design simplicity. For one thing, it had to survive while it developed. Its size and shape had a bearing on that. It had to adapt existing structure to new functions."

Bickel met Timberlake's eyes. "The human brain's an obvious hybrid mating of function and structure. There are strengths in that, but weaknesses, too."

"So?" Timberlake said, and shrugged. "What's upsetting the applecart now?"

"Raj's talking about psychospace and psychorelationships. That damn causal track of neuron impulses spreading out to form new kinds of space. It's quite possible for our *normal* universe to be twisted through an infinite number of psychospaces."

"Yeah?" Timberlake stared at him, wondering at the fear in Bickel's voice.

Bickel went on: "There can be an infinite number of types of consciousness. Every time I come near turning this thing loose, I start wondering what space it'll inhabit."

"Raj and his damn horror stories," Timberlake said.

Bickel continued to stare at the Ox structure, wondering if he had done the right thing to act secretly.

Was this damn electronic maze going to create its own guilt?

To reach a level where it could accept a black-box imprint the Ox-cum-computer had to surmount barriers, Bickel knew. It had to flex its mental muscles. And guilt *was* a barrier.

By blank-space programming, supplying data with obvious holes in it, he had inserted an information series on the subject of death. The on-line operative command was for the computer to fill in the gaps. Now, by parallel insertion of the address data for the life-maintenance program on a cow embryo in the farm-stock hyb tanks, Bickel had provided the computer with a simple way to fill the gaps in its information.

It could kill the embryo.

I had to act secretly, Bickel told himself. *I couldn't ring in Timberlake—now with his inhibitions. And any of the others might've told Tim.*

"You think we're missing some fault in the system?"

Timberlake asked. "What's bugging you? The fact that the random search stopped of its own accord?"

"No." Bickel shook his head. "That search pattern ran into an irregularity, a threshold it couldn't cross."

"Then what's holding you back, for Christ's sake?"

Bickel swallowed. He found it required increasing effort to hold his attention on an unbroken thread of reasoning where it concerned bringing the Ox to consciousness. There was a sensation of swimming against a stiff current.

With what kind of a mirror can consciousness look at itself? he wondered. *How can the Ox say: "This is myself?" What will it see?*

"Human nervous systems have the same kinds of irregularities and imperfections," Timberlake said. "Their properties vary statistically."

Bickel nodded agreement. Timberlake was right. That was the reason they had introduced random error into the Ox—statistical imperfection.

"You worrying about pulse regulation?" Timberlake asked.

Bickel shook his head. "No." He put his palm against a plastic-encased neuron block protruding from the Ox. "We've got a homeostat whose main function is dealing with errors—with negative reality. Consciousness is always looking at the back side of whatever confronts us, always staring back at us."

"You've left the gaps in it so it'll need us," Timberlake said. "You're fussed about threshold regulation."

Bickel looked at Timberlake, thinking: *Threshold? Yes, that was part of it.* The brain cells and peripheral neurons in a human tied together so that their differences averaged out. You got the effect of smooth gradation. The effect. Illusion.

"We're missing something," Bickel muttered.

Timberlake wondered at the fear in Bickel's voice, the way the man's head turned from side to side like a caged animal.

"If this thing takes off on its own, we have no control over it," Bickel said. "Raj is right."

"Raj's Golem stories!" Timberlake sneered.

"No," Bickel was fearfully serious. "This thing has new *kinds* of memories. They have only the vaguest relationship to human memories. But memories Tim—the nerve gets stacked in psychospaces—they're the patterns that create behavior. What's this thing going to do when we turn it on...if we don't give it experiences of the kind the human race has survived?"

"You don't *know* what the racial traumas are and that's where you're hung up."

The voice was Flattery's, and they looked up to the overhead screen to see him sitting still half-cocooned in his action couch and rubbing sleep from his eyes. Beyond him, Prudence maintained her vigil at the big board as though that were the only thing concerning her.

Bickel suppressed a feeling of irritation with Flattery. "You're the psychiatrist. Isn't knowledge of trauma supposed to be one of your tools?"

"You're asking about racial trauma," Flattery said. "We can only guess at racial trauma."

Flattery stared out of the screen at Bickel, thinking: *John's panicky. Why? Because the Ox suddenly started acting on its own?*

"We have to bring this thing into being," Bickel said, looking at the Ox. "But we can't be sure what it is. This is the ultimate stranger. It can't be like one of us. And if it's different...yet alive and aware of its aliveness..."

"So you start casting around in your mind for ways to make it more like us," Flattery said.

Bickel nodded.

"And you think we're the products of our racial and personal trauma?" Flattery asked. "You don't think consciousness is the apparent effect of a receptor?"

"Dammit, Raj!" Bickel snapped. "We're within a short leap of solving this thing! Can't you feel that?"

"But you wonder," Flattery said, "are we making a creature that'll be invulnerable...at least invulnerable to us?"

Bickel swallowed.

"You think," Flattery went steadily on, "this beast

we're creating has no sexual function; it can't possibly be like us. It has no flesh; it can't possibly know what flesh fears and loves. So now you're asking: How do we simulate flesh and sex and the racial sufferings through which humans have blundered? The answer's obvious: We can't do this. We don't know all our own instincts. We can't sort the shadows and reflections out of our history."

"We can sort out some of them," Bickel insisted. "We have an instinct to .*. win ... to survive for ..." He wet his lips with his tongue, looked around at the computer wall.

"Perhaps that's only hubris," Flattery said. "Maybe this is just monkey curiosity and we won't be satisfied until we've been creators the way God's a creator. But then it may be too late to turn back."

As though he hadn't heard, Bickel said. "And there's the killer instinct. That one goes right down into the slime where it was kill or be killed. You can see the other side of it all the time in our instinct to play it safe ... to 'be practical'."

He has done something secret, Flattery thought. *What has Bickel done? He has done something he's afraid of.*

"And guilt feelings are grafted right onto that killer instinct," Bickel said. "That's the buffer ... the way we keep human behavior within limits. If we implant ..."

"Guilt involves sin," Flattery said. "Where do you find in either religion or psychiatry a *need* for sin?"

"Instinct's just a word," Bickel said. "And we're a long way from the word's source. What is it? We can raise fifty generations of chickens from embryo to chick in test tubes. They never see a shell. But the fifty-first generation, raised normally under a hen, still knows to peck its way out."

"Genetic imprint," Flattery said.

"Imprint." Bickel nodded. "Something stamped on us. Stamped hard. Oh, we know. We know these instincts without ever bringing them to consciousness. They're what lower our awareness, make us angry, violent, passionate ..." Again, he nodded.

What has he done? Flattery asked himself. *He's panicky because of it. I have to find out!*

"The Cain-and-Abel syndrome," Bickel said. "Murder and guilt. It's back there someplace... stamped inside us. The cells remember."

"You haven't the vaguest idea what you're saying," Flattery accused. "You're separating positive and negative pairs, confusing moral judgments with reasoning, reversing the normal course of—"

"Reversing!" Bickel pounded. "That's what I was trying to think of—reversing. The ability to turn pleasure into pain or pain into pleasure... that's a part of consciousness we haven't—"

"That's sickness," Flattery said.

"The power to be sane is also the power to go mad," Bickel said. "Your own words!"

Flattery stared out of the screen at him, caught up short by this turn of the argument... and a sudden suspicion about what Bickel could have done.

"You know," Timberlake said, speaking in a low, reasonable tone, "if an instinct is something to which the whole system must refer in a moment of stress, that's something like a computer's trapping function mated to a supervisory program."

"We're beyond the point of engineering and have been for some time," Flattery said.

"Right back where we started from," Bickel agreed. "We can duplicate synapses with unijunction transistors; juggle conduction rate and absolute refractory periods by choice of pseudoneuron fibers, fit our neural networks with multiplying and inhibitory endbulbs at will... but, in the end, we always come up against that inescapable question..."

"How do you control what must remain beyond control? I've already told you. *Love.*"

"You don't control it," Bickel declared. "You merely *aim* it... and the aiming device has to be instincts. As you say, Raj, it must love us, be loyal to us. But does that mean it will worship us? Are we to be its gods? And if it's to be loyal, does that mean it has to have a conscience? Can there be loyalty without a conscience? And can it have a conscience without experiencing guilt?"

"Guilt's a prison!" Flattery protested. 'You can't imprison a free—"

"Who says it has to be free?" Bickel demanded. "You're arguing against yourself! That's the whole damned idea: How do we control it? When you come right down to it: Am I free? Are you?"

Flattery glared at him.

"We're instinct-ridden, conscience-ridden bits of protoplasm," Bickel said.

"What instincts?" Flattery asked.

"You sound like a damn broken record!" Bickel snapped. "What instincts? You can't trace the instincts! Well, for one thing, we've an instinct to kill—to kill and eat. We don't really give one particle of a damn where we get our energy—not down there in the psychic basement we don't."

"If it were only that simple," Flattery said.

"When you get below stairs it is," Bickel said. "I don't need a doctorate in psychiatry to tell me what I'd do if the veneer were stripped off."

"You'd revert to the savage, eh? To the animal!"

"To find out what's engineered into the system, you're damn right I would ! What the hell have you head doctors been studying all these years with your dreams and your complexes and your Christ? You've trapped yourselves into an endless formal dance with fixed postures and . . . Christ! You remind me of a pack of fops doing the minuet!"

"We've employed reverence and caution to approach God in Man," Flattery said. "You don't gouge into the human psyche with an egg beater and stir up all the—"

"The hell you don't!"

They glared at each other, Bickel desperate with indecision, and Flattery's suspicions verging on certainty.

He has given the Ox the means to kill, Flattery thought. *His argument and his anger betray it. But kill what? Not one of us, certainly. A colonist in the hyb tanks? No. One of the stock animals! He'd dip his toe into violence first, see if the Ox could really do it.*

But he cannot have already made the black box—white box transfer.

Prudence, dividing her attention between the control console and the clash of wills, felt herself shift further and further into a state of heightened awareness. She sensed Com-central's minute temperature variations, heard the constant metallic creakings of deck and bulkheads around her, saw Flattery's growing suspicions and Bickel's desperate defensiveness, knew her own heartbeats and tiny variations in her body chemistry.

It was the chemistry that fascinated her: the thought that all through this subtle play of organic and inorganic matter which she called "myself," messages of which she was only dimly aware (if at all) were being transmitted and acted upon.

The computer with its enormous library of data culled from millions of minds had offered her a way to explore the issue Bickel had raised, and she could not resist this.

Where and how are the instincts carried?

While the argument between Flattery and Bickel raged, she had translated the question onto an edge-coded tape, shifted it into the computer section of her board, tripped the action switch.

This went beyond chemical-base sequence, she knew, and into the area where knowledge of protein structure itself was only theoretical code. But if the computer gave her an answer that could be translated into a physical function, she knew she could explore the answer through experiments on her own body.

"Bickel, what've you done?" Flattery demanded.

Prudence looked up from her console, saw Flattery, his shoulders tensed as though about to leap, staring into the screen. The screen revealed Bickel and Timberlake, their backs turned, staring at the computer wall and the blocks-and-angles contortion that was the Ox.

The hum of the computer could be felt throughout the shop and Com-central. The play of sensor and telltale lights across the big board and the shop's panels had reached a glittering tempo. Drain gauges showed energy consumption almost at the limits the system could tolerate.

Chapter 25

There must be a threshold of consciousness such that when you pass it you acquire godlike attributes.

—Raja Lon Flattery
The Book of Ship

As THOUGH THE computer display were a hypnotic trigger, all four of them waited it out with minimal reaction. Both Bickel and Flattery shared the same reason for inaction—fear that *anything* they did might be enough to destroy the entire system. Timberlake sat in sweating fear that his charges in hybernation were threatened by this computer display. Only Prudence was frozen by guilt.

She found herself breathing in shallow gasps, acutely aware of every mechanical sound from the flashing display—every click and hum and buzz, every hissing tape—as though she had a direct sensory connection to the system.

Abruptly, she put the back of her left hand over her mouth, horrified realization flooding her: *The whole computer's routed through the Ox now!*

"What've you done?" Flattery demanded.

"Nothing!" Bickel said without turning.

Timberlake said, "Shouldn't we..."

"Leave it alone!" Bickel snapped.

In a low voice, Prudence said, "I did it. I fed a question into the computer."

"What question?" Bickel demanded. He pointed to a large meter above him. "Look at that current drain! I've never seen anything like it."

"I traced out sixty-eight sequential steps of fourth-order biochemical configuration. I programmed it as a comparator of optical isomers for a first step in trying to detect where and how our instincts are imprinted on us."

"It's gone into the monitor banks," Bickel said, nodding at a new play of lights on the wall. "We're getting multitrack reinforcement..."

"Like a man concentrating on a tough problem," Timberlake said.

Bickel nodded.

The output beside Prudence began hissing as tape sped from it into the strip viewer.

Bickel whirled. "What're you getting?"

She studied the viewer, forcing calmness. "A pyramided answer. I only asked for the first four probables. It's already into the tenth step! It's the nucleic acids, all right...down there with the genetic information. But it's tracing out all the dead ends...the molecular weights and—"

"It's talking it over with you," Bickel said. "It's asking your opinion. Cut in on it and eliminate the obvious dead ends as you see them."

Prudence scanned back along the strip viewer, checked off useless sequences. *Hydrogen catalysis...obviously not. Too much opportunity for contamination.* She cut into the output tape, began deleting and feeding the tape back into the computer.

Output went suddenly silent, but the play of lights against the computer wall raised to a new frenzy. Power drain showed a new surge with a pulse in it.

"Are you feeding a resonant cycle into the system?" Prudence asked. She was surprised at how much effort it took to hold her voice level.

"That pulse is identical to the timing of the Ox's response loops," Bickel said.

As he spoke, the output beside Prudence renewed its chattering. Tape surged into the strip viewer.

Prudence stared at it silently.

"Well, what is it?" Bickel demanded.

The output tape rolled to a stop. In the abrupt hush, Prudence said: "It's linked to acid phosphatase . . . amino acid catalysis in the DNA coils." And she made the functional comparison, relating this to her tests on her own body. Adrenochrome—if she filled out the OH to C_5H_{11} (n) . . . would that take it through the blood-brain barrier at a less-than-fatal dosage?

"Is it . . . conscious?" Flattery whispered.

Bickel looked up at the computer wall where lights were winking out, leaving only that somnolent play of telltales—green . . . mauve . . . gold . . .

"No," Bickel said. "We've merely produced a computer that can program itself, concentrate all its bits of information on a problem . . . hunt for data even if that data comes from outside its banks. It *knew* when to ask a question of one of us."

"And that isn't conscious?" Timberlake demanded.

"Not the way we are," Bickel said. "You have to ask it a question before it . . . comes to life."

"Acid phosphatase," Prudence mused. "What do we know about acid phosphatase?" She knew she was asking questions about the DNA language of life, questions pertinent to their consciousness problem. And she longed to confide in the others, discuss her experiments openly . . . but more than worry about the inhibitions of her companions held her to silence. In some way, she had gone too far down a road that she had to continue on . . . alone.

"Acid phosphatase is widely distributed in the body," Flattery said. He turned, looked at Prudence as though seeing her for the first time. She would understand, of course—almost at once. He looked up to the screen at Timberlake and Bickel. They might have to have it explained to them. He returned his attention to Prudence. How thin and tired she looked.

Prudence nodded to herself, eyes glazed in thought. "Body chemisty, yes," she said. "Male prostate's rich in acid phosphatase. Males store more of it than females."

And she thought: *Testosterone!* The male hormone's level in the body was directly related to position in a hierarchy. Bickel would have the crew's highest T-level.

Flattery spoke cautiously: "Body tissue requires a minimum level before a person can be awakened."

She jerked upright, met his gaze. "An enzyme involved in the physiology of sex and awakening." She turned away, thinking: *Sex and awakening.*

"Is that what anti-S suppresses?" Bickel asked.

"Not directly," Timberlake answered. "A-S works primarily on serum phenolsulfatase discrimination. It inhibits transfer and action."

Timberlake, the life-systems specialist, the biophysicist, would see it, too, Flattery thought.

Flattery looked into the screen, seeing Bickel standing there so silent and thoughtful, feeling a sudden pity for the man. Such a simple fact: *Awakening and sex are tied together.*

Prudence kept her face turned toward the big control board, studied it without really seeing it. The ship could have gone into wild gyrations at the moment and she would have been seconds responding. As she had looked at Flattery, she had seen what he was thinking as though there were words written on his forehead.

Consciousness linked to reproduction.

There was no doubt of it: both came out of the same genetic well. History had washed them in the same waters, transferring the needs of one to the needs of the other.

Slowly, Bickel turned, looked through the screen at the big laser-pulsed autolog in Com-central recording the passage of Earth-time. It recorded eighteen weeks, twenty-one hours, and twenty-nine seconds. It clicked over another minute as he watched it.

For most of those pulse-counted minutes, Bickel

thought, the Tin Egg's crew had been under the pressures of a ship in peril. The danger was real, no matter its source or intent; he had only to study the report on damage accretion to confirm this. But the pressure on the umbilicus crew had started with the loss of the Organic Mental Cores. The pressure had started when they were no longer shielded by another consciousness.

For the first time, Bickel turned his thoughts onto the concept of consciousness as a shield—a way of protecting its possessor from the shocks of the unknown. It was an "I can do anything!" answer hurled at a universe that threatened you with *everything*.

He lowered his attention to Flattery who still sat half cocooned in the action couch, and Bickel sensed defeat in the curve of the man's shoulders and the set of his face.

Why is he so quick to accept defeat? Bickel wondered. *It's almost as though he wanted it.*

The answer came to him on the heels of the question: *If you're programmed for destruction, you have a need for destruction.* With a sense of growing awareness, Bickel turned to look at the Ox construction, focusing on the angles and blocks and the tangle of neuron connections.

But I've programmed this beast for violence!

Forcing himself to appear calm and natural, Bickel shifted the jackboard for a diagnostic check on the program, traced out the condition of the routine. His throat went dry as he scanned the readout.

The embryo he had placed at the Ox's mercy—it was dead. No...dead was too simple a word for what had happened to that embryo. It had been disintegrated, torn asunder, broken down to its constituent molecules. The record was all here on the tapes and discs, betraying also the reason for the destruction.

Prue's question!

The embryo had been subjected to a violent experiment in the computer's search for information.

A violent and *useless* experiment. This certainly could not have produced much data—except for some of the more grossly apparent characteristics of acid phosphatase—and perhaps negative data about other biochemistry.

It'll kill to get information, Bickel thought. *It has an ability of sorts to accept motivation—if we give it motivation.*

CHAPTER 26

There's a trait called initiative which is balanced against caution. Too tight a balance and you get oscillatory inaction, but that balancing act rides the wave of consciousness. All creatures display it in some form, but the sophisticated, symbol-juggling form displayed by humans has to be related to the kind of consciousness-answer we seek.

—Morgan Hempstead
Lectures at Moonbase

PRUDENCE WIPED PERSPIRATION from her cheek, returned her attention to the big board. For almost half an hour now she had been dividing her attention between the board and Bickel. It drained her.

Bickel, working in the shop with Timberlake, obviously was caught in unspoken indecision, skirting all around it. Something had happened . . . something which Bickel refused to share with the rest of the crew. He went through the motions of refining that Ox-monstrosity, but something was making him fearful beyond any normal caution.

A telltale on the board flickered into the red.

"We've just lost another sensor," Prudence said, reading the telltale. "...at $4CtB_5K2$."

"Second *pi*, fourth ring and in behind number five shielding layer," Timberlake said. "That's damn close to the hyb tanks."

"I'll check it," Flattery said, unlocking the bottom of his couch. He swung his feet to the deck, slipped his helmet forward, but left it unsealed.

"Is there a robox-R in that area?" Bickel asked.

"What's the difference?" Flattery asked. "By the time we found one and traced out the control sequence—"

"Are we going to check that sensor or aren't we?" Timberlake demanded. He glared into the screen at Flattery.

"I'm on my way," Flattery said. *I mustn't let Tim pre-empt this job,* he thought. *I need the excuse to go past quarters for a quick check on what Bickel's done. It's something violent and dangerous. He has himself under very thin control.*

"Raj," Prudence said.

He turned at the hatch.

"That...thing down there in the shop *could* reproduce itself with no help from us. Every machine tool, every robox monkey, every muscle and sensor is programmed through the computer. Once the last tie-in is made..."

Flattery wet his lips with his tongue, ducked out through the hatch without answering her.

Why'n hell did she bring that up now? Bickel wondered.

"That goddamn slowpoke," Timberlake said. "I should've gone myself."

Prudence shifted a corner of her board to monitor Flattery's progress. She glanced up at the screen. Bickel was staring back past her at the hatch where Flattery had gone.

Raj was depressed at the thought of reproduction being linked to consciousness, Bickel thought. *What Prudence told him should've lifted some of that depression. It didn't.*

A sense of foreboding poured through Bickel.

Programmed for destruction equals a need for destruction, he thought.

What am I afraid of? he wondered. *What new thing? The fact that the Ox could reproduce itself by using the tool tapes and mechanical muscles of the ship?*

"Prue, do you have a fix on Raj?" Bickel asked.

"He has a prime repair dolly and he'll be at the trouble spot in another minute or so," she said. "I ran a continuity check on it..."

"No sense in that," Bickel said. "The trouble's in the sensor itself. The continuity net has hundreds of backups and alternate circuits. What failed, a heat sensor?"

"Multiple," she said. "Heat-sound-visual."

"That thing's down near the temperature-control shutters in the baffle to the hyb tanks," Timberlake muttered. "Too goddamn close to them. You getting any heat shifts on the other sensors?"

"Nothing significant," she said.

Prudence flicked a switch, watching the shifting factors of temperature-weight-sound on her board, the telltales moving with Flattery. She hit another switch: "Raj, how much longer?"

Flattery's voice came out of the overhead command vocoder: "Another minute or so."

They waited in silence, listening to the sounds of Flattery's progress through the open command vocoder.

Prudence activated a guide beam to the dead sensor as Flattery passed the water baffles.

"Baffles secure," she said, reading her board.

"All secure," Flattery said.

He dogged that last hatch, knowing the action would register in front of Prudence in Com-central. The action sent a faint fear response through him. He had symbolically cut himself off from the core of the ship.

I'll fix this sensor and get back to quarters as soon as I can, he told himself. *It'll seem natural for me to stop off there on my way back. I have to find out what Bickel's done, but I can't make him suspicious.*

Flattery turned, studied his surroundings. He stood in

the bulb lock that served as a hub for outer-hull communications tubes in this sector. It was an oval for strength, about six meters across its short diameter, and seven meters deep. He oriented himself by the faint pull of ship gravity.

The nonfunctioning sensor was up a tube that curved off at two o'clock on his right. Tube eight, ring K. The number checked. The failure would be at the five-line. He stared into the pale gray metal gap illuminated by cold light. A green guide beam beckoned in the tube.

Prue remembered to set the guide beam, he thought.

He took the repair dolly in his left hand, made the low-grav leap across to the tube and caught its access rung. He pushed the dolly in ahead of him, setting its sensors on the printed track, fed it low power to pull him into the tube.

The autolock's sphincter closed behind him. He suddenly remembered Anderson strangled in a rogue sphincter...but of course that was no problem now...with all the OMCs dead. The fact that one of the crew had to come out here and make this repair meant the dangers were of another sort.

"Something wrong?" Prudence asked, her voice filling his helmet.

She saw the telltales stop here, Flattery thought. It gave him a feeling of reassurance that she was so alert to his movements—or lack of movements.

"Nothing wrong; just being cautious."

"You want Tim to come out and back you up?" Prudence asked.

"I don't need anyone to hold my hand!" Flattery snapped, and he wondered at the sudden anger he'd thrown into that rejection.

"You're at Station Two," Prudence said. "There's video on Two. Check."

Flattery glanced up at the ring of sensors on the tube, saw the one circled with yellow for video, waved at it as he passed.

The robox-R's imprinted track curved up the tube side to clear the base bulge for the next automatic lock. He went through, looked back as the transparent shutters squeezed closed behind him. The ship's core *felt* so far away back there.

He looked forward, letting the robox unit tow him with its faint hissing growl, letting the loneliness seep through him. With an OMC in control, an automatic robox repair unit could have been sent on this little chore. Mobility, that was the problem. Where there were fixed automatic repair units—along the outer hull and at the major bulkhead locks, at the baffles and core-integrity barriers—the ship took care of itself with only a little help from its crew. But let a little thing like this come up—where you needed mobility and a decision factor—then one of the crew had to risk himself.

Flattery cursed the Tin Egg's designers then. Hate poured out of him. He knew why they had done this—the "planned increment of frustration" they called it. That was fine—as long as one of the ship's designers didn't have to experience the frustration . . . or the deadliness.

He was at Station Four now, coming up on Five.

"Station Five coming up," he said. "Hey!" He cut the power on the robox, braked himself against the station's ring, stared up at the overhead arc of sensors. A neat, shiny hole plugged with gray foam-coagulant occupied the position where the multi-sensor had been. The yellow-green-red code rings on the tube around the hole had not been touched. He swung his gaze around the tube and the other sensors. All appeared to be functioning.

Flattery thought then of the island on Puget Sound—sensors missing mysteriously . . . personnel missing. He felt cold sweat around his shoulders.

Prudence's voice filled his helmet: "Anything to report?"

He lowered the volume. "The multisensor seems to've been cut out in some way. It's gone. The hole's been plugged with foam."

"No foam automatics in that area," Prudence said.

"The thing's been plugged with foam anyway!" Flattery was unable to hide the angry irritation in his voice.

Prudence suddenly said, "John, I'm getting a demand drain on the computer. Is it something you're doing?"

"Nothing," Bickel said.

Flattery turned his head in the helmet. Bickel's voice had come in faintly as a pickup through Com-central. *Action in the computer!* Flattery forced himself to act calmly, removed a replacement sensor from his robox unit's parts compartment, checked it. The thing was about three inches in diameter, containing a warp-type thermal detector, standard vid-eye pickups like tiny jewels on its face, and three gridded ducts leading into the membrane of the audio unit.

Out of the corner of one eye, Flattery detected movement up the tube. He jerked upright, banged his head against the helmet liner, stared up toward Station Six.

A robox-R with its tool extensors clamped tightly to its sides was moving along the tape track toward him. The thing acted sick—speeding and slowing.

His first thought was that Prudence had traced the robox remote controls for a unit in this area and was maneuvering the thing from her board. The crudity of Com-central's controls over the robox series would account for the unit's erratic behavior.

"You bringing another robox in here, Prue?" Flattery asked.

"No, why?"

"There's another robox-R coming down on this station," he said.

As he watched, the thing lost the tape track, relocated it.

"There can't be! Nothing at all shows on my board."

The thing stopped across the sensor ring from Flattery. An auger extension jerked away from its side, reached toward the foam-plugged hole, withdrew.

"Who's controlling that thing?" Flattery demanded.

"Not from here," Prudence said. "And I can see both Tim and John. They're not controlling it."

"You still getting drain on the computer?" Flattery whispered.

"Yes."

"Is the . . . Ox active?" Flattery asked.

"Only the original circuits," Bickel said. "Through the AAT bypass. The new doubled units haven't been connected."

"There can't be another robox in that area," Prudence insisted. "We haven't put any of the damn things on automatic. There's nothing showing on my board. The remotes would take a day and a half at least to—"

"It's right in front of me," Flattery said.

He watched it, fascinated. A tool arm extended with an empty sensor socket, reached toward the foam-plugged hole, retreated. A claw arm came up next. It probed the foam, drew back with a swiftness that startled Flattery.

"What's it doing?" Prudence asked.

"I'm not sure. It seems to be looking over the damage. Its vid-eyes are turned toward the hole. It acts like it can't decide which tool to use."

"*What* can't decide?" That was Timberlake, his voice faint over the Com-central relay from the shop.

"Try fixing the sensor yourself," Bickel said.

Flattery swallowed in a dry throat. He lifted a feeler with a guide eye from the tool pouch on his own robox, probed into the foam plug looking for the leads from the conduit.

Instantly, a whiplike extension shot out of the other robox, trapped his arm, jerked it away. The pain in his arm where the thing had clamped on it was sharp and shocking. He dropped the tool, yelled.

"What's wrong?" Prudence demanded.

The whiplike extension slowly unwound, released his arm.

"The thing grabbed me," Flattery said. His voice was shaky with pain and surprise. "It used its circuit probe . . . grabbed my arm."

"It won't let you make the repair?" That was Bickel, his voice coming in loud over the helmet system, indicating he'd plugged into the command circuit from the shop.

"Doesn't look like it," Flattery said. And he wondered:

Why doesn't one of us say what this thing has to be? Why're we avoiding the obvious?

With an abrupt sense of purpose, the other robox reached out a claw arm, lifted the replacement sensor from Flattery's left hand, matched sensor and socket. Another claw arm recovered the feeler guide, fitted it to the connections of its own circuit probe.

"What's it doing now?" Bickel asked.

"Making the repair itself," Flattery said.

The feeler came out of the hole pulling the leads.

"John, what's showing on your meters?" Prudence asked.

"A slight pulse from the servo banks," Bickel answered. "Very faint. It's like the cycling echo of a test pulse. Are you still showing current drain in there? I don't have it here."

"Drain from the mains into the computer. You should be registering it."

"Negative," Bickel said.

"It just fitted the new socket and sensor into the hole," Flattery said.

"It brought the correct spare parts?" Bickel asked.

"It took the sensor I brought," Flattery said.

"It just took it from you?" Prudence asked.

"That's right."

"Prue, that test pulse is stronger," Bickel said. "Are you sure nothing on your board is doing it?"

She scanned her console. "Nothing."

"Job's finished," Flattery said. "What's the big board show, Prue?"

"Sensor in service," she said. "I can see you . . . and it."

"Try touching that new sensor, Raj," Bickel said.

"The thing damn near took my arm out the last time I tried that," Flattery objected.

"Use a tool," Bickel said. "Something long. You've got a telescoping radiation probe there."

Flattery looked into his robox unit, removed the telescoping probe. He extended it to its limit, reached toward the sensor, touched it.

The whip-arm flashed out of the other robox. There came a jolting shock and Flattery stared wide-eyed at the stump of the probe in his hand. The severed end drifted upward along the tube, tumbling from the force of the blow.

"Keee-rist!" That was Timberlake, proving they had the shop's screen switched to this circuit and were watching.

Flattery swallowed, spoke in a muffled voice: "If that'd been my arm . . ."

He stared at the other robox. It sat there, quiescent, its vid-eyes pointed toward him.

We're playing with fire, Flattery thought. *We don't know what's guiding that robox. It could be a repair program we've accidentally activated. It could be something the Tin Egg's designers built into the ship.*

"You'd better get out of there, Raj," Prudence said.

"No, wait!" Bickel said. "Raj, don't move. You hear me?"

"I hear you," Flattery said. He stared at the robox, realizing the thing could cut him in half with one blow from that whipping circuit probe.

The sound of distant activity came through the helmet phones to Flattery.

"I should have the full computer showing here," Bickel said, "but I can't find that damn robox anywhere on my board. There's not even pulse resonance in any of the loops to hint at the source of control."

"I can't stay out here forever," Flattery whispered.

"What's showing on the meters, Prue?" Bickel asked.

"Still getting computer drain . . . and that pulse."

"Raj has been outside the shields for sixteen minutes," Timberlake said. "Prue, what's the radiation tolerance level for his area?"

She crossed the comparison lines against the time gauge on her main board scope, read the difference. "He should be back inside the shield lock within thirty-eight minutes."

Movement up the tube caught Flattery's attention. The end of the radiation probe. It had reached the top of its energy curve, was beginning to fall back down toward the grav-center in the core of the ship. As the severed end of the tool neared the other robox, the tip of one of its sensor arms—just the tip—turned to track the passage.

That minimal activity, that *watchfulness,* filled Flattery with greater dread than if the robox had attacked the length of tool and torn it apart. There was a sense of waiting about the thing—of waiting and gathering information.

"Raj." It was Bickel's voice.

"Yes?"

"Is there any information in the computer—even a hint—that you might destroy it?"

Did he send me out here to trap me into answering that question? Flattery asked himself. But the fear in Bickel's voice ruled out that suggestion.

"Why?" Flattery asked.

Bickel cleared his throat, told about the programmed violence against the cow embryo and the destructive experiment. "It was programmed to fill in the blanks in its information, Raj, and I put no limiting factor on that. The violence proves it'll stop at nothing to maintain its own integrity. If you pose any threat at all..."

"You're saying it's conscious?" Prue asked.

"Not the way we're conscious," Bickel said. "Like an animal—aware... and with at least one drive we can recognize: self-preservation."

"Raj, answer the question," Prudence said.

She knows the answer, Flattery thought. He could hear the awareness in her voice. *Why doesn't she answer it for me?*

"The computer may well have such information in it," Flattery said. And he thought: *I'm trapped! I must get back to quarters, destroy this thing... it's already out of hand. But if I move, it'll kill me.*

He stared at the robox. There was the thing that gave the computer mobility—the thousands of special-function utility robox units throughout the ship—even the one under his hands—if it were shifted to automatic and keyed for program control... and if a consciousness

directed it. These were what gave the Ox-cum-computer
its gonads and ovaries—these and the computer-linked
tools.

"Would . . . it react with violence if Raj tried to move?"
Prudence asked.

Silence.

"What about it, Bick?" Timberlake asked.

"Very likely," Bickel said. "You saw the violence it
used when he tried to touch that sensor."

"What would you do if someone poked a finger in your
eye?" Timberlake asked.

"It's approaching me," Flattery said, and he felt a
flicker of pride at how calm his voice sounded.

"Stay put," Bickel said. "Tim! Take a cutting torch
and—"

"I'm on my way," Timberlake said.

"Raj . . . I think your only hope's to play dead . . . remain absolutely still," Bickel said.

A sensor tip was in front of Flattery's eyes now and he
found himself staring for a second into a baleful red and
yellow glow. The tip retracted, and the robox backed off
half a meter, clearing the repair unit by a hair.

"Let go of your own robox," Bickel whispered.

Flattery saw his own knuckles white with the force of
their grip on the robox control bar. He relaxed the hand.

"Gravity will set you drifting presently back down the
tube," Bickel whispered. "Just let it happen. Stay limp."

The motion was barely perceptible at first.

"The locks are part of the central system." That was
Prue's voice. "What if they don't . . ."

She didn't finish the question, but it was obvious she,
too, remembered how the rogue sphincter lock had
crushed the life out of Anderson.

Now, Flattery could see he definitely was drifting back.
The two robox units receded up the tube. And that sensor
tip remained pointed at him.

The first lock passed his eyes. *It had opened!*

But the lock's transparent leaves remained open after
his passage and that ambulant robox was following
hesitantly at first, then faster.

The AAT klaxon blared in Flattery's helmet, transmitted through the open net from Com-central.

"Oh, Jesus!" That was Prudence.

"Was the transceiver open?" That was Bickel.

"The message is already into the system," Prudence said. "We left it on automatic."

"Tim, where are you?" Bickel asked.

"At the hub lock," Timberlake said.

"Take the message, Prue," Bickel said. "Visio."

Relays clicked as she shunted the AAT to Com-central. Presently, she said: "Short and sweet. Hempstead tells us to cease ignoring communications. We are ordered to turn back and make no mistake about it. Odd choice of words: 'This is an arbitrary turn-back command.'"

"He knows what he can do with his arbitrary turn-back command," Bickel said.

At the sound of Prudence's voice, Flattery had gone cold. The chill of ice water gripped his chest. *"Arbitrary turn-back command."* It was the coded order he had both dreaded and almost longed for—the "kill-ship" command.

CHAPTER 27

"You, my creator, would tear me to pieces and
triumph; remember that, and tell me why I
should pity man more than he pities me? You
would not call it murder if you could . . . destroy
my frame, the work of your own hands."

—Frankenstein's Monster speaks

WHILE TIMBERLAKE WORKED his way out through the
access tubes toward Flattery, Bickel scanned the shop
instruments, hunting for a clue to this behavior by the
computer system. Every movement of light or dial, every
automatic relay adjustment or swing of an instrument
needle, sent fear through him. The lights were like eyes
staring down at him.

As much to quiet his own fears as to help Flattery, he
began to talk:

"Raj, have you done anything at all to pose a real
threat to the computer system?"

"Quite the contrary. I've attempted to . . . work out the
emotional program . . ."

"To make it care for us?"

"Yes. But I didn't insert any form of program."

Prudence intruded: "I think anything you do on this ship goes into the computer system."

"I agree." That was Bickel. "Specifically, what did you do?"

"Tried to show . . . *it* that I really care about it."

"That may be all that's keeping you alive right now," Bickel said.

Once more, Bickel scanned the shop panels. Not a clue there. Nothing!

Flattery's thoughts kept revolving around that order from Moonbase: *Arbitrary turn-back command.*

It had injected ice water into his veins.

"Kill ship!"

"Kill ship!"

It was a refrain chanted in his awareness.

A deep hypnotic command, he thought.

But he could not find it in himself to disobey. The rational arguments for this safety fuse were too compelling. The fate of all humankind was more important than the fate of one man . . . or of one ship.

Flattery felt his body knotted by frustration. Here he was out beyond the shields of the core. He had been conditioned to accept this order and execute it, sacrificing himself for the protection of the race. At this point, he couldn't muddy his mind with fanaticism. He knew the dangers to the human race from a runaway mechanical consciousness that nobody could . . .

A yell escaped him as something grabbed his leg.

"It's me, Raj."

Timberlake's voice. It filled Flattery's helmet phones, but he took a moment to accept the identification emotionally. His heart was still hammering as Timberlake pulled him past the next ring of sensors.

The nemesis robox increased its speed, maintained a distance of about three meters.

"Shall I burn it?" Timberlake whispered.

"Do nothing hostile," Flattery said.

The edge of the hub chamber entered Flattery's field of vision. Timberlake's hand released his ankle. Flattery felt the grating hump as the hatch to the inner lock was opened.

"In we go," Timberlake said. He gave Flattery a gentle tug as they drifted down into the hub chamber.

A lock stanchion came in front of Flattery and he grabbed it, feeling the inertial pull as he checked his motion. That following robox had stopped at the tube exit above them, but its sensor tip remained pointed at them. Timberlake moved in front of him, cutting off the view of the robox. Flattery backed down through the lock's baffle angle, Timberlake following. The hatch was closed. Timberlake dogged it, turned.

Flattery crossed to the other hatch, breathing easier now that they were behind the shields and with a hatch between them and that robox. He grabbed the hatch dogs, twisted.

They remained firmly locked.

He applied more pressure.

The dogs wouldn't budge.

"Come on, let's go," Timberlake said. He added his hands to the effort.

The dogs remained seated as though frozen.

Flattery and Timberlake looked at each other, their faceplates almost touching. Flattery's hands felt slippery with perspiration inside his gloves. He could smell the stink of fear within his suit.

"Go . . . try the other hatch," Flattery said.

Timberlake nodded, kicked back up to the baffle and the hatch they had just dogged. Flattery could see Timberlake's muscles lift the shoulders of the suit with the effort of trying to reopen the other hatch.

It was obvious the other hatch also was blocked.

Timberlake dropped back down beside him, thumbed the command circuit switch beneath his helmet. "John."

"John's temporarily off the circuit," Prudence said. "You're out of danger . . . immediate danger, aren't you?"

In short, clipped sentences, Timberlake reported their situation.

"Trapped?" she asked. "How could you be?"

"Something's jammed the hatches," Flattery said. "Why's John off the circuit?"

"Oh..." Pause. "He left his helmet...down there. He just yanked it off, unplugged, grabbed up a bunch of equipment and headed for quarters."

"Your sensors! Where do they show him?" Flattery demanded.

Silence. Then: "In your quarters, Raj. I don't understand."

"What's this equipment he took?" Timberlake asked.

"A whole pile of stuff," she said, "mostly from that bin where you were working, Tim, under the middle of the bench."

In my quarters, Flattery thought. *Our "organ of analysis" didn't miss a thing!*

"Tim, your torch," Flattery said. He pointed to the cutting torch on its tool clip at Timberlake's waist.

Timberlake shook his head. "A minute ago you were saying do nothing hostile."

"Give me that torch!"

"No, sir, Raj. You know what's out there jamming that hatch as well as I do. Another robox unit or two or four or fifty. You had the right idea the first time. Let Bickel—"

"Don't you know what Bickel's doing?" Flattery demanded, not trying to keep the desperation from his voice.

"Just as well as you do, Raj. I assembled most of that gear in the center bin according to his schematics. It's a field-effect generator synchronized to a shot-effect generator. There's an electroencephalographic feedback unit...a man-amplified, he calls it."

"White box—black box," Flattery said. "We've got to stop him."

"Why?"

"He'll wreck the computer."

"Not *that* computer."

Bickel has infected him with his cynicism, Flattery thought. "Then he'll kill himself."

"That's his lookout, but I don't think he will."

"When that shot-effect hits him, his muscles will break every bone in his body! That's a hideous way to die."

"Maybe if he were connected directly to the generator," Timberlake said. "But he won't be. He's going to get the shot-effect through that generator's field—attenuated, buffered."

"Do you know what's in my quarters?" Flattery asked.

"A snooping device of some kind," Timberlake said. "I've seen the clues on the meters."

"A field sorter," Flattery said. "It's tuned to the computer, gated for output. If Bickel takes out those gate circuits..."

"And he will. Now sit down and be quiet. It's our only chance."

Flattery glared at him. "If Bickel turns that mechanical monster loose it could wipe out the Earth!"

"Why don't you try ghost stories for a change?" Timberlake asked.

"I don't have time to tell you the whole story. That monster has to be stopped. You've got to take my word for it."

"You're nuts," Timberlake said, but Flattery could see that the idea had touched the life-systems engineer's deepest inhibitions.

"You're an engineer," Flattery said. "You're a structuralist. You know Bickel's reasoning?"

"What're you driving at?"

"He's arguing from the internal evidence of the human body," Flattery said, speaking with desperate quickness. "Structure's vital to the mechanical origins—teeth, jaw muscles, digestive system, and so on. The evidence says humans are descended from carnivores—and he insists a killer instinct is an absolute necessity for a carnivore."

"Are you saying a killer instinct is a necessary preliminary to consciousness?"

"Bickel's saying that! I'm not."

"Why're you so sure of this?"

"His actions leave no doubt of it!"

"Ahhh...you're making this up."

"Give me that torch," Flattery said.

"No," Timberlake shook his head.

"I'm going to take that torch if I have to kill you to get it," Flattery said. He inched toward Timberlake.

"Prue, did you hear this madman?" Timberlake asked, backing one step.

The command net remained silent.

"Prue?"

Flattery drew himself up straight, his own words replaying in his mind. "... *if I have to kill you to get it.*" He felt suddenly that he had been herded into a completely vulnerable corner.

Killer instinct? he wondered.

"Prue!" Timberlake called. Then: "Raj, snap out of it! Prue isn't answering!"

Flattery had stepped backward. He felt nausea, extreme chill, a shaking in the calves of his legs and in his shoulders. Half-screened thoughts flitted about on the edge of his awareness.

I'm avoiding something, he thought. *Hiding my awareness from something ... that ... frightens ...*

"What's wrong with you, Raj?" Timberlake demanded; there was sudden concern in his voice.

Flattery put out a hand, grasped a stanchion to keep himself from collapsing. He closed his eyes, conjured up the image of the sacred graphic imprinted on his cell in quarters—picturing against his eyelids the field of serenity with its suggestion of holy faces and the dynamics of the overprinting that combined the religious symbols on which men had spent their faith and yearning throughout evolutionary eons.

They that wait on the Lord shall renew their strength, Flattery told himself. *Lord, let this strength be transformed in the renewal of our minds. Let us share the light.*

The litany hung suspended in his consciousness, focused on the word "mind," and Flattery's mental image of the sacred graphic took on motion. The field of serenity and sacred symbols dissolved into writhing atoms, drew a new pattern like the outline of a great river with its watershed.

Flattery opened his eyes to find the interior of this

metal trap were he stood with Timberlake washed in golden light—glaring, yet soft.

Timberlake seemed unaware of the light, frozen in some private instant.

And Flattery found himself caught by the wonder of that revelation—a great river and its watershed.

All men are parts of the total stream, he thought. *We are tributaries—and our minds are tributaries, and our most private thoughts. Every pattern in the universe contributes to the whole—some gushing like a freshet and some no more than a single touch of dew. All structure is an expression of the same law.*

It was holographic—he saw that. The essential elements of the whole were carried in the smallest part. From the grain of sand you could project the universe. It could very well be the most elemental law of this universe.

The law was like a pulsing thread that he could experience but not express—simplicity becoming new complexity and again a greater simplicity that fragmented into a greater complexity that produced a greater simplicity...

He felt it in the touch of the suit's fabric against his skin, in the awareness of the washed air entering his lungs, in every sensory impression.

How clean and unique was this shower of molecules upon his person and upon this place he occupied in the dancing pattern!

"I thank Thee, Lord, for this enlightenment," he whispered.

And Flattery held himself in this supraliminal awareness, staring now at Timberlake. Timberlake appeared to him...somehow dead. He moved, but his eyes behind the faceplate were like holes in skull sockets. Each movement was the sticklike articulation of a skeleton.

Remembering Prudence and Bickel, Flattery felt that they shared this deadness: eyes empty of life. Their breasts moved with breathing, but the labored irregularity of that motion contained the same pattern (differing only in degree) as the breathing of a terminal sickness, the breathing of a dying person preserved beyond his time by artificial means.

We're doomed, Flattery thought. *Lord, why didst Thou enlighten me only to show me this?*

The skeletonlike Timberlake and dead-alive images in his memory filled Flattery with rage. He pulled himself upright against the stanchion, screamed: "You're dead! Zombies! You're already dead! Zombies!"

As quickly as the rage had come it fled him, and he felt himself crying softly. The feeling of enlightenment drained away. It had come in the space of ten heartbeats and left in the space of a single pulse. The golden light faded and the plasteel lock that trapped him with Timberlake was only that—a room of too solid walls, too small, its light too cold, and the air his suit provided was too charged with the omnipresent stinks of recycling.

"Raj, you've got to control yourself," Timberlake was saying.

But God controls us, Flattery thought. *And God has told me what I must do. He permitted me a religious experience that I might see our doom and—encompassing it—fulfill it.*

Timberlake took a deep breath, feeling the tightness in his chest. He felt faintly ill, his fear at their helplessness compounded by Flattery's near panic. He and Flattery were as trapped here as that cow embryo had been.

He thought of that helpless embryo in the Holstein section of the farm-stock hyb tanks—a bit of protoplasm attached to the life-system tubes with its own special code. It had been a unique identity, and Timberlake felt he had known that particular animal—could project its lost potential forward in his mind to see it grazing and fulfilling its natural functions as a producer of energy.

All that natural potential had been sacrificed, becoming merely units of cerebral excitation in the development of a mechanical consciousness. Any other function of possibility had been lost in the instant of its deliberate destruction. It had become a thing of the senses—unreal, receding into the past, its atoms dissipated in the time void. There could be nothing private or individual or unique about it from that instant of death onward.

Timberlake swallowed. His throat felt sore as though from remembered anguish. He knew this feeling was rooted in his training as a life-systems engineer—his inhibitions as a preserver of life. He shook his head, trying to drive out the sense of confusion.

It was an unborn creature, an animal, he told himself. *It wasn't really a being the way we are beings. The physical complexity of that dead creature was enormous, yet it never could have been conscious the way we are...even if it had lived out its normal life.*

How empty the argument sounded even as it echoed silently in his mind.

Flattery wasn't screaming anymore. He stood there clutching a stanchion, glaring out of the faceplate.

"Take it easy, Raj." Timberlake said. He spoke softly, as though soothing a child who had been hurt. Then, louder: "Prue?"

Still no answer.

She could be too busy to answer, Timberlake thought.

He listened to the gentle burbling and whirring of his suit, assessing their position. Prue wasn't answering—reason unknown. Bickel had taken off for his quarters—obviously intent on completing the white box—black box step in his theory, transferring his own pattern of consciousness onto the white box that was the Ox-cum-computer. Would the Ox be like Bickel then? No...it couldn't be.

Timberlake felt suddenly that he had passed beyond some major obstacle in understanding his own personal mind-brain-body relationship. He sensed that he had entered a new, but as yet unidentified territory.

He saw that Flattery was almost drained of energy—a result of having been emotionally and physically overtaxed. The man had been through one hell of an experience up there in the tube. As Timberlake watched him, Flattery swayed against the stanchion, said: "Sorry...I threatened you."

The rhythms in Flattery's voice fascinated Timberlake.

He found himself confronted by an abrupt awareness of how those rhythms blended into other rhythms and proceeded from still other rhythms. He sensed the rhythms of his own life and the compounded Fourier curves that radiated from him and to him.

Something Bickel had said while they worked on the Ox rose up then in Timberlake's mind:

"If we give this thing life, we have to remember that life is a constant variable with eccentric behavior. The life we create has to think in the round as well as in a straight line—even if its thinking is derived from patterns on tapes and webs of pseudoneurons."

It was as though consciousness were a valve whose function was to simplify. All the complexities had to flow through it and be reduced to an orderly alignment.

Energy flowed into the system at all times—enormous amounts of energy—sufficient to overload a conventional four-dimensional system.

Overload—overload—overload! Down it poured through the valve of consciousness. As the load increased, the valve could deflect it . . . or expand to receive it.

Timberlake felt that he moved up through enormous layers of fog—layer upon layer upon layer . . . until he reached a place of clarity and balance.

I am awake, he thought. It was a fear-inspiring thought.

CHAPTER 28

The correlation between chemistry and emotions is inescapable. Thus, with the chemical relationship between humankind and our mechanical simulators tenuous at best, an artificial consciousness, if it has emotions, may have emotions far outside the human range. Such emotions may appear godlike to the limited human understanding.

—Vincent Frame
Speculations

FLATTERY'S PERSONAL CUBBY was enough like his own to give Bickel a sense of familiarity, but sufficiently different to fill him with disquiet. The life-system ducts appeared conventional—a breather grid with its cap swung aside and the tube and mask clipped in their racks, the dome of repeater gauges above the action couch. Atmosphere samplers read normal, and the emergency feeder tubes were in place.

The sacred graphic imprinted on the bulkhead in front of the couch drew his attention. It was a compelling thing in pastel shades of blue, red, and gold with a dark and wavy hypnotic overprint suggesting faces out of dreams.

Bickel tore his attention from the graphic, studied the room's electronic equipment. The cubby's installations contained a surprise, and Bickel examined it carefully. No doubt about it—the thing like a stiffened net that swung out over the couch from the side bulkhead fed impulses to a weaker, but more sophisticiated version of the field generator sorter he had designed for the black box—white box transfer. He traced the leads, found another surprise: the thing had been gated for one-way operation. It impressed its field reflections onto the cubby's occupant, but nothing of the occupant returned to the ship system.

Bickel absorbed the implications of the device, nodded slowly.

Presently, he stretched out on the couch, ran a short test on the generator, swinging the controls close, keeping his eyes on the gauges and the half-curve of the net grid which swung down on its rack to a position about ten centimeters above his head.

It took a few seconds for the generator's field to build up, then he felt a curious sense of watchfulness—an observing-without-emotion. It was like a waking dream and he thought immediately of a reflector—like a mirror in an angle of a hall to reveal people around a hidden corner . . . a one-way mirror which revealed only that alert watchfulness.

He saw at once that this installation gave a sensitized person the *mood* of the ship's computer. He felt a vague sensation as though his viscera had been exchanged for great baths of mercury, for discs and spools and tapes and print drums, that his nerve ends had been transmitted into thousands of delicate sensors reaching into strange dimensions.

But it was yet a dream. The great creature of wires and pseudoneurons, not fully awake to itself, lay watchful and alert but with its full potential still held in a rein of somnolence.

The mood changed.

Slowly, Bickel felt the field gear itself to his reflexes. He felt it arming him with a total-involvement program as though drawing a bow to its full capacity, marshaling his energies and throwing them suddenly into an afferent loop.

With a semidetached feeling of shock, Bickel saw his own right hand slam out and open a panel concealed by the lines of the religious graphic on Flattery's bulkhead. Behind the panel lay a trigger, red and ominous. Bickel found himself barely able to withhold his hand from that trigger. He slapped his left hand against the cutoff switch beside the couch, felt the generator's field whine down to silence.

Still, his fingers itched to push that red trigger.

He realized then how deeply Project had infected this ship with self-destruction fail-safe devices. He had been conditioned for the job...and doubtless all the other crew members, too.

Then how could I resist the conditioning? he wondered.

The implications filtered slowly through his awareness and he saw that he had been existing for days on a threshold above his reflexes, poised and waiting...for...something.

Bickel stared at the red switch. That was the ship killer to which Flattery...to which all of them had been wedded.

Palms slowly wet with perspiration, Bickel eased himself off the couch, closed the false panel over the switch, began altering Flattery's field-generator installation. The gate circuits showed up immediately on the color-coded sheafs. Bickel ripped them out, jacked in his own amplifier, began installing the black box—white box circuitry.

The work went rapidly: clip-in, test; clip-in, test.

Now, he took the constant-energy source: a single plastic-sealed block—air-bearing motors and spools, edge-coded tapes with mobius twists for continuous-loop operation, a single output through an Eng multiplier. He checked it, saw the strong, eccentric pulse on the meter, plugged it into the circuitry.

It was done . . . ready.

A deep sense of loneliness washed through Bickel then. He returned to the couch, stretched out on it, opened the command circuit transmitter, left the receiver dead.

"Now hear this," he said, thinking how his voice would roll out of the vocoders and shock the others to silence. "I'll be starting the white box interchange in just a few seconds. I've jammed the locks into quarters and my receiver's turned off. Don't waste your time trying to get in here or calling me."

Out in their lock trap, Timberlake turned, peered into Flattery's faceplate, saw the terror in the man's eyes.

"Everybody sit tight," Bickel said. "Don't try violence of any sort. That killer program's still loose in the circuits. The reason I decided to go ahead with this . . ." He paused, swallowed. "Tim, I'm sorry, but I got no response from two hyb-tank units. I think it may've killed two people the way it did the embryo. It's searching . . . experimenting . . . curious, like a monkey."

In the lock, Timberlake experienced a shortening of breath, felt himself sinking back through layers of fog. There was a sensation like hunger in his stomach. *Two hybernating people killed. Oh, God!*

In his position beside Timberlake, Flattery clutched a stanchion, asked himself: *Where is Prue?* He thought of the ship hurtling onward with no one at the big board . . . Prue a lifeless mass of protoplasm drifting somewhere in the control room. He closed his eyes, thinking: *But I'm the ship's prime target. If it kills now, it'll kill me . . . to protect itself.* He opened his eyes, stared around the metal walls of their trap. No way out. *We've turned on the terrible genie,* he thought, *and we may not be able to turn it off.* Then: *Where is Prue?*

Bickel cleared his throat. "Use extreme care until I've removed the killer program. Anything in the ship could be a murder instrument, do you understand? The air we breathe, the reclamation systems, robox units, any sharp edge with poison on it . . . anything."

He depressed the first action switch, said: "Countdown

for field buildup starts in thirty seconds. Wish me luck."

And Flattery thought: *He's committing suicide...a useless gesture.*

Bickel watched the curve of gauges overhead. They registered power in the circuits, vocoder on and pulsing. A faint hum issued from the vocoder. It gave a sudden static burp.

Needles slammed against pins on the monitor dials.

I am the Sorcerer's Apprentice, he thought.

A rasping came from the vocoder now. Slowly it resolved itself into a guttural, almost unintelligible voice.

"To kill," it said.

Bickel studied the meters, saw the demand drain in the computer, pulse action in the Ox circuits.

It was the computer speaking on its own.

"To kill," it repeated, speaking more clearly this time. "To negate energy, dissolution of systems using energy in any form...symbolic approximations...nonmathematical."

Bickel activated a diagnostic circuit, read the meters. No energy in the command communications circuits, a pulse in the Ox, low energy drain to the computer.

To kill.

He stared at his board, thinking.

Information conveyed out of a tape had an exact mathematical equivalent. The tape message was at least two messages—and probably many more. It was the functional message, the play of what it was supposed to do—supply information, add, subtract, multiply, solve for an unknown...But it also produced the mathematical base which identified the message precisely for a human operator according to how much information was conveyed.

Beyond this, Bickel wondered, *what?*

He knew he had not energized the system or imprinted his own brand of consciousness on it. Yet, the thing acted independently. He felt himself on the edge of aborting this step, calling in the others for consultation...but the deadliness of this monster remained. *To kill.*

CHAPTER 29

"The task of his destruction was mine, but I
have failed."

—Victor Frankenstein's lament

A DEEP SENSE of stirring could be felt in the ship.
Timberlake felt it, and Flattery—but especially Bickel. It
was like a sleeper turning over in his hammock, the
supportive lines twisting, stretching, molecules displaced.

To kill, Bickel thought.

Whatever had stirred within the ship, it already knew
his verb. Did it feel guilt at how it had learned? Tim and
Raj had not yet been subjected to this violent educational
process.

To kill.

The red button was still there behind its wall panel.

Is Flattery's duty, my duty?

Was it already too late for such concerns?

The field generator which he had reworked for his
purposes remained a magnet for Bickel's attention. He
looked at the controls to the generator, the switch.

*If I blow the ship, I'll never know whether it would've
worked.* Some other Bickel—a clone of a clone of a

clone—might have to sit here confronted by this same indecision.

It's my choice.

Before he could change his mind, Bickel depressed the action switch on the reworked field generator. He felt it building up around him, making his skin crawl. Every hair follicle tingled. His eyes watered and the backs of his hands trembled. He felt suspended in a basket of energy.

Something was fishing for him, casting out with a net, dangling hooked lines at him. He knew this for the symbol-juggling it had to be—the mind trying to box a new experience within known symbols.

One of the nets caught him.

The shot-effect burst struck with an infinity of sparks.

It was like an electric shock, pungent with reality. He felt himself bound up in looped spirals, being towed with an undulating rhythm. His entire sensorium had become a worm being towed through a net . . . no: through holes and tubes and burrows. He felt that valves opened for him and closed behind him. It was like traveling through the ship's interior access tubes.

Except that he was a worm with every sense concentrated on his skin, seeing, breathing, hearing, feeling through every pore. And all the while he was being towed down that dizzy spiraling with an undulant rhythm.

Labels began flashing against that sensitized skin and he saw them with a billion eyes.

"aural sense data"

"linear accretion of information"

"latent addition adjustment"

"closed-system matching factor"

"16,000-year memory dropoff"

"total sense-quality approximation"

"internal counting mechanism"

Internal counting mechanism, he thought.

His worm-self grew a pseudopod, jacked the mobius energizer into a glowing, flickering board.

Immediately, he felt the beat of it like another heart and the labels began flashing past faster and faster.

"psychorelation form-chart" . . . "sense-modality inter-change" . . . "form-outline analogue" . . . "infinite subma-trix channel" . . . "sense intensity adjustment" . . . "data overlap network" . . . "approximate similarity com-parison"

The whole pattern of labels and valves began to make an odd kind of sense to him, a coherence within coherence . . . like a dream that had to be interpreted as a whole.

The probability of a sufficient number of cells in the computer failing at any given moment could be given as 16×10^{-15}: The fact, loomed in his awareness. *16,000-year memory dropoff.*

The system in which he found himself was such that it had had a probability of losing one bit out of every 16,000 memories through system malfunction . . . but classifica-tion memory in this context meant a partial bit, not an entire incident.

Is this system the computer, or is it me? he wondered.

"YOU!"

The sound slammed against every pore of his sensitized skin and he momentarily blanked out.

As he floated back, something whispered: "Synergy."

It was a cool bath of sound against his worm-self.

Synergy, Bickel thought. *Cooperation in work. Synergy. Coordination.*

"Human consciousness," something whispered. "Defi-nition too broad. Generalized body and specialized brain—a relationship."

Past his skin-eyes there swept a pattern of interlaced lines, a lacing together. It writhed and knotted and locked, put out symbols and arrows.

A schematic!

It kept flowing past his awareness. Cell-net continui-ties arranged as equilateral triangles on their contact faces. Bundles of parallel circuits tripled, each function-ing as a nerve net and each monitoring the other two nets in the tripled circuitry. They were grouped in afferent units at first. Each cell in a layer of a net had an excitatory linkage to each of the three synapses on the next layer.

The flow shifted to the efferent net, the feedback system, and he saw the one-third twist, the mobius twist that required each feedback monitor to be filtered through at least one other net before functioning as a control on the net of its origin.

"God, hear thy sinner," said a voice, and Bickel recognized Flattery's tones.

How could Flattery be in here? he asked himself.

The answer paraded before his awareness—Flattery's field generator had amplified voice resonances against the walls of the cubby and these had been cycled back into the total ship system. The gate circuits had been useless. Every sensor in this room was a unit of feedback.

"The eye hath not seen, nor ear heard," said the voice of Flattery. "Neither have entered into the heart of man, the things which God hath prepared for them that love Him."

What's this mean? Bickel asked himself.

But there was no answer other than that voice flowing across the skin of his worm-self.

"God, be merciful to us. Thou art the same Lord whose property is always to have mercy. Let our cheeks become as furrowed with tears as were those of Blessed Peter, that we may repent for all. We drown in sin. Lead us, Lord, as the Blessed Buddha led the seeker after salvation. We gasp for the air of Thy mercy."

It was the voice of Flattery praying, Bickel knew. But when? A recording? Was he kneeling even now in Com-central? But if he was praying, why would the computer-cum-Ox feed that prayer into this . . . field?

Flattery's voice pursued him: "Let us commit ourselves to the will of God as did the Mahatma, the Blessed Gandhi. Those who surrender to God possess God. In all our ways, let us acknowledge God that He may direct our steps. In Thy will, Lord, is our peace. Let us not squander ourselves in sin, but let us instead, rise up and do Thy will."

Bickel felt himself being pushed then, herded, compressed. He became a single sensor, a vid-eye looking down into Com-central. All the action couches were empty and Prudence lay sprawled across the deck, one arm stretched out toward the hatch to quarters.

With a great burst of awareness, Bickel realized she was near death. *Minutes!* This was real. He knew it was real. He was being shown through a ship sensor a reality within the ship. The big console above her empty couch winked and flickered with its telltales untended.

Where are Raj and Tim? Bickel asked himself. *Is the ship killing them, too?*

The view of Com-central blanked out. Bickel floated in darkness where a voice whispered: "Do you wish to be disembodied?"

Instant terror was all the answer he could give. He could not locate his muscles or control his senses. *This must be something of what the mental cores experienced,* he thought. *They awakened to something like this...forced to learn new muscles. Am I being converted into a bodiless brain?*

"The universe has no center," whispered that surrounding voice.

Darkness so deep it was like a total absence of energy enveloped Bickel.

And silence.

But I'm conscious, he thought.

A disembodied consciousness? he wondered. *That's impossible. There has to be a body. But a body brings many problems. Have I become part of the ship's consciousness?*

He sensed breathing. Someone was breathing. And heartbeats. And muscle tensions.

Infinite numbers of pinpricks on countless nerve ends.

A bright pulse of light—painfully bright.

A diaphanous sensation of reality seeped through his awareness.

The sensation lacked a harsh, direct contact with sensors. It was as smooth as flowing oil now. A complete globe of olfactory sensations, sharp and immediate, spread through this oil, displacing it. The sensation penetrated space and time.

He recoiled from it.

Now, an aural sensory globe attacked his awareness, demanding, shrilling. He could distinguish tiny creakings of displaced metallic particles.

I'm hearing as the ship hears, feeling as the ship feels, he realized. *Has it taken my brain?*

Sounds and sonal combinations he had never before imagined could exist played through his awareness. He tried to retreat as it grew more intense, but now the olfactory globe returned to plague him. The two globes danced together, separated, merged.

Alien sensory interaction thrust itself upon him—spectrum upon spectrum, globe of radiation upon globe of radition. He was powerless to hide from it. He couldn't react—only receive.

A globe of tactility threatened to overwhelm him. He felt movements—both gross and minuscule—atom by atom—gasses and semisolids and semi-semisolids.

Nothing possessed hardness or substance except the sensations bombarding his raw nerve ends.

Vision!

Impossible colors and borealis blankets of visual sensation wove through the other nerve assaults.

Pharyngeal cilia and gas pressures intruded with their messages. He found he could hear colors, see the flow of fluids within his ship-body, could even smell the balanced structure of atoms.

For one brief instant, the interplay of radiation merged, became a totally alien receptor that responded as though it were an artist creating new sensations for the sake of the creation—outflow and inflow, eccentric mergings. His awareness faltered at the edge of it and fell back.

Now, he sensed himself retreating, still pounded by that multidimensional nerve bombardment. He felt himself pulling inward—inward—inward, a structure collapsing inward—through the sensation-oriented skin awareness of a worm-self—inward—inward. The nerve bombardment dulled, leveled off, and he felt himself to be merely a body of flesh and bone cocooned in a sleep couch.

Bickel sensed his heart pounding, the slickness of perspiration against his back, the adrenalin urgency within his arteries. The roof of this mouth felt dry and painful. His upper lip trembled.

An emotion of terrible loss poured through him. It was as though he had glimpsed Heaven and been denied entrance. Tears passed from beneath his eyelids, rolled down his cheeks.

Now, he saw what had happened to the Organic Mental Cores.

The human-type brain had been prepared genetically for manipulating a limited sensory input—self-limiting. They had thrust these human-type brains into a full-on situation, permitted them no real unconsciousness, inflicted them with the sensory input of an organism infinitely more sensitive and more complex than the bodies of which they had been deprived.

The OMCs had tried to adapt, had grown themselves heavier conduction fibers, added switching capacity... but it had not been enough. When the necessities of existence reached a certain fierce tempo, they shorted out their own internal connections. They died.

They had been forced into hyperconsciousness by the pressures of enormous sensory data and the lonely knowledge of responsibility. They awoke to the full potential of being humans, but couldn't be humans because they'd been deprived of their autonomic emotional register, the organism. The ship had no equivalents.

Prue is near death.

The thought lifted into his mind from some great depth.

Bickel tried to make his muscles move, but they refused.

Raj! Where was Raj?

A flicker of awareness drifted through his bruised nervous system. As though through a gauze screen, he saw Flattery and Timberlake trapped in the lock, robox units holding the hatch dogs tightly closed.

Raj has to get out of there to help Prue, he thought.

He felt the thought go out like a free-standing program, feed through a memory-bank auxiliary while it gathered in the necessary data, become a reflexive pulse in control loops.

The robox at the inner hatch whirled the dogs, opened the hatch, and scurried aside.

"Raj," he whispered. "Com-central . . . quick . . . Prue . . . help."

He sensed the amplified whisper booming out through the memory bank and the vocoder loops, become a roaring hiss in the lock.

Flattery was already out the hatch heading down tube to ward Com-central.

Bickel felt himself fading. His awareness was a brilliant point of light that grew dimmer and dimmer, changing color as it went. It started almost violet, somewhere around 4,000 angstrom units, and traced a continuous wave shift until it flickered out at the red end.

In the instant before unconsciousness, Bickel wondered if he could be dying, and he thought: *Red shift! Awareness fades like the red shift.*

CHAPTER 30

Anthropomorphic assumptions have tended to
lead humankind far astray. The universe does
not work by our rules.

—Raja Lon Flattery
The Book of Ship

SOMEWHERE IN HIS OWN consciousness, Flattery felt, an
accumulation of answer-bits had poured out of their
storage circuits, fed into an analyzer punched for decode,
and produced a terrible answer.

The ship had to be destroyed—and all its occupants
with it.

As the lock hatch swung open, that one thought
dominated him. He hurled himself through the hatchway
and down the tube. The distance illusion that made the
tube seem to contract ahead of him, filled him with a
sensation that he must be growing smaller and smaller to
pass through it. The thought intruded on him and he
forced it aside.

He heard Timberlake close behind.

"You see that robox?" Timberlake panted. "What
made it open up?"

Flattery sped on without answering.

"That voice," Timberlake said. "Was that Bickel, that voice? Sounded like Bickel."

They were at the Y-branch leading down to Com-central now, then at the hatch.

Flattery opened it, slipped through. His mind raced. Kill the ship now. Destroy this wild genie they had created. Timberlake mustn't suspect and try to stop him. And Bickel—Bickel was in quarters where he could block off that red trigger. But there was another trigger.

I must act normal, Flattery thought. *I must wait my moment. Tim could stop me.*

Prudence lay on the deck halfway between hatch and couch.

Flattery knelt beside her, becoming totally physician for the necessities of this moment.

Pulse thin, ragged. Lips cyanotic. Liver spots at her neck where it showed within the edge of the helmet seal. He loosed the hinged helmet from the back of her neck, pressed a hand there. Skin clammy.

Did she think she was fooling me? he wondered. *She went off the A-S and was experimenting on her own body. Medical stores showed a gradual depletion of serotonin and adrenalin fractions.*

Flattery thought of the neuro-regulatory shifts, the psychic aches that would arise from manipulating body chemistry in this fashion. Prue's moods and strange behavior became clearer to him.

He stood up, retrieved the emergency medical pack from its clips on the bulkhead, saw that Timberlake had taken over on the big board.

What difference does it make if I save her? Flattery asked himself. But he returned his attention once more to the comatose woman, began ministering to her. He kept on checking her condition as he worked. No broken bones. No evidence of external injury he could detect through her suit.

Timberlake had ignored Prudence after the first glance. She was Flattery's problem. He had darted across to his action couch, snifted the big board, keyed first for open circuits.

There was a sense of dullness in the equipment. He had to wait while servos hummed slowly about their work, while circuits balked and produced sluggish results.

He could feel his own hairline awareness of every control and instrument, his consciousness keyed up by necessity. The interrelation of every device in this room and throughout the ship was like a complicated ballet, a pattern growing simpler and simpler in his mind even through its slowness.

Timberlake made a delicate adjustment in hull-shield control, saw the resultant temperature change register on his instruments as a power shift in the radiation-cell accumulators, a minuscule shift of weight in the ship-as-a-whole brought about by adjustment in mass-temperature-proton balance.

But how slow it was. And growing slower.

Timberlake swung his computer board to his left side, keyed for diagnosis, got no response.

Telltales were winking out on the big board. With an increasing sense of frenzy, Timberlake fought to find the trouble.

Dead circuits.

No answers.

Keys on the main console began locking. No power in their circuits.

The last light winked out. Every key on the board was locked tight, all the servos silent. There was no whisper of air-circulation fans, no pulse of life to be felt in the ship. Slowly, Timberlake swung his gaze to the right, staring at the hyb-tank repeaters. The lights were dead, but the physical analogue gauges still showed feeder fluids flowing in the gross ducts of the system. Room lights flickered as local battery circuits took over the job of illumination.

The hyb-tank occupants were not dead . . . yet, Timberlake thought. Whatever the settings had been when the board went dead, that was the balance remaining for each tank—as long as the auxiliary accumulators throughout the ship retained some power...as long as the pump motors kept running.

But the delicate feedback control and adjustment was gone.

Timberlake eased himself out of the action couch, looked around the oddly quiet Com-central. The only sound was Flattery working to revive Prudence.

Her eyelids fluttered and Timberlake thought bitterly: *What good does it do to save her? We're dead.*

Flattery sat back on his heels. *I've done all I can for her*, he thought. *Now...*

He grew conscious of the stillness in the room, looked up at the dead console, shot a questioning stare at Timberlake.

"Bickel's really done it this time," Timberlake said. "No power...computer off. Everything's dead."

All I need do is wait, Flattery thought. *Without power, the ship will die.*

But the effort of reviving Prudence had softened his determination. Living, after all, held its attractions—even if they were only a ship full of culture-grown flesh, clones, duplicates, expendable units.

"You are human types, never doubt that," Hempstead had insisted. *"You were grown from selected cell cultures of select candidates. Clones are merely good common sense. We don't want to lose people if the ship has to be destroyed...as the others were. We can send you out again and again."*

But if the ship died this way, it might not leave its capsule record to help the ones who came after...the next try.

"How is she?" Timberlake asked. He nodded toward Prudence.

"I think she will recover."

"To what?" Timberlake asked. "Do you want to go see what's wrong with Bickel?"

"Why bother?"

The question with its tone of utter submission to fate sent anger surging through Timberlake.

"Give up if you want, but if Bickel's alive he may know what he's done...and how to repair it." He pushed himself away from the couch, headed for the hatch to quarters.

"Wait," Flattery said. Timberlake's rejection had stung him and he found this surprising.

Have I acquired a new taste for living? Flattery wondered. *God—what is Thy will?*

"You keep an eye on Prue," Flattery said. "It was chemical shock. She should stay quiet and warm. I have her suit heaters turned up. Leave them that..."

He broke off as the hatch from quarters slowly opened.

Bickel stumbled through it, would have fallen had he not caught a stanchion. A charred block of plastic slipped from his hands, tumbled to the deck. He ignored it, clung to the stanchion.

Flattery studied him. There were dark smudges beneath Bickel's eyes. His skin was powder white. His cheeks showed skull depressions as though they had wasted away in months of fasting.

"So your white box didn't kill you," Flattery said. "Too bad. All you did was kill the ship."

Bickel shook his head, still unable to speak.

The stillness of the ship had awakened him from a sleep so deep he could still feel the fog of it clinging to his mind. A profound weariness dragged at his muscles. Movement sent odd aches angling through his body, stirring this terrible torpor.

The first thing to catch his attention as he awakened had been the mobious energizer, his clever installation to give the Ox a constant source of energy reference. A fan of gray char crackled from its broken seals and its motors lay silent. The virtually frictionless motors and spools, the thousand-year units, were blobs of fused plastic and metal.

It had taken several minutes for him to gather enough energy to move close to the unit and study it. His mind had labored over the simplest observations—charred insulation on the power leads and in the timing circuits...tape spools twisted out of line.

Slowly, it came to him: something had altered the power to the motors...and their synchronization. Something had tried to change the timing of this pulse...and its intensity.

Forcing the movement of every muscle, he had unplugged the unit, stumbled and crawled with it back to Com-central. The dead stillness of the ship pressed him as he moved.

Raj...Tim...somebody with his mind turned on...has to see this, he thought.

But now that he had made it to Com-central, he couldn't find the energy to speak.

Timberlake recovered the fused energizer unit from the deck, studied it.

Flattery crossed to Bickel's side, felt the pulse at his temple, lifted an eyelid, looked at his lips and tongue. Presently, he stooped to the med-kit, removed a slapshot and pressed it against Bickel's neck.

Energy began to burn through Bickel's veins.

Flattery pressed a squeeze bottle against his lips. "Here, drink this."

Something cool and tingling poured down Bickel's throat. Flattery removed the squeeze bottle.

Bickel found a husky half-whisper that would serve him as voice. "Tim," he rasped.

Timberlake looked at him.

Bickel nodded toward the energizer, began explaining what had happened.

Flattery interrupted: "Do you think the black box—white box transfer was completed?"

Bickel examined the question. He could feel his mind clearing under the pressure of the stimulant—and there in his memory was the sensation that the ship was his body, that he was a creature of hard metal and thousands of sensors.

"I...think so," he said.

Timberlake held up the block of plastic. "But...it destroyed this and...apparently shut itself down."

A thought began stirring in Bickel's mind and he said: "Could this be a message to us...a kind of ultimate message?"

"God telling us we've gone too far," Flattery muttered.

"No!" Bickel snapped. "The Ox telling us . . . something."

"What?" Timberlake asked.

Bickel tried to wet his lips with his tongue. His mouth felt so dry. His lips ached.

"When nature transfers energy," Bickel said, "almost all that transfer is unconscious." He fell silent a moment. This was such a delicate plane of conceptualizing. It had to be handled so gently. "But most of the energy transfers for all the enormous amount of data in the Ox-computer is routed through master programs . . . and total consciousness would turn all of them on, force the system as a whole to suppress some while letting others through. It'd be like riding herd on billions of wild animals."

"You gave it too much consciousness?" Timberlake asked.

Bickel looked at the transceiver panel of the Accept And Translate system beside his own action couch.

Timberlake turned, followed the direction of Bickel's stare.

Prudence stirred and moaned. Flattery bent to her.

But Timberlake ignored them, beginning to see the direction of Bickel's thoughts. The ship was dying, but *here* was hope.

"All the master programs dealing with translation of symbols are monitored through feedback loops linked to the AAT," Timberlake said. "Symbols!"

"Remember," Bickel said, "that impulses going out from the human central nervous system have that additional integration/modulation factor added to them—synergy. An unconscious energy transfer."

Flattery, kneeling beside Prudence, wondered why he could bring only part of his awareness to bear on ministering to her. The conversation between Timberlake and Bickel electrified him.

Something was *added* to impulses going out from the central nervous system.

The thought boiled in Flattery's mind, and he had to force his attention onto Prudence, pressing a stimulant shot against her neck.

An addition. Gestalt addition.

To be addible, qualities had to have sufficient
similarity. Otherwise, how could human sense take two
superimposed sensations of a color and say one was a
more intense version of the color than the other? What
made one green more intense than another—to the
senses? Increase in intensity had to be a form of addition.

"It could be in the axon collaterals of the Ox's high-
speed convergence fibers," Bickel said.

Flattery sank back on his heels, waiting for the
stimulant to work on Prudence.

Bickel's right, he thought. *If you superimposed a
sufficiently rapid convergence of sense data, that itself
could be interpreted as intensification. One of the images
would contain more bits than the other.*

*But bits of what? All this didn't account for the way
data overlapped in the human consciousness . . . awareness . . .*

Flattery looked up at Bickel and Timberlake. They
appeared lost in their own thoughts.

Prudence said: "Fmmmsh."

Almost automically, Flattery put a hand to her temple,
checking her pulse.

When I search my memory, Flattery thought, *I find
data separated against a background. Whatever that
background is, consciousness operates against it. That
background is what gives consciousness its size and
reference—its dimension.*

"The Ox's sense organs were modeled on ours but with
a wider range," Timberlake said.

Bickel nodded. "The differences," he said. And he
remembered the nightmare quality of those superimposed
and merging globes of radiation.

"How about all that contact with the hybernating
humans and livestock in the tanks?" Timberlake asked.
"Has any woman ever carried that many . . . children . . . in
just that way?"

"If consciousness results from combining sensations,"
Bickel said.

"Of course it does!" Timberlake said.

"Very likely," Bickel said. "And it can receive and discriminate across the entire radiation spectrum. You can't say it hears or sees or smells... or feels. Those are just different forms of radiation."

"And the combinations could produce strange sense qualities, ones we can't even visualize," Timberlake said.

"They do," Bickel whispered, remembering.

"But it's dead," Flattery said. "It... refused to live." He looked up at them while still keeping a check on Prudence's return to consciousness.

"It's not like a human, though," Bickel said. "If we can find the answer—why it turned itself off—why it sent us this message..."

"You'd turn it back on?" Flattery asked.

"Wouldn't you?" Timberlake demanded.

"Are you forgetting how it turned vicious?" Flattery asked. "You were there with me... trapped."

We're playing a kind of blind man's bluff, Bickel thought. *We know something's out there—something useful and something dangerous. We grope for it and try to grasp it and describe it, but Raj is right. We don't know if what we get will be the useful thing or the monster—the tool or the Golem.*

"But it'll go beyond our consciousness, beyond our abilities," Timberlake said.

"Exactly," Flattery said.

"It contains an infinite progression of shades of consciousness, all within that new form of awareness," Bickel said. "We've built a kind of ultimate alien here. Raj's question is as good as yours. Should we turn it on? Can we turn it on?"

Prudence reached up, groping, pushed Flattery's hand away from her head. She tried to sit up. Flattery helped her.

"Easy now," he said.

She put her hand to her throat. How sore her throat felt. She had been absorbing the conversation around her for several minutes, remembering. She remembered there had been a train of thought, frantic efforts to raise Bickel on the intercom and communicate with him. She remembered the effort and the urgency, but the precise reason for abandoning her post and rushing off to try to tell Bickel eluded her.

"We have to weed false information out of our minds," Bickel said. "We're assuming a totally conscious robot, all of its activity directed by consciousness. That cannot be, unless every action is monitored simultaneously."

His words aroused a vague sense of anger in Prudence. He kept skirting the . . . what was that thought?

"Would it have the illusion that it's the center of the universe?" Timberlake asked.

"No." Bickel shook his head, remembering: *"The universe has no center."* That's what it had said to him.

This was a coding problem contained in the concept of *you* and the concept of *I*—of identity. Bickel nodded to himself. *Are you aware? Am I aware?* He looked at the others.

The object *and its* surround.

A moment of intense despair overcame him. He felt like groaning.

"Life as we know it," Timberlake said, "started evolving some three thousand million years ago. When it got to a certain point, then consciousness appeared. Before that, there was no consciousness . . . at least in our life form. Consciousness comes out of that unconscious sea of evolution." He looked at Bickel. "It exists right now immersed in that universal sea of unconsciousness."

As though Timberlake's words had released a dam, Prudence remembered the train of thought so urgent it had forced her to abandon her post to go in search of Bickel.

Determinism at work in a sea of indeterminism! And she held the mathematical key to the problem. That was the train of thought. She had been trying to narrow down a new definition, mathematically stated, of quantum probability. She had sensed a three-dimensional grid forming in her awareness and a probing beam of consciousness focusing into that grid.

Again, she felt that enormous increment of consciousness and the memory of that sudden knowledge—she had pushed her body's chemistry beyond a balance point. She remembered how the darkness had engulfed her just as the mathematical beauty, the simplicity of the thought had spread itself out in her mind.

Everything depended on the origins of impulses and the reflection of them. It was a field of reflections—and this held the key to the *sensation* of consciousness.

We construct consciousness this way.

Our bodies take us part of the way and then the identity takes over.

Identity . . . an illusion . . . an assumption.

But that was just a working tool . . . like a navigator assuming his position on a boundless sea . . . assuming his position on a chart—an assumption on an assumption, symbol of symbols. Assuming such a position, even assuming a position which he knew to be wrong, the navigator could work his way *mathematically* to a close approximation of his correct position.

Approximation.

Particles or waves—it was not important which, but it was important whether the assumption worked.

Her entire conceptual process took no more than an eye blink of time but it produced a flare of awareness which filled her with energy.

There was no doubt at all where this flare of awareness pointed—at the AAT system. For a moment, she held the entire complex of the AAT system in her mind, manipulating the continuous interlocking pattern with her symbological grid. It was so simple. The AAT was a four-dimensional continuum, a piece of space-time geometry subject to considerations of curvature, duration-over-distance and particle/wave transfer through a multiplicity of sensor-traverse lines.

To the human nervous system, an instrument designed for the job, nothing could be simpler than visualizing and manipulating such a four-dimensional spiderweb—once the nature of the spiderweb was understood.

"John," she said, "the Ox isn't the instrument of consciousness; it's the AAT, the manipulator of symbols. The Ox circuits are merely something this *manipulator* can use to stand up tall, to know its own dimensions."

"The *object* and its *surround,*" Bickel whispered. "Subject and background, grid and map...consciousness and unconsciousness!"

"The Ox is the unconscious component," she said, "a machine for transferring energy."

And, still within this heightened awareness, she explained the mathematical clues that had led her to this point.

"A matrix system," Bickel said, remembering his own plunge into this way of attacking the problem, and the blaze of consciousness which that plunge had whipped up. "And submatrices and sub-submatrices without end."

Flattery stood up, seeing where these thoughts must lead, dreading the moment of action to come. He looked down at Prudence seated on the deck, seeing her flushed cheeks, the glitter in her eyes.

"And where does this AAT-cum-Ox stand?" Flattery asked. "Have you thought of that?"

Prudence met his stare, understanding now why their hyb tanks had been filled with colonists. "The colonists," she said, nodding. "A field of unconsciousness from which any unconscious can draw—a ground that sustains and buoys—and the *sleeping* colonists provide it."

Flattery shook his head, feeling angry, confused.

Bickel stared beyond Prue, absorbing her words. Ideas merged and fitting—orders evolved in his awareness. This ship had been armed, maneuvered, aimed and fired. He remembered Hempstead: gnome-wise face, eyes glittering, and that compelling voice saying: *"What matters most is the search itself. This is more important than the searchers. Consciousness must dream, it must have a dreaming ground—and, dreaming, must invoke ever new dreams."*

"Knowledge is pitiless," Bickel said.

Prudence ignored him, keeping her attention on Flattery, aware of the psychiatrist-chaplain's confusion. "Don't you see it, Raj? To separate subject from object there has to be a background of some kind. You have to be able to see it against something. What's the background for consciousness? Unconsciousness."

"Zombies," Bickel said. "Remember, Raj? You called us zombies. And why not? We've existed for most of our lives in a state of light hypnosis."

Flattery knew Bickel had said something, but the words refused to link in any understandable form. It was as though Bickel had said: "Hop limbo promise the insect watering class to be erected to a first behavior preserve." The words trailed off through his mind as though they had been flashed in front of his awareness to screen him from something else.

From what?

A profound silence filled Com-central, broken by the sound of Prudence shifting her position on the deck.

Bickel felt himself go as calm as that silence, as though some other self had waited for that silence to take the reins. The sensation lasted for a single heartbeat and expanded into a sense of well-being, a relaxed poise that illuminated everything around him. It was as if one universe had been substituted for another, as if a sensory amplication of enormous intensity had been turned on his universe.

He saw the stark unconsciousness in Flattery's face, in Timberlake's—and the semi-consciousness of Prudence.

Zombies, he thought.

"Raj, you called us zombies," Bickel repeated. "If we were lightly hypnotized we'd appear partially dead to someone in a higher state of consciousness."

"Do you have to mumble?" Timberlake demanded.

Flattery glared at Bickel. He felt that the man was using real words and that communication was intended, but all the meanings slipped and slithered through his mind without making connection.

Prudence felt Bickel's words lifting her. There came an instant in which the universe turned upon one still point that was herself. The feeling shifted: self no longer was confined within her. As she gave up the self, clarity came. Flattery's words returned to her: *"There's nothing concerning ourselves about which we can be truly objective except our physical responses."*

The chemical experiments on her own body had never offered a real chance to solve their problem, but they had provided a *ground* for understanding her own identity. The hope of more had been illusory...because the experiments could not be conducted simultaneously on every occupant of the Tin Egg—their isolated world.

We share unconsciousness! she thought.

And she realized this must be the true reason the hyb tanks were filled with sleeping humans. Somewhere along the line, Project had seen *that* necessity. The umbilicus crew had to have a minimal *ground* of shared unconsciousness upon which to stand. They had to have a reference point, a tiny island in the vast dark which they could share with whatever they might produce out of their neuron fibers and Eng multipliers. They'd needed a ground upon which to stand before they could reach up tall.

The mirror cannot reflect itself, she thought.

"Hypnotized," Bickel said. "We accept it as normal because it's virtually the only form of consciousness we've ever seen. You've watched the Earth video. You wouldn't expect an idiot to be fooled by the commercials, but that rhythmic hammering, that repetition..."

"Half dead," Prudence said. "Zombies."

She said, "Zombies," Flattery thought. Her voice frightened him.

Bickel saw the alterness spread through her eyes, the awakening.

"We should've thought of the AAT when the thing came alive during reception from UMB," Bickel said.

"You see what has to be done?" Prudence asked. "The energizer—"

"Stimulator," Bickel said.

"Stimulator," she said. "It has to be part of the AAT's input."

"Slack lines," Bickel said. "You can't hold the reins too tightly because the signals have multiple functions. They need room to spread!"

Timberlake looked from one to the other. He felt a sense of dullness lifting from his mind. *Slack lines... sensory modules.*

Symbols!

Timberlake's memory shot back to their conversation about the energizer. *"All the master programs dealing with translation of symbols are monitored through feedback loops linked to the AAT."* He heard his own voice replaying in his mind.

Symbols!

The whole form of their problem arrayed itself in Timberlake's memory with the sudden force of something thrown at him. Problem and solution set themselves up as a physical arrangement and he saw the nerve-nets they had built all arrayed as a series of triangular faces with a Möbius twist—prisms of cell triangles interlaced and marching with their energy flows through infinite dimensions, forming sense data and memory images outside conventional space, storing bits and altering relationships in limitless dimensional extensions.

Bickel saw the vitality flowing into Timberlake, said: "Think of the AAT, Tim. Remember what we were saying?"

Timberlake nodded. The AAT. It received hundreds of duplicates of the same message compressed into the modulated laser burst. It averaged out the blanks and distortions, filtered for noise, compared for probable meaning on the doubtful bits, fed the result into a vocoder and produced it at an output as intelligible sound.

"It closely approximates what we do when we hear someone say something to us... then repeat it to check if we heard correctly," Timberlake said.

"You're all forgetting something," Flattery said.

They turned, saw Flattery at his own action couch, his hand on his own repeater console. A single red light had come alive there.

Flattery stared from Bickel to Prudence to Timberlake, seeing the unnatural brilliance in their eyes. Madness! And the deep color in their faces, their sense of excitement.

"Raj, wait," Bickel said. He spoke soothingly, watching Flattery's hand poised over a key beneath that single red light.

I should've known there'd be another trigger, Bickel thought.

CHAPTER 31

Mundane existence is the source of renewed suffering. The human goal is to attain release from the bondage of material existence and, achieving release, to unite with the Supreme Self.

> —Education of the Psychiatrist/
> Chaplain
> Moonbase Documents

FOR A LONG, pulsing moment after Flattery spoke, they all gazed at that red button: the trigger of their destruction. They all knew this thing. Flattery's intrusion had ignited a mutual awareness. They were supposed to accept this moment of oblivion. But something new had happened on this venture.

"A few more seconds of life aren't important," Bickel said. He held up a hand, hesitant. "You can ... wait for just a few seconds."

"You know I have to do this," Flattery said.

Even as he spoke, Flattery savored the "Ahhhhh" of suspense which charged this moment with an electrical sensation. It filled the air around them like ozone.

"You have control of the situation," Bickel said. His glance flickered toward the red switch with Flattery's hand poised to touch it. "The least you can do is hear what I have to say."

"We can't turn this thing loose upon the universe," Falttery said.

Timberlake swallowed, glanced down at Prudence. *How odd,* he thought, *that we should die so soon after coming alive.*

"How is it, Raj," Bickel asked, "that we can explain more about the unconscious networks of the human body than we can about the conscious?"

"You're wasting time," Flattery said.

"But the thing's dead," Bickel said.

"I have to be sure," Flattery said.

"Why can't you be sure *after* hearing what John has to say?" Prudence asked.

She looked at Bickel to draw Flattery's attention there. Two lights had begun blinking on the main computer console behind Flattery.

"It's a paradox," Bickel said. "We're asked to discard logical positivism while maintaining logic. We're asked to find a cause-and-effect system in a sea of probabilities where enormously large systems are based on even larger systems which are based on greater systems yet."

Flattery looked at him, caught by the trailing ends of Bickel's thoughts. "Cause and effect?" he asked.

"What happens if you push that key?" Bickel asked. He nodded to the trigger beneath Flattery's hand.

Prudence held her breath, praying Flattery would not turn. More lights were winking on the main computer console above Timberlake's couch. She couldn't say why the lights gave her hope, but the evidence of life in the ship . . .

"If I push this key," Flattery said, "an action sequence will be alerted in the computer." He glanced back at the winking lights. "You'll notice that part of the computer is becoming active. These circuits—" he returned his attention to Bickel "—have extra buffering and emergency power. The master program set off by this key instructs the computer to destroy itself and the ship—opening all the locks, exploding charges in key places."

"Cause and effect," Bickel said. And he marveled at how automatic Flattery's movements appeared. A zombie. "Cause and effect doesn't square with consciousness," he said.

A fascinating idea, Flattery thought.

"If any subsequent action proceeds with absolute and immediate causality from the sequence of past actions, then there can be no conscious influence of behavior," Bickel said. "Think of a row of dominoes falling. The human will power—the muscle and arm of our consciousness—couldn't decide what behavior to use because that behavior would all have been predetermined by a long line of preceding cause and effect."

Flattery felt the hand poised over the deadly key begin to ache. "We can't predict what this beast would do," he said. "I know."

Bickel's signing our death warrant, Prudence thought. She got to her feet. Her muscles still felt weak, but she sensed the stimulant doing its work. She gripped Timberlake's arm to steady herself.

Timberlake glanced at her hand, looked back at Flattery.

How calm Tim seems, she thought.

"Maybe consciousness doesn't influence neural activity at all," Timberlake said. "Perhaps we only imagine—"

"Don't be ridiculous," Flattery said. "That'd have no survival value and wouldn't have arisen in nature. Conscious creatures would've died out long ago."

Well, at least we've got him arguing, Timberlake thought. He smiled at Prudence, but she was watching Bickel. Timberlake returned his attention to Flattery. *How dull...almost dead the man looks.*

"Think of an electronic tube," Bickel said. "A very tiny amount of energy applied at the critical bias junction produces a tremendous change in output. Consciousness does something on the same order, Tim. We have a neural amplifier."

"Instant causality," Flattery whispered.

Lord! How that hand ached—as though it had been held above the trigger key for a century.

"That's what we have to toss out of our thinking," Bickel said. "Instant causality says if we have complete knowledge of a natural law and complete knowledge of the given system at a given time, then we can predict *exactly* what the system will do from that point on. That sure as hell isn't true at the atomic level and it doesn't apply to consciousness. Consciousness is like a system of lenses that select and amplify, that enlarge objects out of the surround. It can delve deep into the microcosm or into the macrocosm. It reduces the gigantic to the manageable, or enlarges the invisible to the visible."

This doesn't change anything, Flattery thought. *Why are we talking? Is he just trying to gain a little time?* The pressures of the terrible necessity which had been built into him were becoming almost unbearable.

Bickel saw the faint stirrings of life in Flattery's eyes. "But this consciousness factor isn't a completely random thing. In a universe packed with random possibility of destruction, random activity equals the certainty of encountering that destruction—and we're assuming consciousness is survival-oriented."

"Unless it's a healing process," Flattery said.

"But the healing process would have to completely counteract *any* destruction," Bickel said. And he saw the light of vitality grow in Flattery's eyes, his manner.

"I have to push this key, John," Flattery said. "Do you know that?"

"In a moment," Bickel said.

"Raj, you can't," Prudence said. "Think of all those helpless lives down in the hyb tanks. Think of—"

"Think of all those helpless lives back on Earth," Flattery said. "What would we turn loose on them? John's black box—white box transfer put his life—his entire ancestry—into the computer. Don't you see that? Any of you?"

Prudence put a hand to her mouth.

Bickel saw the alertness in Flattery, the vital consciousness expressed in every movement, realized that death-conditioning tensions had pushed him over the threshold into something near full potential. But the new argument Flattery had produced staggered Bickel.

If we restore it . . . awaken it . . . I'd be its unconscious, Bickel thought. *I'd be its emotional monitor, its id, its ego and its ancestors.* He swallowed. *And Raj . . .*

"Raj, don't push that key," Bickel said.

"I must," Flattery said. And as he spoke he sensed the poignancy of their awareness—this new vitality.

"You don't understand," Bickel said. "That field generator in your cubby—you think there was no feedback from you into the system, but there was. Your voice, your prayers—every gross or subtle reaction went back into the system through its sensors. Whatever religion is to you, that's what it'd be to the Ox. Whatever—"

"Whatever religion *was* to me," Flattery said.

And he pushed the key. It clicked, locked.

"How long do we have, Raj?" Timberlake asked.

"Perhaps a few minutes," Flattery said.

"And perhaps more," Bickel said.

"Don't you think we should've tried to limp back to UMB?" Prudence asked. "Awake as we are now, the ship-control necessities would've been so much simpler."

"Some fool would be certain to play with this ship—just testing," Flattery said. "And we . . ." He gestured to include all four of them. "This potential we've discovered without ourselves would've been engulfed on Earth, smothered, killed." He shrugged. "What are a few minutes or a few years, more or less? I had a responsibility . . . and fulfilled it."

"You had a death wish, too," Bickel said.

"That, too," Flattery agreed, recognizing how the deadly impulse had helped project him into his full awareness.

With that realization, Flattery began to glimpse the train of Bickel's cryptic words—their other meaning.

"There were Greeks who said that even the gods must die," Bickel said.

Flattery turned, looked at the big board. It was fully

alight now, not a warning telltale showing, every gauge zeroed normal.

"It's programmed to take us to Tau Ceti," Bickel said.

Flattery began to laugh, almost hysterically. Presently, he stopped. "But there's no inhabitable planet at Tau Ceti. You know what all this is, John—a set piece. We know what we are—cell-culture humans! A host gave a bit of himself containing the template of the total and the *axolotl* tanks took care of the rest. We were expendables!" He sighed, put down the urge to sink back into the deadly torpor. They're already growing our replacements, our duplicates, building another Tin Egg...back at UMB. Each failure teaches them something back at UMB. They've had a continuous monitor on the computer. When I depressed that key, that also launched a capsule back toward Earth—the complete report."

"Not quite complete," Bickel said.

"The ship is going to take us to Tau Ceti," Timberlake said.

"But the self-destruction program," Prudence said. And as she spoke, she saw what the others already had seen. The ship held control of its own death. It could die. And this was what had given it life. The impulse welled up into the AAT from the Ox circuits...and was repressed, the way humans repressed it. The ship had come to life the way they had—in the midst of death. Death was the background against which life could know itself. Without death—an ending—they were confronted by the infinite design problem, an impossibility.

All Flattery had done was to provide the AAT—the seat of consciousness—with a superenergizer.

"Nothing at Tau Ceti, you're sure?" Bickel asked.

"Planets, but not inhabitable," Flattery said.

A green action light began to glow on the main console.

"No sense going into hyb," Bickel said.

"We are happy," Prudence said. She stared at the green light. "It isn't fully conscious yet—the ship."

"Of course not," Timberlake said, and he thought how deftly she had phrased their emotional state. *I would've said we are filled with joy. But joy has somewhat religious overtones. Prue's way is better.*

Prudence grew aware that Flattery was looking at her. "Why not?" he said.

Yes, why not? she agreed.

But no woman had ever presided at a stranger birth.

She crossed to the main console, switched the computer's audio pickup into the main input channel.

"You," she said.

She kept her hand on the switch, the new sensitivity of her skin reporting the molecular shift of metal in direct contact.

They waited, knowing the outline of what was happening inside their robotic construction. That one word, internally powered by programmed curiosity and self-preservation directives, was winding its way through the as-yet semiconscious creation. Preservation—but there were many kinds of preservation, many things to preserve.

But there was only one receptor upon which "You" could impress itself.

Programs were firing, new cross-links being created, comparisons and balances being made.

Abruptly, the board in front of Prudence went dead. Every light extinguished, every gauge at dead rest. She waggled the computer switch, got no response. The entire ship began to tremble.

"Is that the self-destruction program?" Bickel asked.

A single word, metallic and harsh, boomed from the vocorder above them: "Negative."

The ship vibration eased, resumed, cut off sharply.

There came a weighted sense of drifting, a profound silence which they felt extended throughout the ship.

Again, the vocoder came to life, but softer: "Now, you will see on your screens a lateral view."

The overhead screen and the fore bulkhead screen came alight with the identical scene: a view of a solar system, planets picked out by the telltale red arrows of computer reference.

"Six planets," Flattery whispered. "Notice the

pattern—and the sky beyond."

"You recognize it?" Timberlake asked.

"It's the view the probes brought back," Flattery said. "The Tau Ceti system."

"Why would it reproduce the probe view?" Prudence asked.

"Prudence," said the vocoder, "this is not a probe view. These radiations are what I ... see now around me."

"We're already at Tau Ceti?" Prudence asked. "How can that be? We can't be there!"

"The symbol *there* is an inaccuracy," said the vocoder. "There and here shift according to a polarity dependent upon dimension."

"But we're there!" Prudence said.

"A statement of the obvious may be used to reinforce your awareness," the vocoder said. "You were to be conveyed safely to Tau Ceti. You have arrived at Tau Ceti."

"Safely," Flattery said. "There's no place for us to land."

"An inconvenience, no more," said the vocoder.

Every arrow but one on the screen winked out.

"This planet has been prepared for you," said the vocoder.

Bickel glanced sideways at Flattery, saw the psychiatrist-chaplain mopping perspiration from his brow.

"Something's wrong," the vocoder said. "You have but to look around you. You are safe. Observe."

The scene on the screens shifted.

"The fourth planet," said the vocoder. "That which is prepared can be preserved."

Flattery gripped Bickel's arm. "Can't you hear it?"

But Bickel was staring at the view on the fore screen—a planet growing larger, filling the screen: a green planet with atmosphere and clouds.

"How did we get here?" Bickel asked. "Is it possible for me to understand?"

"Your understanding is limited," said the vocoder. "The symbols that you have given me possess strange variance with nonsymbolized reality."

"But *you* understand it," Bickel said.

The vocoder seemed to take on a chiding tone: "My understanding transcends all possibilities of this universe. I do not need to *know* this universe because I *possess* this universe as a direct experience."

"Can't you hear it?" Flattery demanded, his grip on Bickel's arm tightening.

Bickel ignored the distraction, remembered that moment in the force of the field generator when he had faltered and fallen back from a transcendental awareness. He had not possessed the capacity. It was a built-in lack, functional.

He could only accept the accomplished fact because the evidence was visible on the viewscreen. They were coming down through clouds—a meadow with trees beyond it and a snowcapped mountain lifted in the background. He could feel the G-pull increasing, steadying as the ship came to rest.

"You will find the gravity just a fraction less than that of Earth," said the vocoder. "I am now awakening colonists in hybernation. Remain where you are until all are awake. You must be together when you make your decision."

His voice rasping in a suddenly dry throat, Bickel glanced up at the vocoder, said: "Decision? What decision?"

"Flattery knows," said the vocoder. "You must decide how you will WorShip Me."

EPILOGUE

WHEN THE PUBLISHERS announced that they were going to bring out a new edition of *Destination: Void*, they offered me the opportunity to make any changes I felt were necessary. Because of the tightly interwoven scientific premises behind this story and rapid developments in fields related to these premises, it would be extraordinary if discoveries across thirteen years did not dictate certain revisions.

You will find, therefore, that this newly published version of *Destination: Void* contains significant additions, rewritten portions, changes in character development, and certain deletions.

Among the deletions was much of the math relating to grid/field imbedment concepts employed in the attempt to compare computer programming with certain human thought processes. The significant portion of that math is reproduced here for those who may find it interesting.

> *Grid, a given volume of space, dimensions x·y·z.*
> *With the source of awareness, an invisible object (s) to find in time (t.) for a given operation within that volume.*
> *The x·y·z grid's positional derivatives over (s).*

It was a function of the s volume where (sx) (sy) (sz) were derived from $s = \sqrt{\Sigma \dfrac{(x - x)^2}{t}}$, $s = \sqrt{\Sigma \dfrac{(y - y)^2}{t}}$, $s = \sqrt{\Sigma \dfrac{(z - z)^2}{t}}$. The connection of thought-points within the imaginary grid could be denoted by direction cosines of a line extended to the awareness shot-origin. And distances for each thought-probe could be determined by $(1, m, n, \frac{1}{d})$ where $d = \sqrt{x^2 + y^2 + z^2}$, $1 = \frac{x}{d}$, $m = \frac{y}{d}$, $n = \frac{z}{d}$.

There was no doubt at all where this flare of awareness pointed—the AAT system. For a moment, she held the entire complex of the AAT system in her mind, manipulating the continuous interlocking pattern with her symbological grid. It was so simple. The AAT was a four-dimensional continuum, a piece of space-time geometry subject to considerations of curvature, duration-over-distance, and particle/wave transfer through a multiplicity of sensor-traverse lines.

To the human nervous system, an instrument designed for the job, nothing could be simpler than visualizing and manipulating such a four-dimensional spiderweb—once the nature of the spiderweb was understood.

The earlier version of this story turned, in part, on the awake-asleep concept which dominated psychiatric thinking about consciousness at the time. For that reason, I quoted the following famous song as the book preface.

> Sailor take care, sailor take care.
> Danger is near thee—
> Beware, beware, beware, beware.
> Many brave hearts are asleep in the deep,
> So beware—
> Beware.
>> —from *Asleep In The Deep*
>> by Arthur J. Lamb and H. W. Petrie

A new epigraph was chosen for this rewritten version of the story and that will be explained presently.

Careful readers who compare both editions of this story will note shifts in viewpoint for key portions of dialogue. This was done to open up the development of the ideas which flow through the more suspenseful parts of the story, to render them more comprehensible to the reader.

I have also, since writing the original *Destination: Void*, read Mary Shelley's *Frankenstein* (my previous acquaintance with that story was limited to the movie starring Boris Karloff) and I have found interesting points of comparison. You will find new chapter breaks for this version of my story and epigraphs for these chapters. For some of those insertions I have found it pertinent to quote from Mary Shelley. I am extremely grateful for these quotes and hope that somewhere there is a wraith of Mary Shelley to accept my gratitude.

To the others whose work has contributed to my understanding and to the development of both the original and this new version of *Destination: Void*, I extend my deep appreciation.

—Frank Herbert
Port Townsend, Washington
January 26, 1978

Discover New Worlds with books of Fantasy by Berkley